THE GRIPPING BEAST

A Novel by Peter Craigie

Published by Peter Craigie

Copyright © 2012 Peter Craigie

ISBN 978-0-9559864-4-4

## PRELUDE

He leaned forward, staring through the shimmering wet of the windscreen. The headlights carved a reassuring tunnel into the sleet-filled night but beyond the bright cone of light he knew there was nothing but darkness; high cliffs and the sea below. McNaughton gritted his teeth and tried not to think what the result of a mistake might be, steering with elaborate care, concentrating on the line of low hummocks that marked the edge of the narrow coast road. A blast of wind, gale-force and sudden surged out of the blackness and a hot panic shot through him as the car veered across the road. Just in time he regained control. He realised that he was trembling. "Relax," he said out loud. "Just relax; but concentrate." He scowled. "How the hell do you do that?"

Archie McNaughton had very few illusions left in life and when it came to his own driving ability, none at all. He had been almost fifty when he had first dared to drive and though as with so many late-life romances, he had then become completely captivated, he knew his limitations. Coached by Norman, his new young friend, and aided by the magic of automatic transmission he could negotiate the quiet island roads safely, at least during daylight hours. In summer that meant most of the time this far north. But on a dark winter night in appalling weather, it was very different.

1

His concentration strayed for a moment as he glanced at the clock on the facia before him. Eight o'clock! Hell, he thought, he could be standing in a warm pub with a dram in his hand doing what he did best--- holding forth to an admiring audience about the iniquities of the land-owning classes or the case for penal sanctions against the oil and nuclear industries. A bleak smile flitted across his square truculent face. He had become a cult figure within the party and he relished the thought.

He was hated in some quarters too. He knew well enough that some of his more belligerent speeches had made him enemies and the high-profile legal cases he chose to handle on issues like land tenure or pollution meant that his enemies were powerful enough to do him serious damage. But he always had his insurance. His eyes flickered towards the battered briefcase on the seat beside him. Then abruptly he peered back into the wet darkness. Just concentrate, he thought. That was what Norman was always nagging him about. His head jerked back involuntarily as a savage sweep of rain slashed across the windscreen.

The twisting narrow road was unwinding before him in a hypnotic succession of illuminated cameos. No, he thought, his mind drifting again, he had no shortage of enemies. Norman laughed at him and said he had become paranoid in his old age. Well, the boy didn't know everything, he thought sadly. But McNaughton was a realist and he knew that he had information that could embarrass, even destroy, some of the most powerful men in the land. He also knew what those people could do if they thought he was too much of a threat.

So he walked a dangerous line. Not that he had cared about the risk, at least until he met Norman Orr. Luckily there was little these men knew about his private life and nothing they could use against him. For there were some who would not hesitate to ruin him if they dared. McNaughton laughed out loud, at his image in the windscreen. For he'd made sure the ones who knew the most were not in a position to reveal anything about Archie McNaughton.

Still, the threat was there. That was why he had started to carry the revolver with him when he was alone in the car. The gunsmith in Thurso had recommended a .357 magnum. "An excellent weapon for self-defence". Not that Archie expected to have to use it. It was just a precaution, as he told the police. Travelling about the country late at night, speaking at public meetings, a legal personality and with his high political profile and living in a remote place like Scarisby, it made sense.

McNaughton scowled silently, remembering how he had agonised about allowing them to use the house at Scarisby. Well, what was done was done. At least he had been careful never to be there when they had their get-togethers. But it had gone against the grain to let them use the old place. Then he had realised that what went on there could be made to cut both ways, if that ever became necessary. Now he had a favour or two that he could call in when the time was right; from men who knew how to keep the lid on almost any scandal. Men with more to lose than himself.

He grinned malevolently at the thought and wriggled his heavy-set body closer to the wheel, squinting into the darkness ahead of him. Soon he would be home with Norman. It was only the thought of Norman that had made him rush to catch the ferry on a night like this. For that boy had changed his life, unlike the many before him. McNaughton winced at the thought of the succession of young men who had filled his life down the years. But this time it was different.

Another sudden gust of wind struck the car, pushing it sideways. To his right the land fell away rapidly beyond a shallow ditch, down across grassy slopes to the high cliffs. Instinctively he clung a little closer to the land-side edge of the road, steering into a tight bend around a head-high mound of fluttering reeds. For a brief moment he lost sight of the road completely, his headlights arcing into the night sky. Then he

3

sensed rather than saw the dark shape in front of him.

A blaze of light leapt out at him and with an oath McNaughton slammed his foot heavily down onto the brake-pedal. The car slithered awkwardly to a halt on the wet road. Who the hell was parked here on a night like this? Carefully he put the gear lever into neutral and pulled the hand brake on, just as Norman had taught him. The engine ticked over quietly.

A tall figure in a long coat glistening wet in the headlights loomed up before him, a deep collar turned up against the wind and rain hiding the face in deep shadow. Yet it seemed to McNaughton that there was something familiar about the figure. He lowered the window and squinted out into the wind and sleet, staring up in astonishment as the light fell on the man's face. "What the hell are you doing here?" he said. "And that's a bloody stupid place to stop, if you don't mind me saying so."

Without a word the man whipped his right hand across in powerful back-handed blow and a small weighted leather blackjack struck McNaughton on the right temple above his ear. He slumped forward unconscious but still held in place by the seat-belt. The man calmly walked around to the other side of the vehicle and opened the passenger door. Reaching towards the glove compartment and fumbling awkwardly at the catch with his gloved fingers, he removed McNaughton's revolver. Then he picked up the leather brief-case and leafed rapidly through its contents. After scanning the documents he selected a few and thrust them into his coat pocket.

He returned to the open driver's window and jerked McNaughton back in his seat. Coolly he studied the weal where his blackjack had struck. Looking around to ensure the isolated road was still clear of traffic, he slid off the safety catch and placed the muzzle of the revolver carefully against the bruise. When he squeezed the trigger he stood well back to avoid the spray of blood and matter that splattered across the interior of car.

Pulling open the driver side door he dropped the revolver on to the floor by McNaughton's feet. Then he released the hand brake and slid the gear lever into the drive position. The car moved slowly forward and leaning his weight against the door frame, the man steered the car off the road and bumped it over the shallow ditch on to the smooth hillside. With a final heave he slammed the door shut and stood back to watch as the car gathered pace, bouncing crazily away towards the cliffs, headlights illuminating the hillside in an unnatural green.

For an instant the lights hung as if suspended in space, twin beams blazing into the rain-filled night sky. Then they vanished completely. The man waited for the sound of the crash. But the only noise was the shriek of the wind and the distant surge of the sea. He pulled the papers from his pocket and examined them by the light of his car headlights. With a smile and a sudden jerk of his arm he scattered them into the dark night.

# CHAPTER 1

The fog took me completely by surprise, rolling in swiftly and silently under a brilliant blue sky. Of course, I should have known better. But that was something I had been saying a lot recently. Though in fairness, as I rigged Tom Drever's little day-racer that morning the sun had been high and hot, with only a gentle breeze from the south-west. Orkney had looked like the Greek Islands. It was a notion that turned out to be very deceptive.

The sudden boom from the twin foghorns on the Pentland Skerries sounded quite unreal in the bright sunlight and glancing around I saw that to the west a solid wall of white fog had sealed off the Firth. My first reaction was to outrun it and as I put the helm over the boat came about gracefully. A quick look at my watch told me that high water was approaching and I would have the assistance of a strong tidal flow running east into the open North Sea. So at that stage I wasn't worried.

But the fog was closing fast. Still, even in these light airs Tom's yacht moved beautifully and I was close enough to see the tall cliffs of Hoxa Head, only a mile or two away to the north-east. Once safely past the Lowther Beacon and its nasty ragged reefs I had only to clear Old Head and from there it would be an easy trip back to the mooring, with a gentle offshore breeze helping me on my way. I stared across the rapidly darkening waters at the long line of silent cliffs and imagined that I could see the ancient Scarisby tomb against the skyline. It was hard to believe that a few weeks ago I had known nothing about it and its legacy of death.

But the fog was moving much faster than I had imagined. Within minutes the first wisps were coming drifting into the boat. Then the sunlight died completely away and the air became damp and cold. I shivered, cursing, and remembered the sweater I had left behind. What had possessed me to set out with light cotton trousers and only a shirt under my life-jacket?

On the other hand, as I had slipped off the mooring that morning with the heavy scent of wild meadowsweet drifting languorously over water all had seemed well with the world and I was in a mood to relax. After all, I had just completed another assignment for Odin Investments, though God knows how. And had not the melodramas of the past few weeks been resolved like the plot of a Wagnerian opera? The beautiful love goddess had found her flawed hero, she had won the magic necklace and the villain had been cast down. A morality tale? Well, that would be going too far. But at least I had survived.

Now I crouched over the tiller, peering out across a glassy swell into ever thickening mist. The cliffs faded briefly from sight, reappeared for an encouraging moment and then vanished totally. Visibility was down to a few hundred yards and getting worse and the tell-tale ribbon on the mast-head fluttered fitfully as the breeze died away. Above me the sun had been transformed into a pale watery globe, drifting vaguely in and out of clouds of fog. Then it vanished completely and in an instant my world became just the wooden rail of the boat and a few feet of heaving dark water.

A cold white shroud of mist folded in on me and now I started to worry. I knew I had been heading roughly south-east and on course to clear the reefs when someone had thoughtlessly switched the lights off. In fog the wind can change direction completely and with no sun to steer by and only a fluky wind I could only try to hold my last known course and hope for the best. I tried to recall exactly how the currents ran around this dangerous coastline. OK, I thought, let's reason it out. The flood tide will push me south and out into the open sea, if I was lucky and didn't hit something hard, like the Lowther Reefs or any one of half a dozen small islands.

And if I was unlucky? I gritted my teeth and tried not to think about what happened to people who ran on to rocks in these cold waters. I cursed again. What was I doing here anyway? I could have been cruising around San Francisco Bay in the sunshine on my step-father's gin-palace. Or better still, sitting on the deck at Sam's in Tiburon, drinking a beer and watching the sun go down. Or coming up, or whatever the hell it was supposed to be doing at the moment. Still, I thought brightly, I always tell my clients that the first step to solving a problem is to know that you have one. Well, I had a problem and I knew it. What I really needed was a solution. Or a stroke of pure luck. Then through the fog I heard the sound of a power boat engine heading towards me. Hallelujah, I thought. The famous Lennox luck has done it again! But as it turned out, I was wrong about that too.

Looking back on the whole thing I have no excuses to offer. I mean, I learned the golden rules at my mother's knee. The first rule if you are going to make a precarious living as a management consultant is that you should always be perfectly clear who your client is. It sounds obvious, I know. But sometimes it gets to be complicated and getting it wrong can be a fatal error. Though not usually in the literal sense. The second rule is to make sure you end up collecting your fee from somebody. Or maybe that's the first rule. I normally get that part right.

But this time I very nearly got them both wrong. Because I forgot the third and most important rule; always know when to say 'no' to an assignment.

It all began about nine o'clock on the fourth of July on a grey morning of the type that passes for summer in Edinburgh. I knew it was the fourth of July because I had just received the annual offer from my step-father to join him in his political lobbyist firm in California. Since my mother died he has sent me the same offer every year on Independence Day. I think it's the American idea of whimsy. In truth he was lonely. And so every year I gave it more thought. For it was a tempting offer and I knew that I owed him a great deal. He had been kind to me when he acquired me, along with my mother, as a kind of job lot some thirty years earlier. He had met her in Paris when she had gone there to her people after my own father died. Later he helped me find my first job when I left business school in the States and of course my dual nationality was due to him.

Then when I was drafted for the US military he offered to pull strings to keep me out of Vietnam and when I refused his help he gave me some good advice. "They'll be able to use your language skills in Intelligence, so volunteer for Special Services as soon as you can. With any luck it will all be over by the time you've finished your training. That way, if you do get involved in any unpleasantness you'll be working with professionals. That way there's less chance of being shot by some frightened kid high on dope from your own side."

So I took his advice and they taught me to speak Vietnamese, use explosives, handle a small boat and do some rudimentary unarmed combat. Very useful for a management consultant. Now though, I don't tell people about Vietnam. It doesn't seem relevant somehow. But I was there right at the end when things were collapsing. Very occasionally someone sees my curriculum vitae and asks me what I was doing there. "You've heard of the first of the few?" I say. "Well, I was the last of the many." The experience left me with a dislike of Chinese food, a deep suspicion of US foreign policy and the desire to return to my father's roots in Scotland.

So there I was, sitting alone in the kitchen of my Edinburgh New Town flat, listening to the slow movement from Mahler's Fifth Symphony and stared at my coffee mug with the zodiac signs, wondered about alternative careers. It was music to commit suicide by and that mug always depresses me anyway. It has a lot to say about Capricorn character traits and what your ideal line of work should have been. It's all very dispiriting and I keep meaning to throw it away. But it doesn't say anything about being decisive.

The truth was that I was bored. Now, there was no way I should have been bored. I mean, I was head-hunting a key fund management appointment for an important client who would give me a hard time if I didn't produce the goods. The client wasn't boring either. Apart from anything else, Hans Grieder was the only big time client who had stayed with me when I set up on my own account. So I needed to hang on to him for sordid financial reasons but also, damn it, for the sheer prestige of working for Odin Investments.

People find it reassuring when you tell them you act for a high-profile organisation like Odin, though just why Grieder gave me his work was a mystery to me. Usually clients like Odin Investments prefer to have someone who is worth suing in case the assignment goes wrong. So the client certainly wasn't boring. The truth was it was the candidates who were boring. For the credible contenders were all turning out to be actuaries and talking to actuaries is a pretty dull way to spend the day, even the relatively lively ones who run multi-million pound pension funds.

My other problem was that the money scene is incredibly incestuous and it seemed almost impossible to keep my search confidential. I was starting to have an uneasy feeling that everyone I contacted was expecting my phone call. Of course, members of the Faculty of Actuaries do all know each other and I was beginning to think the bastards might have decided amongst themselves who was going to get the job. So they were probably sitting out there, choosing a short-list for me and making jokes about my head-hunting technique. Or what passes for jokes with actuaries.

Then I sighed. At least I'd found a few who could do the job and had sent them away to think things over. So for now there wasn't much more I could do until I was free to divulge their identities to Grieder. In the meantime, I thought, I might as well go sailing. I reached for a newspaper to check the tides at Granton Harbour and started to flick through the pages. Then my slender sense of duty reasserted itself.

Careful, I thought, your super-ego is slipping its clutch--- you have work to do. I was just about to close the paper when I saw a strange little story tucked away at the foot of an inside page. 'Break-in at Police Headquarters' was the headline. Now that really was odd enough to waste time on. The story was short and non-committal; 'Police sources confirmed that persons unknown had broken into the Headquarters of Lothian and Borders Police earlier in the month and that an investigation was underway. Nothing of value had been taken.'

That does it I thought and tossed the paper aside. The world has really been turned upside down. As far as I know, people didn't usually break into police custody. I was still sitting there, trying to summon up enough enthusiasm to phone Grieder with a progress report when the telephone rang. I picked it up. "Terry Lennox," I said.

A crisp masculine voice answered me. It was mostly cultured public school Scots but with an underlay of something else; something harder and more commercial. "Good morning, Lennox. This is Anthony Raven, of Raven and Thompson."

This was my day for surprises. Someone once said that Edinburgh is more a large town than a small city. So I knew Raven. Though his firm had never been clients of mine or even business contacts. But there was the small matter of Raven's wife, Patricia. Well, it had been almost a year since we were seriously involved. Although for a while, after the relationship was over, she had a habit of reappearing from time to time, usually when I least expected her. I suppose it was to check out whether I was pining and still receptive and available. Usually I was, at least two out of the three.

But then who wouldn't have been receptive? Patricia was simply the most beautiful woman I had ever seen. She somehow generated an air of calm elegance and a remote ladylike image that made her seem far out of the reach of mere mortals. Which I suppose is why what happened so devastating. For a time, I mean. A long time.

I still can't explain it. One moment of relaxation, one casual, sociable kiss and she had melted astonishingly into my arms. The cool facade was gone and she clung to me with a desperate need. The sudden transition from icy control to helpless surrender had exited me beyond reason. Yes, that was exactly what it had been--- beyond reason. The whole affair had been beyond reason. But the contrast between her public face and how she acted in private had held me in a kind of thrall. Was it all a just game to her? Well, I didn't think so at the time and if it was a game it was one I enjoyed playing. Of course it didn't last and she had drifted away. But then each time she would reappear with some more or less plausible explanation for her behaviour. So we would end up in bed again.

But each time it ended the same way, watching her dress and hurriedly repair her make-up and hair before she rushed home to host some polite dinner-party for her husband, promising to call me soon. Which sometimes she did and I would almost begin to believe in her again. Then eventually she didn't. Until the next time she appeared, that is. Then it would start all over again.

So when I heard Raven's voice I did some rapid thinking.

12

How much did he know? Well, who can tell what goes on inside a marriage? Especially one as strange as theirs seemed to be. Not that Patricia would ever say much about him, out of a strange kind of loyalty I suppose. But somehow she gave me the impression that Raven had no interest in her as a woman and that he didn't care much what she did in her spare time, just so long as the public image was maintained. Did I really believe that? I had certainly wanted to believe her. But was it likely? Or was I part of some strange game they were playing out between them.

Still, it had been a long time since her last visit to my flat. So when I heard Raven's voice I had a clear conscience. Well, more or less.

CHAPTER 2


Raven went on briskly. "Listen Lennox, I want to see you. quite quickly please. I have some things I'd like to discuss with you. An assignment for a client of mine, principally. Sorry for the rush. But I'm going up north tonight on a short trip and I'd like to get things started. Can you come to my office immediately after lunch? That would suit me best."

Something about him irritated me. It was nothing personal, of course. "I'm very heavily committed, Mr Raven." I said coolly. "It might be some time before I could do anything for your clients, and of course it would always depend on whether I thought I could help."

"Oh, it's the sort of thing you do," he said breezily. "But rather not discuss it on the telephone. Confidential. You know the sort of thing."

I knew the sort of thing only too well. Maybe a client wanted a successor for somebody before that somebody knew they were leaving the organisation. Sometimes there were excellent commercial reasons for keeping an appointment like that under wraps. After all, it never hurts to keep the competition guessing. But Raven's assurance grated with me. I suppose it was the calm assumption that I would come running as soon as he called. "Of course I appreciate that re-scheduling some of

14

your existing work may cause some additional expense," he went on smoothly. "So if it is a question of cash I assure you that my client will cover any costs you may incur in taking on the assignment." He paused. "Fees are unlikely to be a limiting factor."

Hey, I thought. Maybe I'm being over-sensitive. "Just a moment," I said, pretending to check my diary. "Well, as it happens I could see you this afternoon around two-thirty. Where exactly is your office?"

He gave me an address near, but not in, the most prestigious part of Edinburgh's New Town. It was only about a half-a mile or so from my flat. "Excellent!" He sounded really pleased. "Our name is on the front door."

"By the way," I said before he could ring off, "I don't think I have ever acted for you before." I grinned at my image in the mirror, choosing my words carefully. "How did you get my name?"

There was a pause. Then I heard him give a laugh. "My dear chap," he said. "You'd be surprised! I know a great deal about you, one way and another. This is a small town after all! Until two-thirty then." The line went dead leaving me staring back at my reflection in the mirror. Ho hum, I thought.

I was still wondering exactly what he had meant when the telephone rang again. I groaned, please God, don't let it be Grieder. I hate it when he has to call me for a progress report. You really have to keep the initiative with a man like him or he'll run you ragged. If Hans Grieder was a gardener he'd be the kind who pulls up the plants each day to see if the roots are growing.

"Lennox," I said briskly, trying to sound like a man completely on top of events.

"This is Donald Lynch. Are you all right? You sound

15

strange."

Donald Lynch! I visualised him, plump and glossy as a well-fed partridge, probably lounging back with his feet on his desk, waistcoat unbuttoned, his insipient paunch bulging out over the well cut trousers and his prematurely bald head gleaming under the office lights. Donald was one of the best young corporate finance strategists I knew. He was ferociously bright, with a mind like a steel trap. We had been colleagues once and we stayed in touch, swapping assignments and business information in a complex system of barter that we settled periodically with an expensive dinner, charged to whichever of our lucky clients we thought deserved it most.

"I'm OK," I said and glanced at my watch. Donald's firm was based in Boston and it could be no more than five o'clock in the morning there. Which was early even by his workaholic standards. "Hey, what time is it in Boston?" I asked.

There was snort and then a pained sigh. "I'm not in Boston, Terry. I'm in London. What's wrong with you?" he went on, "I thought you were supposed to be a leading head-hunter. In touch with every tremor of the web, the ebb and flow of world business talent. Don't you even read the F.T?"

"No comment," I said brightly. "And by the way, that was a mixed metaphor."

"Very amusing," he said. "I'm beginning to see why you have to keep picking my brain. Ever considered a career change? I hear there are great opportunities in Edinburgh for rent-boys. You'd be good at that, with all your high level contacts." He seemed to think that was very funny.

"Listen," I said, "At least once a day I consider a career change. But being a rent-boy wouldn't be that much of an improvement, not with the ass-holes I have to deal with."

16

Donald hooted with delight. But I knew him well enough to recognise the ritual dancing. He had called to ask my advice about something, and that didn't happen every day. But when it did it meant he had a big problem. "So tell me, what are you doing in London?" I asked.

"Up-date that confidential file you keep on me, old son. I'm now Director of Strategic Development for the Irving Group."

I searched my memory for information about the group. As far as I could recall, they were a medium-sized mini-conglomerate, family owned, with a respectable but not very exciting profit record. "You mean, acting Director?" I assumed he had been seconded from the corporate finance house, probably on some profit-improvement project.

"No," Donald said. "I've left the firm. I'm actually an executive director on the board of the Irving Group."

More surprises! I had always imagined that Donald was locked into merchant banking by golden chains that would hold him for the rest of his natural life. The Irving Group must have come up with something special to attract him. "Tut!" I said. "You don't mean you've made a career move without consulting me, Donald. What were you thinking about?"

He was suddenly quiet. "That," Donald finally said sheepishly, "is what I want to speak to you about. I think I may have made a mistake."

I sat up straight in my seat. Things must be bad. Donald didn't make mistakes and if he did, he didn't admit to them. "Right," I said quickly. "Do you want to talk about it now? Or would you rather meet me some place?"

"I'd prefer to talk face to face. Some of this is--- well, delicate to put it mildly." He laughed grimly. "I'm coming to Scotland next week to talk to our chief institutional investors. I'm

17

supposed to take them through our new strategic initiatives. Maybe we can meet then?"

"Of course. Just call me when you get here."

"Thanks Terry. And it's my turn to buy dinner." Now I knew he was in trouble. Before he could ring off I asked him if he knew anyone who could handle a big fund management appointment.

"How much?" he asked succinctly. I told him the package was flexible but negotiable well into six figures. He rattled through all the questions I expected. "Assets?" I told him the fund had about half a billion pounds under management. "Too small," he said instantly. "Who's the client?"

I hesitated. "Asian and European Asset Management."

Donald hooted again, this time with derision. "You don't mean you're still working for Odin and that bastard Grieder? You are a glutton for punishment, Terry." He thought for a moment. "Tell him to merge it with the rest of his UK asset management group. I think he has a similar operation in London. Then he can cut out the overheads, close one of the offices and get rid of all the bums. It just might be a viable business then."

I smiled quietly. Good old Donald. He had just described precisely the unwritten brief for the job. "But the money sounds reasonable," he went on. "Not enough for me of course. But send me the background notes. I'll probably find somebody for you. Just make sure you tell Grieder the operation needs radical change." He went on breezily. "Listen, I can't afford to give you any more free advice, Lennox. I'm going to have to start charging you." Then he paused, "I'll send you the background on the Irving Group and we can discuss it next week. And, Terry---thanks."

After he rang off I sat thinking for a while. He was right,

of course. Grieder was unusually difficult to deal with. But then nothing about Grieder was usual. For a start he had built Odin Investments into one of Europe's largest business virtually from scratch by a series of shrewd and sometimes ruthless acquisitions. Now the group was his personal creature; a powerful financial and information services complex with a stake in most of the key business sectors. Its core was insurance and fund management, plus a solid foothold in merchant banking and currency and derivatives trading.

Recently he had moved into the highly lucrative and influential business of information distribution, using world-wide computer networks to control and process the data on which modern commerce depended. Through his fund management operation I knew that Grieder had also made several strategic investments in important high technology companies and that he had a place on the board of a large computer hardware company and a string of software firms at the cutting edge of new developments. Everything Grieder did was aimed at only one end, the accumulation of information and through that, of power. So Odin Investments was huge. But what made it really unusual was that Grieder still controlled it totally and personally, with the meticulous attention to detail of the obsessional neurotic he almost certainly was. Grieder was not just unusually difficult. He was also unusually rich and powerful.

Apart from that I knew very little about him. Nor I think did anyone else. Oh, there were occasional profiles in the financial press or in Der Spiegel or Paris Match. But no-one seemed to know anything about his personal life; only that he had never married and that there was no known female connection. That figured, it seemed to me. From what I knew about him, he probably got his kicks reading consolidated profit and loss accounts.

When he wasn't at the Odin head office in Brussels he spent his time inspecting his subsidiary companies around the globe. When he wasn't doing that, it seemed that he lived alone somewhere in the Swiss mountains near Interlaken, in a huge mansion that he had named "Asgard". I looked up the reference once. Asgard was the home of the Gods in the Norse Sagas.

Grieder's version was apparently almost as inaccessible as the original. It had a private aerial tramway system which was the only way in or out. Not that Grieder encouraged visitors and very few people were ever invited to Asgard; only some very privileged business contacts coming to seal a particularly important deal or to ski with Grieder. Skiing appeared to be one of his few passions. That, and controlling money and people.

Needless to say, I had never been invited to Asgard. For Grieder was always polite with me but cold; cold and strangely distant. After five years of working with him on some of his most critical appointments he still called me 'Mr Lennox' as if we had just met for the first time. No matter how successful I was or how much I knew about his businesses, he remained always stiff and formal, at best showing only a grudging respect for my professionalism. Perhaps he knew no other way.

But each time we met he would stare at me fiercely and repeat his usual mantra, as if I were some kind of novice. "Mr Lennox," he would say, "you must understand that only the best is good enough for Odin Investments. Only the very best." I always knew what was coming next; I had heard it so often that I could have sung along with him. "I want you to understand the standards I require. For unless you do understand, you will fail me. And if you fail me, I shall have no further use for your services. I hope I make myself clear."

Grieder was totally convinced that he was surrounded by idiots who would inevitably let him down. In a rare moment of emotion he once explained to me why he couldn't delegate responsibility to anyone in the organisation. I had been summoned to his private office one evening to discuss an assignment. One moment he was seated calmly across the table from me outlining his plans. Then I made an innocent comment about the need to delegate. Well, not so innocent really, for I was curious to see how he would respond.

Grieder leapt from his chair and towered over me, tall, fair haired and athletic. He fixed me with his glittering eye--- in his case literally eye singular, for he had lost the other one in a skiing accident. Glaring down at me, his lean and tanned face working strangely, it was clear that for once he had lost all his control. His good eye glowed with a deep self-righteous anger that I found slightly scary.

"People tell me I should delegate, Mr Lennox!" he shouted. "I know you think that too!." I tried to look non-committal, just in case he had totally flipped and had an axe handy. But Grieder didn't really care what I thought, though I had clearly struck a raw nerve. He ranted on for twenty minutes while I sat there, clocking his performance with surreptitious glances at my watch and trying to look interested.

"But how can I delegate when no-one will accept responsibility? Tell me that, Mr Lennox!" I nodded in what I hoped was a sympathetic way. "I cannot find the executives I need--- the men of real quality I can trust to run the group as I would. This is why I take so much personal responsibility. This is why I must monitor my executives so closely. I must ensure that my standards are met--- the very highest standards." He spoke in perfect English, with just a trace of Swiss-German in his accent. At least he said he was Swiss. Sometimes I wondered. They never did discover what happened to Martin Bormann. It didn't seem a good idea to remind him that all his senior executives were appointed by him personally. For the truth was that apart from a few masochists who thought of him as a challenge, the very best executives--- the ones he really did need, simply refused to work for him. It was a dreadful kind of self-fulfilling prophecy.

But on the other hand he paid extremely well and he owned some high quality businesses, so there was usually

21

someone willing to take him on in spite of his reputation. After all, a year or two with Odin Investments looked good on a cv. At least, that's what I told the candidates.

From the beginning he made it clear that he didn't think I would be much of an improvement on the other incompetents he had used in the past. But to date I had confounded him by completing every assignment. OK, I had sweated blood over them and when I die they will probably find "Odin Investments" written on my heart. But what the hell! He was a multi-millionaire in Swiss francs and he paid his bills promptly. So why should I complain? Besides, I suppose I thought of him as a kind of challenge. Now what did that make me?

For in a peculiar way I did enjoy his funny little ways. I knew of course that he was only waiting for me to screw up so that he could despise me as much as he did the rest of the world. But I made damn sure nothing went wrong. It was a secret game we played whenever he was in the mood for another round; the conflict that dare not speak its name. I suppose we both knew that in the nature of things sooner or later I would fail and that this would confirm his view of humanity. I'm not sure what would have happened then. I never did understood what made Grieder tick. Not even at the end, after everything that happened.

Get your retaliation in first, I decided and I telephoned his Brussels office. But he wasn't available of course. I left a message with one of his personal secretaries outlining my progress on the search and I hoped it sounded convincing enough to keep him of my back for a week or so.

Then I cooked an omelette fine herbe and ate it with some rather nice wholemeal bread from a local health food shop. What a busy morning, I thought, and completely forgot about the break-in at police headquarters.

# CHAPTER 3

Just after two o'clock I strolled past the sober facades of Edinburgh's New Town and found Raven's offices half way round a stylish crescent overlooking small private gardens full of mature trees and thick shrubs. I mounted the steps and pushed open the heavy front door. My footsteps rang on the marble floor of a lofty Georgian entrance hall. An elaborately painted ceiling covered with decorative plasterwork arched high above me. In the centre of the hall stood two tall columns, crowned with formal neo-classical capitals and trying to look like marble. I tapped them as I passed and was pleased to hear the sound of hollow wood. How very Edinburgh, I thought. In one corner of the hall a flight of stone steps with a fine mahogany hand rail and heavy cast iron ornamental balusters led upwards. On the wall was a board bearing the Raven and Thompson name and an impressive list of companies registered at this address.

I took a few moments to study the list. These were businesses the firm represented in some way and the list was impressive. There were some international corporations, mostly in property-related businesses to judge from their names; a couple of building and construction companies, a property development company, a hotel and leisure corporation, something called Thai Entertainment Developments in Bangkok and a US-registered group of restaurants and casinos. I frowned. It didn't sound quite right for Edinburgh. But I had heard that Anthony Raven was far from a conventional solicitor, dealing in conservative wills, family trusts and house conveyancing.

An arrow pointed mutely upwards and on the first floor I found a pigeon-hole with a sliding glass screen and a middle-aged receptionist who seemed to spend most of her time saying, "Raven and Thompson" into the office telephone system. She peered at me questioningly from behind metal-framed spectacles and when she heard my name she nodded shortly and indicated a large door opposite. "Please have a seat in the boardroom. I'll let Mr Raven know you are here."

I gave her my best smile and the full Lennox charm--- on the principle that it does no harm to have an ally in a client's office. "Shall I be meeting Mr Thompson as well?" I enquired ingenuously.

She looked at me pityingly. "There is no Mr Thompson," she said simply. "There hasn't been a Mr Thompson for many years. Not in my time at the firm."

"And have you been here long?" I ventured.

She looked at me demurely. "Since I left college," she admitted.

"So that must be--- what? Five or six years?" I said brazenly.

She gave me a withering look. "I'll tell Mr Raven you're waiting," she said bleakly and pointed towards the boardroom again. But when I glanced back at her she was watching me with a smile on her face. Hey, I thought, another success!

I opened the heavy panelled door and found myself in a long, elegant Georgian drawing room which was still much as it must have looked in the eighteenth century when the building was new. The ceiling had the original plasterwork or an excellent reconstruction and at one end of the room there was what looked like a genuine Adam fireplace. On the mantle-piece a large marble clock ticked nervously against the silence of the room and in front of the fireplace was a large traditional lawyer's desk, covered with the large traditional bundles of documents.

In the middle of the room a modern boardroom table took up most of the floor space. I don't think Robert Adam would have like it. Nor the odd-looking modern glass-fronted display case that stood between the tall curtained windows. I walked across to the display case and peered in. It was about five feet high, with internal lighting and what seemed to be a sophisticated temperature and humidity control system.

I stared in fascination. The bottom of the case was filled with a mass of succulent fleshy leaves in a rich confusion of shapes and sizes and shades of green. From the base of each clump a long slender stalk reached up towards the top of the case, bearing a spray of the most beautiful and delicate blossoms I had ever seen. Each one was subtly different in colour and shape from the others and yet clearly somehow they were all related. I was so engrossed in the strange exotic display that I was startled to hear a voice behind me. "Ah, a lover of beauty, Mr Lennox? How do you like my Phalaenopsis? Lovely things, aren't they. You've discovered one of my little weaknesses!"

I turned to see Raven close behind me. I don't know when he had come into the room. Certainly I had not heard the door open. He stood for a moment studying me, a curious smile on his lips. It was the first time we had met face to face and I had to admit, despite of a certain reluctance on my part, he was impressive. He was a big man, an inch perhaps taller than me which would make him six one or so, with strong square shoulders and a figure that was still trim and fit looking.

He was wearing brown shoes, with a well-cut grey Prince

of Wales check suit, a pale pink shirt and a slightly countrified cotton tie with a deep maroon paisley pattern. He seemed younger than his fifty years; his hair dark and full, his features pleasantly strong and tanned, his brown eyes clear and frank. Other than the brown shoes, and my prejudices apart, he seemed like a man with whom in other circumstances I might have done business.

Still without taking his eyes from me, he went on, "They are delicate little things. Very beautiful. It's just that they take so much looking after. They need a specially caring environment, you see. They wouldn't survive long in the cold outside world. Do you know much about the orchid family, Mr Lennox?"

I shook my head. He was trying to tell me something, and it wasn't just about orchids. He crossed the room and stood beside me, gazing admiringly at the blossoms, making no effort to introduce himself. "They are so vulnerable, at one level. And yet you know, orchids are one of the most ruthless and successful families in the plant world. They've colonised the entire globe, from sea-level to the high mountains."

"Expensive to keep too, I bet."

Raven glanced sideways at me and smiled his strange little smile again. "You're so right, Lennox. Very expensive to keep. But when you have something rare and beautiful, does cost matter?"

"I suppose that depends on whether you can afford it."

He sighed, "Indeed it does, Lennox. I see you're a realist, as well as a lover of beauty. Come and have a seat." He led me to his desk and gestured me into an arm chair. "You might say that orchids are realists too, Lennox. That's the thing I admire most about them, actually. Not only are they beautiful but they are wonderfully equipped to survive." He rocked back in his seat behind the desk and clasped his hands behind his head. His light brown eyes gazed at me steadily. "You know, with some species of orchids it's not the fittest that survive. It's the most deceptive. Do you like that idea?"

He was starting to irritate me. "They sound a bit like lawyers," I said with a polite smile.

He roared with laughter and leaning forward pressed a switch on his telephone. "Touché," he said. "I knew we had a lot in common." He smiled at me amiably. "Yes, just like some lawyers. Well, like people I suppose. You see, they have learned how to play on powerful basic impulses. Like greed and lust. And fear," he added casually. "You know, they deceive poor insects into helping them to reproduce by making themselves into exact images of female flies or bees, to lure foolish males into attempting copulation and in the process spreading their pollen abroad."

He smiled at me again but this time his dark eyes seemed to turn curiously opaque. "To make it more confusing, Lennox, they also make themselves look like potential enemies and that incites insects into violent attacks. Same result, of course! Sex and violence." He glanced at me dispassionately. "Coffee? Or would you prefer tea?"

I decided right then that Raven was definitely no ordinary Edinburgh lawyer. "Tea will be fine," I said, glancing conspicuously at my watch.

He ordered the tea and leaned forward towards me. "But I mustn't prattle on about my obsessions," he said with a smile. "You're a busy man I understand. Let me tell you my problem. I have a client called Island Developments. It is an investment company registered in Liechtenstein for tax reasons. The exact ownership isn't important at this stage. But I can assure you they will not cavil at paying substantial professional fees. However, they do expect high standards. They have the resources to pay for the best advice and it is their policy to do so."

27

He broke off as the receptionist brought in a silver tray complete with fine china cups and saucers, silver Georgian tea-pot, a matching milk jug and sugar bowl and a platter of biscuits. He cleared a space amongst the papers and she set the tray down reverentially on his desk. "Biscuits!" he said, raising an eyebrow. You're honoured, Lennox. Milk?" he asked, pouring out a cup and sliding it across the desk towards me. I nodded, trying to look as if silver and a china service was my normal style in the afternoon.

"But no sugar," I said, virtuously. "So what do you do for this client, Mr Raven? And how do you think I can help?"

"Oh, we do various things, mostly to do with commercial property transactions." He waved aside my question. "The situation is that recently they acquired an estate in the Orkney Islands."

Orkney, I thought? Good sailing if you know what you're doing and have a boat to suit those rather tricky waters. As it happened, I knew someone who lived there and if he didn't have boat it would be because the whisky had finally got to him.

Raven went on. "The estate is called Scarisby. The plan is to develop it as a leisure and sporting complex, partly commercially and partly for the private use of the principals and their guests. I should tell you that I have counselled against the idea, but my clients are determined to proceed." He rocked back in his seat and smiled at me. "What they need at this stage is an experienced Project Manager to prepare an overall development scheme and to supervise its implementation. So the individual must be qualified technically--- a surveyor most probably--- ideally with experience of developing similar sporting estates and the management ability to handle wealthy, demanding clients. I have a set of notes outlining the situation that I can pass on to you."

28

I felt a real sense of relief as I shrugged and sipped my tea in what I hoped was a genteel manner. "It sounds interesting, Mr Raven. But it isn't really my scene. I know next to nothing about the leisure field. I wouldn't know where to start looking. But I'm sure there are other consultants who can help you, people who specialise in that kind of work. Why not try one of them?

Raven eyed me for a moment. "Good of you to be so frank, Lennox. But I didn't make myself clear. We have already advertised the position in the specialist press and we have a number of potential candidates. What the client would like is your assessment of their managerial competence."

I nodded thoughtfully. "Well, I could certainly handle that for you," I admitted. "But as I said, I'm heavily committed on another assignment that will keep me occupied for the next few weeks. I'm don't think--- "

He cut me off. "Ah yes, the search you're doing for Odin Investments." He saw the look on my face and gave me his knowing little smile. "I did say your activities were well known. You should know how difficult it is to keep a secret in this town."

Ouch, I thought. "So it would seem," I said shortly.

"Well, legal and financial circles do overlap at a number of points, you know." He sounded almost apologetic. "So I had heard something about it." He shook his head sadly. "Edinburgh is an incestuous place. As I said, difficult to keep a secret here!"

Bloody hell, I thought. Now it's not only the actuaries who are organising my assignments. The whole damn town is in on the act. Maybe I should ask him who's going to get the job. He went on easily. "Now I appreciate that you probably have a special relationship with Hans Grieder. I mean, you must have," he glanced at me, "to act for him as frequently as you do."

I did my looking modest bit. "I'm not sure anyone has a special relationship with a man like Mr Grieder." Damn right, I thought to myself.

"Yes, I've heard he's a bit of a recluse," Raven said. "But interesting, none the less." He gazed at me thoughtfully. "Still," he went on briskly, "that's another matter. If there is any way you could fit in my client's work without too much inconvenience to Mr Grieder, well, we'd be most grateful. And of course for your assistance at such short notice we'd be prepared to agree a fee that recognised the extra effort. Something rather more than your normal rate. By the way, what do you charge, normally?"

I thought quickly. For a lot of reasons, not all of them rational, I didn't want to become involved with Raven. I picked my highest daily rate--- the one I use for merchant bankers and other profligates who are spending other people's money. Then for good measure I added fifty percent. I gave him the figure.

He didn't even blink. "That sounds fine," he said. "Suppose we were to double that--- for a total of, say, ten days or so?"

I was tempted. That kind of money would buy me a new spinnaker sail. "It's an attractive offer," I said. "But I think it's unlikely I could fit it into my programme. Perhaps I can get back to you when I've assessed my workload." Get me out of here, I thought, before I find myself working for Patricia Raven's husband!

Raven nodded and glanced at his watch. "Please do. I'm going up to Orkney this afternoon to--- ", he shot a glance at me appraisingly, "to see how things are going. I'll call you from there tomorrow to hear how your plans work out." He stood up, briefly shook my hand and ushered me out to the staircase. As I started down towards the pillared entrance hall he called after me, "If you're really interested in orchidacea you should come and have a look at the collection I have at home. You haven't been to my home, have you?"

I glanced back at him sharply. He was standing above me on the stairs, looking down with that odd little smile on his lips. "I can't say that flowers are a special interest of mine, Mr Raven. But I do envy you. After all, thing of beauty is a joy forever, isn't it? "

The smile faded suddenly. "Ah my dear Lennox. If only it were so easy." He shook his head. "If only it were so easy." He turned away, leaving me standing there alone.

Jesus, I thought. First Hans Grieder and now Raven! Why do all the crazy ones pick on me? I shrugged my shoulders. But at least they were high-paying crazies.

# CHAPTER 4

As I walked back to my flat I noticed that out over the Forth estuary thin torn strips of high cirrus cloud were creeping in from the west. That is where most of our weather comes from and those clouds usually meant a change, probably for the worse, with winds strong enough to make sailing even on the cold estuary more uncomfortable than usual. I was studying the local tide-tables trying to work out whether I could fit in a quick sail before the weather really turned nasty when the telephone rang. I picked it up and the voice at the other end was instantly recognisable, though it had been months since I had seen her. But the low intimate tone, the confidential half whisper, was unmistakeable.

"Hello," she said. "It's me. I'm sorry it's been so long. You must have thought I was dead. Maybe you wish I was. Can you ever forgive me?"

I think it's called defusing righteous anger and it's a great technique. especially if you look like Patricia Raven. I took a deep breath. "I recognise the voice," I said, trying to sound blasé and indifferent. "But could you just remind me about the name."

She gave a throaty laugh. "Oh you men," she said. "You're so inconstant. It's me. The one you said you would love for ever."

"I'm sorry, that really isn't much help. You'll have to be more explicit."

"Pig!" she said mockingly. Then she gave another of her surprisingly unladylike deep and dirty laughs. "But I am quite prepared to be as explicit as you like." I was trying to think of an answer to that when she went on. "I hear you've been speaking to someone I know," she said casually. "What did he want? Is it something you can tell me about?"

Ah, I thought. So that's why she's ringing. Not a guilty conscience, surely? "How did you know I had been to see him?" I asked.

"Oh, I happened to call the office this afternoon about something else. It was quite a shock when the secretary told me you were with him." Her voice became lower and more urgent. "It brought everything back to me. Oh darling, how I miss you. You do understand, don't you? But at times it all seems so useless and I hate to mess up your life again. And yet, when I heard your name---"

Get a grip, I told myself as my head began to swim. You've heard it all before--- a dozen times. I thought of saying something flippant, like "I know. My name has that effect on women. I'm thinking of changing it by deed poll." But instead I heard myself saying, like some conditioned reflex, "I've missed you too".

"Have you, darling? Really?" She sighed. "I wish I could believe that, Terry. I need to believe it, you know. You mustn't say it if you don't mean it. You don't know how much it means to me. Things here are so awful."

Suddenly I found myself reassuring her. Of course I knew that I was being taken for a ride. But to be frank, I didn't care. "Of course I miss you. But you always know where to find me, Patricia. I'm not the one who vanishes for months on end."

"Oh, you do hate me!" She sounded dejected. Then she went on. "But look, I'll make it up to you, Terry. One reason for calling is to say that I have two tickets for the English National Theatre tonight. You see, I'm on my own for a while."

The mice are dancing while the cat is away, I thought. "Yes, I knew that you were going to be on your own," I said. "What's the play."

"The Way of the World." She had the good grace to give a nervous little laugh. Then there was a pause. "Congreve and restoration comedy. Would you come with me tonight? It will be so lovely to do something together. Something public and--- normal."

I knew what she meant. There had been a time when I wondered if she really existed outside my flat. So doing something together appealed to me; ordinary things like buying her a programme and sitting together in a crowded theatre, surrounded by Edinburgh's finest. It seemed to give the relationship, if that was what we had, some kind of legitimacy. And who cared if Anthony Raven heard about it? At least I would avoid his weird assignment. So I said yes, and we arranged to meet inside the theatre foyer at seven fifteen that evening. I hung up the telephone and stared into the mirror. What was she up to? "Damn you Lennox," I said to my reflection. "You and your fatal charm." But he didn't look entirely convinced about it either.

In spite of my all doubts I arrived at the theatre before seven o'clock, in case she was early. The place was buzzing with people trying to buy last minute tickets, finding their way around the grand Victorian foyer, meeting their friends and finding the toilets--- all the things you have to do before a great cultural experience. It always surprised me that in a town like Edinburgh you could stand and watch a thousand people, selected more or less at random from the sentient classes and not see anyone you know. It seemed statistically unlikely. But there it was. Seven fifteen came and went but still no Patricia. I wandered off and bought a programme. Seven twenty-five, and the foyer emptied as the lucky punters who had tickets found their seats and the others drifted off to the pubs.

Suddenly she was there beside me, tall and slim, auburn hair falling over her shoulders and swaying loosely as she approached me, moving with the easy grace of a thoroughbred filly. A long, close fitting skirt of some silky material, boldly patterned in blue and tan, clung artfully to her slender thighs as she walked. It managed to look expensive and informal at the same time. It was probably Escada or Laurel and with it she wore a more formal dark blue jacket out of the same stable and a pale blue silk shirt open casually at the neck. Her skin glowed, tanned and golden from some early summer Mediterranean holiday taken since I had last seen her. Her only jewellery was a simple heavy gold chain around her slender neck. And her wedding ring, of course. I noticed that.

She took my arm, in the same instant reaching up to give me a chaste peck on the cheek in the approved social manner. When she wasn't around I somehow forgot how beautiful she was. Well, to be truthful I tried not to think about it. But the sight of her fine high-boned features and full lips, the wide-spaced, almond-shaped eyes; large, tawny brown and at times almost yellowish in colour, struck home and I was hooked again. "I'm sorry I'm late," she murmured. "We'd better go straight in."

Our seats were at the end of a row. Patricia seemed strangely nervous, looking around anxiously as we settled down. I handed her the programme. She smiled graciously at me and flicked through it in a half-hearted way. We had arrived just as the house lights dimmed and the audience noise died away. Any moment now the curtain would rise. She leaned close to me and said quietly, "Do you really want to see this play? Or would you rather go somewhere more private?"

She never failed to surprise me--- that was one of her charms. But what was this all about? I remembered my Congreve. "Women are like tricks by slight of hand, which to admire we should not understand."

"This would be a good time to go, if we're going," I said and we made a hurried exit. By the time the curtain rose we were at the back of the auditorium and ten minutes later we were in my flat. About two minutes after that we were in bed together and it was as if she had never been away.

About half-an hour later I raised myself on one arm and looked down at her. I ran my hand gently down across her flanks, as slim and athletic as a young boy's. A thin film of perspiration coated her skin. "So how did you enjoy the first act?"

She opened her eyes and gave me a dreamy look. "I loved it," she murmured. "I can't wait for the rest of the play."

Much later, as we lay quietly together, she whispered "Thank you, Terry. You don't know how much it means to me to be able to see you like this. I feel clean again. You take everything horrible away."

I frowned and kissed her lightly. "Clean? Horrible?"

"You don't know how wonderful it is to be here with you. You have no idea what life with Anthony is like for me."

It was unusual for her ever to refer to Raven. I frowned at her again. "Is it so very different with him?"

I could feel her mood change. She laughed bitterly and rolled away from me. "You have no idea. You really have no idea, do you?" she said, absently glancing at her watch.

36

Grabbing her by the shoulders I gave her a gentle shake. "Then tell me," I said. "I want to know what's going on."

She lay back and studied me. Her eyes glittered almost yellow through narrow slits. "You treat me like a woman," she said slowly and deliberately. "My husband doesn't."

I shrugged. "Familiarity," I said. "It's not unnatural for a marriage to go cold in that way."

Her eyes flared resentfully. "You won't understand, will you! But unnatural is a good word for Anthony. You see, he likes to play games, nasty little games that give him pleasure. Anthony has his own uses for me; things he expects me to do."

I stared down at her, scarcely beginning to guess at what she was telling me. "Patricia, he can't make you do anything against your will. You can always tell him to go to hell. You don't belong to him, after all."

She interrupted me, angrily. "Oh you don't understand, Terry. You've never wanted to own anyone or anything. But that's exactly what Anthony wants. He wants to own me--- completely and utterly."

"That's crazy," I said, shaking my head. "If you don't like what's going on, leave him. Get out."

She slumped back against the pillow and looked at me from under her eye-lashes for a long moment. Then she gave a half-smile. "You're very sweet, Terry. But you just don't understand. Nothing is that simple."

"From what your telling me it shouldn't be difficult to get a divorce if his behaviour is so--- ," I chose my word carefully, 'peculiar'. Why don't you just clear out?"

She gave an ugly harsh laugh and shook her head irritably. The laughter sounded cruel but I knew it was aimed mostly at herself. "And go where? There's the small matter of money, darling. Money," she said harshly. "Money and---," she paused and looked quickly away. "Other things." She glanced at her watch again. "Anyway, he would never allow me to leave. Anthony never lets go of any of his possessions. Though sometimes he gives them away." She laughed again, resentfully. Then she turned to me and put her arms round me, kissing me gently. Her tawny eyes half filled with tears. "Be glad you don't understand, Terry. I hope you never do. But I don't want to talk about it."

I lay back in bed, watching her dress and repair her make-up and hair. "Let me call a taxi for you."

Peering into my bedside mirror to apply her lipstick she smiled a twisted smile at me. "No need. I left my car round the corner from here on my way to the theatre." So she had planned the whole thing from the beginning. Good old Congreve. She glanced at me. "Are you going to help Anthony?"

I shook my head, "Probably not."

"What a shame," she said casually. "Maybe you should. It would be nice to think you were there somehow; a little closer to me in a way." So she knew he had offered me an assignment.

I walked with her to where her car was parked in a side street that sloped steeply down beside one of the New Town's formal gardens. It was close to midnight and the streets were deserted. The early summer light had finally gone from the sky, the only illumination came from amber streetlamps flickering fitfully through the trees and the noises of the city were stilled apart from the occasional sound of a distant car. It was as if we were walking alone in some lonely country lane. She kissed me briefly and without a word slid gracefully into her car.

As I watched her drive away I realised she had said nothing about meeting me again. I shrugged. Nothing new there, I thought.

"Apart from that, Mrs Raven," I said to myself, "how did you enjoy the play?"

# CHAPTER 5

Next morning I woke early, tumbled out of bed and started to work painfully through those exercises my physiotherapist insists on if I plan to go on walking upright. Then I showered and shaved and started to make coffee, decaffeinated of course. I read somewhere that the real stuff does awful things to your mental processes. In my condition I couldn't take any chances. On reflection though, I decided that after last night I was probably too far gone for a spot of caffeine to do any harm.

I sipped the coffee and thought about Patricia Raven. This was always an enjoyable process, especially the idea that she found me irresistible. But attractive as that notion was I really didn't buy it. I had that old feeling that she was playing a game with me and a game in which I was somehow only a minor player. I headed for the CD-player and some suitable music. The Brahms concerto for violin and cello filled the sunlit kitchen. Balance and harmony, that was what I needed. Life might be worth living after all, as long as I didn't try to make too much of events like the previous night.

My mood was definitely improving. But Patricia's words still nagged at me. At times she seemed absolutely sincere, totally genuine. Having met Anthony Raven now, I knew instinctively there was something very odd about him. I sensed it, although I couldn't quite define it. So did she really need help? Not that she had ever asked for help in so many words. OK, Raven played weird games with his wife--- apparently physically as well as psychologically. Did that matter in the great scheme of things? Did I care if he tied her to the bed-posts and did unspeakable things to her? Did I care if she enjoyed it?

I decided it was time to think about something else. Harmony and balance, that's the thing. That was when my telephone rang. I turned down the music and picked up the receiver. "Good morning, Lennox. How are you this morning? Suitably refreshed, I hope?"

I don't believe this, I thought. It was Raven. And this time when I heard his voice I definitely didn't have a clear conscience. "I'm well rested, thank you," was the best I could do.

"Good, good," Raven said briskly. "Because I'm hoping there's a lot you can do for me."

This is getting worse, I thought.

"I've been thinking about our discussion. My client and I agree it is essential for us to have the best possible advice in making this appointment. I'm authorised therefore to offer you a fixed bonus of ten thousand pounds, in addition to the daily fee rate we agreed. Payable in advance to defray your expenses."

I took a deep breath. Ten grand up front would defray quite a few expenses--- including a new spinnaker for the boat. I started to rationalise rapidly. My Odin search assignment had reached a quiescent stage or at least a natural break. I could put it on hold for a week or so. And enjoyable though Patricia was, it might be no bad thing to keep out of her way for a while. Especially when her husband was footing the bill.

"That sounds interesting, Mr Raven. On that basis I think I probably can help you."

"Excellent," he purred. "I was sure we could make it interesting for you. I'd like you to start immediately. My office is sending you round some paperwork on the candidates and also the project briefing notes. I've done a preliminary sift of the replies to our advertisement and there are a few possibles we'd like you to interview. My secretary has arranged for each of them to visit Orkney and spend a day there. I suggest you see them up there. She will book you into the same hotel as the candidates to make it simple. Tell her if you need anything else. By the way, there is a flight just after four o'clock today. I hope you will be able to make that."

I had the distinct feeling I was being hijacked. But sometimes you have to put the client's needs first; and then there was the matter of the extra ten grand. I spent the rest of the day going through my mail, arranging the details of my trip with Raven's secretary, and leaving another reassuring message for Grieder. "He's out of the country, Mr Lennox," his PA said, "But he'll be pleased to know things are going well."

That wasn't exactly what I had told her, but I decided to let it go. My mail consisted of the good news from the Readers Digest that I had come through the first three stages of a competition I didn't know I had entered. There was also a large brown envelop with a London postmark and inside a set of published accounts for the Irving Group. Donald Lynch had also included an organisation chart showing the principal operating companies and their main activities.

At first glance it looked like a complete dog's breakfast, a classic example of a collection of businesses put together by family owners on a series of whims, with no strategy other than providing members of the family with more or less gainful employment.

There was a Bus and Transport Division which to judge from the Chairman's enthusiastic report was their traditional core business. They probably should have stuck to it. Then there was a fuel distribution business, which seemed to make sense as a diversification. But the rest of the group consisted of a retail electrical chain, a TV rental company and a company providing consumer credit facilities for retail customers--- none of which made obvious sense to me. Turnover was just over twelve million pounds with profit before tax of less than a million. I could see why they had head-hunted Donald. If ever a business needed strategic development it was the Irving Group.

Donald's notes explained that he had taken over as Managing Director of the consumer credit company and was also Group Director of Strategic Development with a seat on the main board. I flicked through the accounts. I don't know what the collective noun for Irvings might be but there was certainly a proliferation of them, all with shareholdings and options and most of them on the board.

Other than that, there wasn't much I could tell from one set of annual accounts, though it was clear Donald would have his work cut out with the credit company, which was barely breaking even. But without detailed trading and management accounting information even a trained accountant would find it difficult to make sense of the figures and I was no accountant.

On the other hand I knew Donald was, and a very good one. He must have studied the business thoroughly before he agreed to join them. So what was his problem? I sighed and tossed the accounts aside. He'd have to explain it to me.

Right now I needed to prepare for a trip to Orkney.

# CHAPTER 6

The slab-sided Loganair Shorts 3-60 squatted on the runway at Edinburgh Airport, looking worryingly like a caravan with wings. But once in the air its traditional prop engines droned steadily on, reassuringly noisy, as the landscape slipped away beneath us. The rivers with their checker-boards of green farmland and then the wild massive bulk of the Cairngorms, mottled and dark like ancient weed-encrusted monsters rising from the deep, drifted past. Then there was a brief stop at Inverness Airport, an oasis of cultivation in the mountains, before the short final flight across to Orkney.

The islands appeared suddenly on the horizon, a handful of low, green mounds scattered across the blue-grey ocean, with here and there a fringe of golden sands. The sky was bright and the sun still high, although far out to the east I could see a long rolling bank of fog on the cold North Sea, held temporarily at bay by the warmth of the land. Then swiftly we were down and taxiing towards the homely little terminal building, a metal-construction with a tiny customs office and incongruous warning notices about drugs. It must have taken me all of ten minutes to get out of the aircraft, claim my baggage and collect a hire car. In twelve minutes flat I was on the road to Kirkwall.

On the flight I had studied the papers Raven sent me. There was a map of the Scarisby estate, which seemed to be located at the extreme end of the most southerly island of the archipelago, linked by a series of causeways to the mainland of Orkney. The house was empty but the keys were held at a nearby farmhouse and I could pick them up there when I wanted to see the place. The candidates for the job had been scheduled at the comfortable rate of two each day over the next three days. Not exactly a back breaking programme and one that would give me time to look the place over early next morning, before I started the interviews.

I thought about an old contact of mine who was living here. He was in fact a local, an Orcadian who had come down to university in Edinburgh during my time there. His name was Tom Drever and I hadn't seen him for years. But during our misspent youth and from time to time since he had been a chum of mine, mainly on account of our shared passion for sailing--- and his phenomenal capacity for whisky. We had kept in touch over the years, although our paths had taken us in very different directions. I went away to business school in the States, while he became a journalist, first on a local Edinburgh paper and later, as his reputation grew, on Fleet Street. Presumably his capacity for drink had been no disadvantage there. Then abruptly it seemed he had given it all up and gone home, tired of southern parts, to take over as Editor of the local weekly. If nothing else, as he wrote to me at the time, it meant he was closer to the distillery.

By seven o'clock I had checked into the comfortable but faintly synthetic hotel Raven's secretary had chosen for me. I found Tom's number amongst the host of Drevers in the slim volume of the Orkney telephone directory and we arranged to meet. "But not where you're staying," he said firmly. "There's a real pub down the street by the harbour. I'll see you there." So just after eight I walked into the pub, past a row of blackened old rum barrels and into the tiny snug at the back of the public bar. Tom was standing with his back to an old-fashioned fireplace where, in spite of the summer weather outside, a coal fire glowed. I decided the locals knew something about the weather.

45

Tom's big round face, pink and gleaming from long hours of sailing and drinking, split in a broad smile. He waved a glass in my direction. "Terry Lennox, you old bastard!" he boomed. "What brings you up here? I thought you were a perpetual jet setter." He seemed to fill the room. But Tom always seemed to fill a room. He was only of average height, maybe five ten at most, but that was all that was average about Tom Drever. I suppose you'd describe him as on the fat side of plump, but his heavy-boned, powerful frame somehow made him seem merely solidly built. With his thick torsoed body, topped by an almost completely round head with cropped red hair, he reminded me of a stone pillar with a cannonball perched on top.

He was almost as indestructible. Tom was one of nature's tight-head props though, thank god, I had never had to scrummage against him. For he was incredibly strong, the only man I ever saw move a full-sized billiard table on his own. Just why he wanted to move it I can't remember. But at the time he had seemed determined to do it--- and it usually wasn't a good idea to stop Tom Drever once had he decided to do something. Luckily, most of the time Tom was endlessly good-humoured.

He stood there now, brown tweed jacket, cords and a pair of heavy brogue shoes with scraps of mud sticking to the soles, and a coarse checked shirt open at the neck, looking every inch a local crofter. But his soft brown eyes surveyed me shrewdly and appraisingly. He grabbed my hand. "What'll you have. You're still a whisky man?" he asked me anxiously in the broad vowels of the islands. He had retained that accent even during his London days.

We sat near the fire and looked each other over. At first sight it was easy to dismiss Tom as a backwoodsman and I knew some who had made that mistake. Certainly, when it suited him, he could play the hayseed as well as anyone. But under the couthy facade I knew there was a quick and sophisticated mind. He had picked up a First in physics at

Edinburgh with no apparent effort and he might have gone on to a career as a scientist or an academic. A glass of Highland Park appeared and I sipped it appreciatively. "Ten years old," Tom said. "None of that ponsy sixteen year old stuff." He grinned at me. "So what brings you up here," he asked again.

I told him the story about Raven, at least the part I could tell. "Well, well, there's a strange thing." He said and leaned back, the chair creaking ominously under his bulk.

I looked enquiringly at him.

"I have a bit of an interest in Scarisby myself," he said. "You know about McNaughton and how he died?"

I shook my head. "Who's McNaughton? And remember, what I told you about the development plans for the estate. They are confidential at this stage. So don't print anything in your paper yet."

Tom Drever guffawed with laughter. "Who's McNaughton, did you say? Why he's about the most exciting thing that's happened here in fifty years! His family owned Scarisby for three or four generations." He looked thoughtful. "Though they were in-comers. They moved up here from the south in the middle of the last century."

I nodded. "So how does Anthony Raven's client come to own the estate?"

"Archie McNaughton was a bachelor with no living relatives. Scarisby was sold by his lawyer to meet the inheritance tax bill plus one or two small legacies." Tom looked at me pointedly. "His lawyer was Anthony Raven."

I raised my eyebrows. "That's interesting, certainly. But not necessarily a conflict of interest, if that's what your thinking. What is it about McNaughton that makes him so exciting?"

Tom rocked back and beamed at me. "Just as I said; the way he died. Quite apart from his life, which was interesting enough. But you'll need to read the book I'm writing about it."

I ordered two more whiskies and settled down for what was clearly going to be a long session. "A book? Come on Tom, tell me! What's the story?"

He shook his head sadly. "I despair of you folk in the big cities. You never seem to know what's going on." He drained his first glass and reached for a full one. "Archie McNaughton was well known in nationalist political circles. A bit of an eccentric in some ways. A keen amateur archaeologist, like his father before him who spent a lot of the family money excavating old stone age sites, tombs and the like on his estate."

"Being an archaeologist, even an amateur one, doesn't seem very eccentric to me."

"No?" said Tom. "But then you are an eccentric!" He roared with delight and slapped his great thighs. I had the feeling he had been waiting for someone to fall for that gag for a long time.

Eventually he quietened down. "The thing is, Archie was more than just a little eccentric. He had a few, well, genuine peculiarities that might have prevented him from going all the way to the top politically if ever they had become known about publicly." Tom squinted at me over his glass. "I did say he was a bachelor? Well, there was absolutely no chance of him having any children, to judge from his sexual habits." Tom shrugged. "Be that as it may, he was on track to be a parliamentary candidate and might even have won the seat. Then there would have been no holding him." He nodded thoughtfully. "Archie was a man of some charm when he wanted to be, and of great ability too, in spite of his oddities.

"So what went wrong?"

"What went wrong was that one wild night last year, towards the end of October, he killed himself. On his way back from a meeting in Sutherland he shot himself in the head and drove his car over a cliff in South Ronaldsay."

I blinked. "In that order? Wasn't that a bit excessive? To say nothing of unusual?"

"Not to say bloody difficult, if you ask me." Tom tilted his head sideways, half in amusement. "A lot of folk thought there was something odd about it. Especially his boy friend, a young lad called Norman Orr who had been living with him at Scarisby." Tom shrugged his shoulders indifferently. "Well, I presume that was the relationship. But whatever, the boy was convinced McNaughton didn't kill himself. Certainly he seemed to have everything going for him at the time, so it's hard to see a motive for suicide. That's what interested me originally. As you know, folk usually drive somewhere quiet if they intend to kill themselves in a car. Though McNaughton was never a man to do anything by half." He glanced across at me. "There are a few strange aspects to the thing. That's why I'm writing the book."

I frowned. "What do you think happened, Tom?"

He grimaced. "The inquest was clear enough. He was shot in the head at close range with a bullet from his own revolver. Then his car went out of control and over a nearby cliff. Luckily it didn't burn, so the evidence was more or less intact, though banged about a bit by the rocks and the sea."

"But still you seem to have some doubts?"

Tom shrugged his shoulders. "Not doubts, exactly. But there were some aspects that interested me."

"Like why he was carrying a revolver in the first place?"

49

Tom nodded. "Yes. Plus the fact that we know of no reason for him to top himself. The authorities made a lot out of his bouts of heavy drinking and periods of depression." He laughed abruptly, "But that isn't exactly unusual in these parts. And his young man, his companion he called himself, says that McNaughton did express fears for his safety. One theory is that he made some powerful enemies in the business world. He was forever championing worthy causes like anti-nuclear protests and land reform, which didn't endear him to the big corporations and the absentee land-owners."

"Sounds as if he had antagonised some influential lobbies," I said thoughtfully.

"Yes, he had certainly done that. There's no doubt he was very effective in pushing objections to developments all over the north. He was a lawyer and a good one, and he didn't pull any punches I can tell you! So he had cost some people a lot of money, one way or another. And he looked likely to cost them more."

"I'm surprised they didn't simply buy him off, if he was causing that much trouble. You know the sort of thing, a consultancy retainer or an appointment as special counsel somewhere."

Tom smiled grimly. "I understand that's exactly what they did try. But Archie McNaughton was a rare animal; a man of integrity. That's what made him so dangerous, and so interesting from my point of view. Or maybe he was more ambitious than that," he added cautiously. "Anyway, I'm investigating the whole thing and putting forward some other theories about his death."

"Murder?" I insisted. "Political assassination? Pretty far fetched, isn't it?"

Tom downed his drink. "Maybe. But according to young

Norman Orr there were papers missing from McNaughton's briefcase--- depositions and statements relating to a claim he was handling against the nuclear industry. The briefcase was found in the car more or less intact. But the inquest decided the documents could have been lost as the car crashed. Norman Orr wasn't convinced, though."

I frowned. "McNaughton would have to be causing a lot of trouble for anyone to go that far. Still," I grinned at him, "it will make a good story. At least I hope so for your sake. By the way, what happened to the young man--- this Norman Orr? I take it he's not still at the house?"

Tom waved for another two glasses of whisky. "No, he's disappeared. He did hang around for a while until all the formalities were over. Then he took off somewhere. Probably went down to London or Edinburgh where he has friends, I understand. With McNaughton dead there was nothing to keep him here. He got a small amount of money from the estate and cleared off." Tom smiled grimly. "I suppose he wasn't in a party mood."

I must have looked puzzled, for Tom went on, "Oh, there have been strange stories about Scarisby over the past year or two. About peculiar parties, with young men being brought in to entertain older men, who were supposed to be here for the fishing. Not that we have much more than rumours to go on. So if there was something odd going on at Scarisby they were very discreet about it. Certainly young Norman Orr had nothing to say about it." He chuckled into his drink. "I just hope trout was all they caught." He looked up at me cannily, "You may know," he said, "the fishing in South Ronaldsay is not that good. Most of the best trout lochs are here on the mainland. Which makes your plan to develop the place as a sporting estate just a wee bit odd too."

I shook my head at him sadly. "What a den of iniquity! And I thought I was escaping from wicked old Edinburgh!"

Tom was beginning to show the signs of his Highland Park. He leaned back in his chair. "Wicked old Edinburgh indeed," he boomed. "At least we don't have folk stealing things from our police stations up here. Now that really was an interesting story!"

I recalled the newspaper report about the break-in at police headquarters and frowned at him. "Come on Tom, what is this all about?"

He laughed and shook his head. "That will have to be another book!" he said. "In the meantime you'll just have to draw your own conclusions. You Edinburgh folk with your rent-boys! I wish you'd keep them down south."

"What are you telling me, Tom?" I asked. But half-a dozen drinks later there was still nothing more I could get out of him. Just after midnight I remembered that I had promised myself a visit to Scarisby early next morning so I extricated myself with difficulty, arranging to meet Tom for dinner the following evening. I tottered along the silent harbour front and fell into my virtuous bed.

CHAPTER 7

Next morning, early and surprisingly bright, I headed over the Churchill Barriers towards South Ronaldsay. The barriers had been built to keep enemy submarines away from the British fleet in Scapa flow and in the process had created a chain of excellent roads linking the southern Orkney islands. In places they had also created sheltered bays with sandy beaches and I knew Tom Drever moored his boat in one of them. With the gentle programme Raven had arranged for me, I had high hopes that at some stage I'd find time for a sail.

The road unwound rapidly through low green hills and fields full of fat cattle. Within half-an hour I came to a small unobtrusive sign for Scarisby and turned down a narrow side road, scarcely more than a track, that seemed to head towards the sea. The ground fell steadily away, becoming damp and marshy. Patches of coarse grass and fluttering clumps of white bog cotton dotted about and pools of water, glistening in the low sun, appeared everywhere. Suddenly I was driving along the side of a shallow loch, half filled with reeds. Dead ahead of me I saw Scarisby and beyond it the sea.

I stopped the car and my first impression was of complete silence. Then I became aware of a light sweep of wind gusting in occasionally from the sea, ruffling the grasses and water of the loch. Even on a pleasant morning the wind had a chill edge as it sang over the loch. From somewhere far off I heard a shrill intermittent cry that sounded eerily across the empty slopes. I hoped it was a curlew. I frowned as I looked the place over. Birdwatchers Anonymous would love it. But to me Scarisby didn't look to be an ideal site for a leisure complex.

Not that there was much wrong with the house, although architecturally it was out of place in the Orkney landscape. At the foot of the little loch, in the only sheltered spot for miles around, it huddled beneath some rising ground that probably backed onto the sea. Indeed as I approached I saw that it was quite an impressive house, off-white in colour, with a long low frontage and a carefully maintained slate roof. But it had an odd, almost eccentric look, the front being dominated by a curiously Alpine-looking porch and a high pointed elaborately carved wooden surround supported by two rustic red-painted tree trunks. Recessed into the porch were big double doors and to each side there was a row of bay windows, firmly shuttered. There was no garden to speak of and only a rough track leading round the side of the house towards what was probably a small garage. I walked all round the building. It looked exactly what it was, a Victorian hunting lodge that would have been in keeping on Dee-side or in rural North Wales. At some stage two wings had been added at the rear of the house, presumably to provide extra bedrooms. It wasn't possible to see into the interior of the rooms but Raven's secretary had arranged for me to pick up the house keys from a nearby croft. I glanced at my watch. There was plenty of time before my first candidate to have a look at the surrounding area.

Behind the house the land sloped steeply up and I followed a well-trodden path through coarse grass and thistles. The smell of salt hung heavy in the air and after about a hundred yards I could hear the waves pounding somewhere below. Then suddenly I was on the edge of a steep cliff that dropped sharply away beneath me in a series of ragged sloping shelves. Here and there were pools of water, trapped and left behind by some recent storm, glinting in a watery sunlight. I stood for a moment looking across the blue-grey water of the Pentland Firth. On land it was a pleasant enough morning but away to the west I could see a bank of low cloud and mist that looked as if it planned to spoil the day. The cliff path led downwards to a small bay, rocky like this whole coast but sheltered from the prevailing winds. Right on the edge of the water I saw a neat little boathouse. Interesting, I thought and started to scramble down the narrow path. As I drew nearer I saw that the boathouse had been recently built, with a strong wooden frame and a solid concrete foundation that sloped down to the water and formed a very handy slipway. At the top of the slipway were heavy double doors, securely padlocked. Somehow it didn't look like the kind of thing the locals would have bothered with and I guessed that it belonged to Scarisby. I clambered on to the concrete surround and peered into the interior. The light was poor but what I saw was a surprise.

Inside was a large motor-boat. But it was not the usual workman-like vessel that the local men use for inshore lobster fishing. This was a sleek powerful, semi-displacement job, twenty-five or more feet in length, with a couple of big in-board engines that would push it along at anything up to thirty knots. There was no sign of a fuel pump, so I couldn't tell if the engines were diesel or petrol. I studied the rakish lines enviously. It was the sort of craft that would have looked the part in the Mediterranean, with accommodation for three or four people--- perhaps more if they were really friendly. I remembered Tom Drever's story of strange parties and smiled. Maybe the passengers were very friendly.

I was on my way back up the track towards the house when I noticed ahead of me on the cliff top, beyond the shelving cliffs, a long low green mound standing out against the sky. Curiously regular in shape, like an upturned boat, it looked distinctly man made. I left the track and inched my way carefully along the smooth grassy slope towards it, keeping well clear of the cliff edge. The mound seemed to grow almost naturally out of the hill on the landward side, but on the side facing the sea it formed a straight rough wall made of large slabs of local rock. In front of this wall was a flat open area of grassy stones and earth. I jumped down onto this to examine the structure more closely.

There was a low entrance in the wall with strong stone lintels and uprights that at some stage had been partly blocked with rocks. I walked the few paces to the edge of the flat forecourt. Then I quickly stopped. The ledge ended abruptly in a steep cliff falling sixty feet or more into heaving dark sea and wet black rocks. The cliffs beneath me formed one side of a deep gorge into which the waves surged relentlessly, their steady thunder magnified by the cliffs and rising powerfully up to me. I have a reasonable head for heights from my rock climbing days but even so I stepped back sharply from the edge. This was no place on a dark night, I thought. An early morning plunge wouldn't be too good either. Not into that maelstrom below.

I turned back to the mound. This must be one of McNaughton's excavations. Well, maybe a tomb could be made a feature of a leisure complex, but off hand I didn't see quite how. Perhaps one of Raven's candidates would be able to tell me. Still, the site was interesting and I wondered fleetingly about who had gone to so much trouble to build it, to say nothing of the person who had gone to the trouble of opening it up again. Archie McNaughton must have been a man of many parts.

I checked my watch once more. The diversion to the tomb meant that I'd have to postpone inspecting the inside of the house until tonight, after dinner with Tom Drever if I was still capable. I stopped off to introduce myself at the farmhouse, a derelict stone-built old building clinging desperately to the edge of yet another shallow loch. Then I headed back to Kirkwall to meet Anthony Raven's young hopefuls.

# CHAPTER 8

The first candidate was so spectacularly wrong for the job that I knew it as soon as I saw him in reception. A tall polished looking young man wearing a dark, too-smart business suit, a shirt with wide red and white stripes and a floral patterned silk tie, he simply didn't look the part. He bounded up as I approached and seized me enthusiastically by the hand. What had Anthony Raven been thinking about? Admittedly I hadn't seen the rest of the applications, so maybe they were even worse. But at least on paper this one had done some of the right things and he had taken the trouble to brief himself well, including having looked at Scarisby. His big idea was that the land around the house could be turned into a golf course. I looked at him with more respect. That was one of the few things for which it might be useful. It would cost a fortune of course. But at least it was an idea.

Unfortunately he was a non-starter. He was all wrong in appearance and style for the place and the people he'd have to work with locally. There's something called "face validity" which can be almost as important as your actual ability. Do you look like the thing you're supposed to be? I wound him down as quickly as I decently could. Fortunately he was bright enough to recognise that this wasn't the job for him and within half-an-hour he withdrew his application. I chatted to him for another fifteen minutes or so, in a desultory sort of way, about keeping him in mind for something more suitable. After all, everyone is a solution to somebody's problem.

The next one was quite different; but much worse. He had been a partner in a small surveying firm and claimed to have experience of development projects, including work on a leisure complex. Unfortunately this turned out to be a local government plan for a children's play park in Birmingham. This somehow didn't seem quite what Raven had in mind--- although I was beginning to have serious doubts if Raven had anything in mind. The candidate's suit had seen better days and so had he, to judge from the pinkish tinge around his eyes.

I asked him a few questions and he opened up with embarrassing eagerness, confiding that he had left his last firm 'by mutual agreement'. Apparently this was to give him time to shake off an unfortunate problem he had developed as a result of too much client hospitality. His eyes told the whole sad tale. After last night I wondered how my own eyes looked, so I did feel bad about rejecting him. But a move to Orkney didn't seem a good idea for someone with a drink problem--- even if he managed to avoid Tom Drever. So I let him down gently and said I'd let him know. Was I simply having one of these days, when nothing and no-one seems right? Or was Raven having a sick joke at my expense?

I decided to think about it tomorrow. I packed up my papers and strolled along the harbour front and onto the busy commercial pier. There I did what any sensible man would do under the circumstances. I leaned on a handy rail, gazed around the little harbour and enjoyed the sunlight. I did briefly think about Raven's assignment and his strange choice of candidates. But then I gave up. Who cares? It beat the hell out of working for a living.

Tied up near a little slipway were a couple of big sea-going cruisers, the kind you could sail around the world if you felt in the mood--- and I was beginning to feel in that kind of mood. I watched the crews enviously as they pottered about on deck. Messing about in boats, I thought; there's nothing quite like it. Especially when you're right across the road from a pub. For some reason that made me think of Tom Drever and I realised it was time to collect him. He had promised to buy me dinner at a restaurant he knew on South Ronaldsey and after that I reckoned I needed to look at the house at Scarisby.

On the way down we stopped at his mooring to introduce me to his boat. She turned out to be a slim beautiful 21-foot Bermudan-rigged sloop, a genuine racing boat with enough keel to give her stability and sleek lines that hinted at how well she would handle. She looked manoeuvrable and fast, just what you need to get out of trouble if the weather changed suddenly, which it did at very short notice in these parts. It was love at first sight. "Take her out when you want," Tom said generously. "I rarely find time these days. She's pining for some action."

The meal was another triumph. The little restaurant looked out across a flat calm sea and the sky was wrapped in a strange luminous light that I had only ever seen before over the lagoons of Venice. The food was just as special. I started with a crab salad that tasted so fresh it must have been scuttling about the floors of silent seas in the very recent past. Then I went on to a fish stew that would have put to shame a chef from Marseille. Only the aioli was missing and here somehow it seemed just right without the strong garlic flavour. With it we drank a bottle of Semillon and nobly refused to consider a dessert. Instead we opted for coffee and a glass of the wine of the country. Tom stuck to his favourite Highland Park while I tried a twelve-year old Scapa malt. He leaned back and beamed across the table at me. "You see how much I miss London."

I shook my head sadly. "It must be hell living here, so far from civilisation."

Tom nodded abstractedly and glanced down at his watch. "There's someone I want you to meet. He's supposed to be joining us for a drink. I thought you should meet him. He may tell you a bit more about Scarisby."

I look at him enquiringly. "What's the angle, Tom?"

"It's a fellow called John Childs. He came up here from the south a few years ago and seems to be semi-retired. Works as a kind of free-lance, part-time museum curator locally, mostly to give him time to write and also access to information, he says. He's a specialist on old Norse culture and well regarded in academic circles, I believe. An expert on the archaeology of the Islands or so he says."

At that moment a small slightly built man came into the restaurant. He had a long narrow face, thinning reddish hair brushed across a balding dome and a ragged beard and moustache of the same colour, framing a soft moist mouth. He held out a limp slender hand and sat down, studying me with undisguised interest. His watery-blue eyes seemed to be too large for the rest of his lean bony features, giving him the air of a permanently startled spaniel. His voice was thin and faintly effeminate, an impression heightened by the way he fluttered his hands as he spoke. From time to time he covered his mouth with one slim hand and shot a weak smiling glance at me, as if eager to see my reaction.

But he seemed likeable enough; a shrewd, intelligent little man. When Tom told him I was doing work for the Scarisby estate he showed even more interest. "Oh," he gushed, "it was so sad about poor Archie. Such a loss. Not," he added, looking at me half apprehensively, "that he couldn't be quite--- well, brusque," he said with a slight toss of his head. "If you know what I mean." I told him I had never met Archie McNaughton. He simply nodded and looked down at his hands. "Ah well," he said non-committally.

Tom ordered another round of drinks that included a double for Childs. "You've a bit of catching up to do, John."

Childs picked up his glass and studied its amber contents thoughtfully. Then, "So what is your connection with Scarisby?" he shot at me suddenly. I explained how I came to be working for the new owners of the estate. When I mentioned Raven's name a flicker of recognition flitted across his face. Then, "Oh yes," he said vaguely. "I think Archie may have mentioned his name to me."

"I understand you and McNaughton had interests in common," I said casually. "Or rather, an uncommon interest." Childs glanced at me a touch coyly. He looked appealingly in Tom's direction and then questioningly back at me. "I mean the archaeology of these parts," I added innocently.

"Well," he smiled, "in that respect Archie was an enthusiastic amateur. But yes, I've written one or two small books on the subject. Are you interested in chambered cairns, Mr Lennox?"

I admitted that it was a subject that had not yet seized my attention. "Oh never mind," he said generously. "It isn't everyone's thing." He raised the glass of whisky in Tom's direction and sank most of it in a single gulp.

"I want you to tell Terry a bit about the place. So he understands what he's dealing with," Tom said firmly.

"Chambered cairns," I said thoughtfully. "I did see something unusual this morning. On the very edge of the cliffs behind Scarisby--- a strange looking mound?"

"Sounds like your bloody tomb," Tom Drever said to Childs. "Maybe you have a convert here after all!"

Childs looked embarrassed but pleased. "Well, it was really Archie McNaughton's tomb." Then he looked at me, shocked. "I mean--- ," he stammered awkwardly.

"We know what you mean, John," Tom interrupted roughly. "Just tell Terry about the damned thing."

Childs took another gulp of whisky and tried to recovered his composure. "What I meant was that Archie McNaughton had most of that excavation done. Actually, he and his father and his grandfather before him." He smiled knowingly at me. "The whole McNaughton family seem to have been amateur archaeologists at one time or another.

I nodded. "So it's a Viking tomb or some such thing?"

Childs laughed and finished off his drink. Tom went to order another round. "Dear me no!" he said. "It's much older than the Vikings. The islands have been inhabited for thousands of years," he said to me pityingly. "Tombs like the one at Scarisby are Neolithic--- which means about 5,000 years old."

"That is old!" I said respectfully.

He nodded. "Yes. The Vikings were here much more recently; only about a thousand years ago. They did stay for quite a while though," he added helpfully, "and they certainly did leave their mark on the place."

"Go on," I said. It was my standard interview response, but I was genuinely interested in what he had to say.

Childs didn't need much encouragement. "They moved into some of the existing settlement sites and it seems they did it surprisingly peacefully, really. In spite of the image we have of them, pillaging and raping. Though they undoubtedly did do a lot of damage; breaking into the old tombs in search of buried treasure and that sort of thing."

"Was there anything of value in these old Neolithic sites?" I asked.

Childs shook his head firmly. "Nothing of real value. Remember, we're talking about a pre-metal society. So the Vikings must have been disappointed. But they did find a lot of good farming land and plenty of fresh water, which is what most of them really wanted."

"What about the beast you mentioned," broke in Tom Drever. "The other night you said something about a beast of some kind being in the tomb. Mind, you were pissed at the time!" he added.

For an instant I thought I saw a flash of fear in the large emotional eyes. Childs stared at Tom blankly and shook his head. "Nothing's been found in the chambered tombs except a lot of bones or an occasional stone tool left by the builders. Or things dropped by would-be tomb robbers wasting their time looking for buried treasure." He glanced cautiously across at me. "But mostly just bones; human and animal bones mixed together in some ritual way we don't fully understand." He glared at Tom. "So the only beasts in the chambered tombs are long dead. I think you must have been pissed," he added tartly.

"I'd like to read up on the subject," I said quickly. I wasn't in the mood for one of Tom's disagreements, which sometimes became a little robust. I checked my watch. It was only nine o'clock and outside it was still as bright as day. "Tom, I want to run down and take a look at the house." I turned to Childs. "Would you like to come with us?"

"No, no!" he said hastily. "I have to be on my way." He gave me one of his shy little glances. "But if you're interested, I'd be glad to explain the tomb to you. I have a few books on the subject you might enjoy." He walked beside me all the way to where I had parked the car. "If you like," he said diffidently as I unlocked the door, "I could meet you at the house tomorrow morning."

I hesitated for only a moment and then nodded my

agreement. After all, he might be able to tell me about more than the tomb. As we drove away Tom slapped me on the thigh. "I think he's taken a liking to you, Terry. Better watch your step!"

"He's gay?" I asked.

Tom shrugged his powerful shoulders. "I suppose so. But as long as he doesn't bother me, why should I care?"

"You said something about gay parties at Scarisby. Would Childs have been involved in that?"

Tom shrugged his shoulders again. "Who knows?" He grinned at me. "Why don't you ask him?" He paused. "Though if you're really interested in that kind of thing there are people in Edinburgh who might be more use to you. I have a contact there--- a journalist pal who knows the local gay scene. He might know of any connection there was with Scarisby."

I stared across at him in surprise and almost missed the turn off for Scarisby. At the last moment we skidded into the narrow track towards the house. "Edinburgh? What has Scarisby to do with Edinburgh?"

Tom shook his head. "I'm not quite sure at this stage. But my pal Morrison is well connected in some dodgy places. He's still short of enough hard evidence to make a real story, but he does have some interesting theories." He glanced at me. "It might be an idea if you knew about them at least. Especially if you're planning anything ambitious for Scarisby."

I collected the keys from the farm and drove on past the little loch. In front of the house I stopped and switched off the car engine, sitting staring at Tom. "What are you getting at, Tom? Is it something you've turned up investigating McNaughton?"

"No," He admitted. " I'm treating McNaughton's death in quite a different way. I don't think it has anything to do with the gay scene. According to young Norman Orr, McNaughton avoided the fun and games that took place at the house and there's no reason I can see why the boy should lie. He doesn't deny their relationship and why should he?" He shook his heavy head. "So McNaughton's death wasn't connected with the gay scene. Either it was suicide as everyone thought. Or just maybe he was murdered. For some reason to do with politics or money. McNaughton made a lot of enemies, one way and another. Of that there is no doubt."

Perhaps that was how it happened, I thought. But the story was resonating with something else, a fragment of information or some casual remark I had heard. But just for the moment I couldn't pull it all together. Which was a pity, because it might just have saved a couple of lives.

# CHAPTER 9

Inside the house heavily curtained against the brightness of the evening light and we went rapidly from room to room opening the shutters and pulling back the curtains. One long corridor ran back through the main part of the house and on each side at the front was one large room. To the right it was a stylish sitting room, well furnished in country house Victorian style, with family portraits and hunting scenes by unknown artists. On the other side was a dining room with a long heavy mahogany table, the type that can be extended to suit a large gathering. It filled the middle of the room and was surrounded by a dozen or so matching chairs. The ceilings were low and the walls painted in muted tones on a rough plaster finish that fitted the rural image.

We followed the dark corridor into the rear of the house. It opened directly into the two wings and where it divided the way was barred by a pair of sturdy wooden doors. The right hand one opened easily and we entered a long narrow passage with windows down one side looking across an area of rough ground to a similar set of curtained windows in the other wing. On the outer side of the passage a row of doors opened into bedrooms, each with a view of the bleak surrounding countryside. The beds had all been stripped and the rooms had the empty impersonal feel of a barrack block after the troops have moved out. "No shortage of accommodation," Tom remarked as we went back to the main corridor.

I tried the left-hand door. It was locked and none of the keys would open it. I shrugged. "More of the same, I suppose." I was rapidly losing interest and increasingly dubious about Scarisby's potential as a site for development.

Once back outside the house we looked around. "Maybe we can get into the other wing through the garage," said Tom speculatively. "Do you have a key for it?" I tried each of the keys. One of them turned easily in the well-oiled lock. We stepped inside. The garage was empty but at the rear there was a small door that should open into the main part of the house. It was locked firmly by an old-fashioned but very effective mortise lock. Tom seized the handle and shook the door vigorously. Then he tried his bulk against it. He looked at me and grinned. "Pretty flimsy--- it wouldn't take much to force it."

I'd seen Tom go through heavier doors than this one. "What are you talking about?" I snapped. "I can't start demolishing my client's property. Anyway, why bother? I've seen enough. Let's get out of here."

Ignoring me, Tom poked around in the dark corners of the little garage. Against one wall was a low bench and on it lay a few old rusting tools, including a pair of pliers that had seen better days. He picked up the pliers and worked them free of rust while he looked about for inspiration. Then he spotted two or three cheap metal coat-hangers hanging on a hook in one wall. They were the kind that dry-cleaners give away, the kind that breed uncontrollably in wardrobes. "I don't know why it is," Tom said grimly. "But I've never liked locked doors."

With a jerk of the pliers Tom straightened out the hook of the coat-hanger. He checked the metal roughly against the key-hole and then bent it into a neat right angle. Inserting this into the lock, he turned it carefully. It spun freely but the door remained firmly locked.

Tom grunted and withdrew the coat-hanger. "Come on, Tom. Let's get out of here," I said impatiently looking at my watch. Tom silently worked at the wire with the pliers again, adjusting the angle of his make-shift key. After a couple of attempts the metal seemed to catch on the lock. Carefully Tom increased the pressure. I heard a soft click and the coat-hanger turned smoothly in the lock. Tom looked at me triumphantly.

"Good God," I said, shaking my head. "The power of the press! I find it very worrying. I suppose breaking and entering is part of journalistic training nowadays?"

Already Tom had pushed open the door. He grinned back at me. "I think you'll find that technically this is larceny, as you legally hold a set of keys. But it's an interesting point." He vanished into a narrow passageway like the one we had seen in the other wing.

"That's good to know," I said to thin air. Then I followed him back into the house. The passageway on this side of the house had fewer doors and they were all locked. Tom did his trick with the coat-hanger on the first door. Inside was so dark that at first we seemed to be in a normal bedroom. I pulled back the window curtains and opened up the shutters. Then I saw that it was a bedroom; but by no means a normal one. For a start it was much bigger than the rooms we had seen in the other wing and in the middle of the floor there was a large king-sized bed. The other difference was that the walls consisted of an unbroken line of tall plate mirrors and there was another large mirror on the ceiling, directly over the bed.

Tom and I looked at each other and I raised my eyebrows. "Curious," I said. "An island tradition?"

We found two more of these intriguing bedrooms. The rest of the passage was taken up by one very large room, furnished as a kind of sitting room with a television set, a video-player and a few large sofas and chairs. But it was not your typical sitting room. Like the bedrooms it too was equipped with mirrors round the walls and overhead there was a mirrored ceiling.

Then I saw the set of metal hooks screwed into the ceiling. My mind isn't prone to boggling. But it was starting to boggle now. "A playroom of some kind?" I said to Tom in wonder. But Tom was busy with his improvised key again, working on the lock of a large wall cupboard. As I spoke, he pulled open its double door. "And here are some of the toys, I think." He peered at a stack of video tapes on a rack. "Scandinavian He-men", he read aloud. "Danger, Boys at Work." He grinned at me. "Fancy a quiet evening at home?"

I raised my eyebrows silently again and opened one of cupboard drawers. Then I held up a tangled set of harnesses and belts, made mostly of leather and strong blue woven cotton webbing. I waved them in Tom's direction. "And," I said, "there are handcuffs in a matching material, for the truly discriminating pervert."

Tom opened another drawer and held up a large solid black rubber object. It looked vaguely familiar but it was on such a monumental scale that for a moment I didn't realise exactly what it was. Certainly I had never seen one that size in real life. In fact they don't come that size. At least I hope not. Tom began to laugh a long slow belly laugh. "I wonder," he said, "if you can get it in white?"

Quietly we locked all the doors again and walked back to the car. "Who the hell was using this place?" I burst out. "You must have some idea who McNaughton's friends were. What's been going on here, Tom?"

Tom shook his head and looked puzzled. "This isn't part of my book. I still think young Norman was telling me the truth when he said Archie wasn't involved in that stuff. This is another story altogether--- and a rather nasty one that doesn't particularly interests me, to tell you the truth. But the fellow I told you about in Edinburgh may be able to tell you more, if it suits him."

I dropped Tom back at his flat and we agreed to try out the boat together the following evening. Then I went back to my hotel. It was midnight but the sky was still light and a red sun was just about to dip behind the hill across the bay. I lay on the bed watching the light fade and thinking about McNaughton and Anthony Raven. What was the connection? Raven said he had been McNaughton's lawyer. But was he something else as well? Did he know about the exotica in the house at Scarisby?

Presumably not, for surely he would not have asked me to come here and risk the story leaking back to Edinburgh? Yet he'd been here only a few days earlier and on the very night that Patricia and I had decided not to watch that play.

Or so he said.

Or so Patricia had told me, a little voice whispered. What was going on I thought hazily? Finally I dropped off to sleep without an answer.

CHAPTER 10

No brilliant solutions came to me in the night and I woke early. The sun was still up there in the same position. But a glance at my watch convinced me that it must be rising, so I decided to do likewise. I worked through my morning exercises and listened to a classical music programme while I shaved. The slow movement from Mozart's 21st piano concerto came drifting into the room, with a studied elegance that almost persuaded me reason and harmony might prevail in this confused world.

Then I realised I had run out of clean shirts. With a curse I pulled on a sweater. There was time to buy a couple of shirts before I started my meetings. But first I had a rendezvous to keep with John Childs at Scarisby. Overnight the weather had broken and low cloud, mist and rain were driving on a stiff westerly breeze as I crossed the causeways. Childs was waiting, huddled in a Barbour jacket by the front door of the house as I drove up. He tossed a waterproof coat in my direction. "Here," he said awkwardly. "Don't say I'm not looking after you. If you stay around here for long you'll learn never to trust the weather."

We struggled up the hill towards the tomb, slipping and sliding on the short wet grass. At the flat area in front of the tomb we crouched down to shelter from the wind. Childs smiled at me. "It's so nice that you are interested in the archaeology of the place. I have some books in the car that you may enjoy. Just let me have them back when you're finished with them."

He pulled some of the stones away to reveal the low entrance. "You can see," he said, panting with the effort, "how much work must have been involved for these Neolithic people. To quarry and gather together enough building material for a structure like this would be a major social project." He straightened up. "A collective effort involving the entire community. I estimate there must be something like 12,000 man-hours of work," he went on eagerly.

I translated that mentally into cash. "That's more or less the cost of a large modern house. Just to bury their dead in a safe place?"

Childs finished clearing the doorway. "On the other hand it was probably used over a very long period. Possibly as long as seven hundred years. So from that point of view it was good value for money, if you care to think of it in that way. More importantly, it seems to have been of great cultural significance to them. Well, it must have been, to justify such an investment of time from people who had a fairly marginal life-style. You'll see more inside."

"Inside?" I gazed at him doubtfully. "Are we going in there?"

Without answering, Childs crawled into the low tomb and showed the way for me with a torch. I took a deep breath and scrambled into the darkness after him. The interior seemed empty and remarkably dry for a 5,000 years old structure. The head high walls were built of neatly laid flat stones, with every few yards a massive upright slab that projected into the space, creating a series of chambers while at the same time acting as roof supports. Childs played the torch beam around the walls and I gasped. In one corner lay a pile of human skulls.

"Just the remnants," Childs said calmly. "That chamber was piled high with skulls when Archie and his father did the first excavation. The curious thing is that each chamber contained a different set of bones. Here were arms," he waved the torch around, "and here the leg bones. We don't know exactly why they split up the skeletons like that. But we think the bodies were first laid out in front of the tomb, on the ledge to allow the birds to pick the bones clean. Then they were neatly interred here. It's not an uncommon form of burial."

I was glad to be out in the clean fresh air again as I dusted myself down. "Terrific way to dispose of your nearest and dearest." I said. "Archie McNaughton did all this excavation himself?"

Childs nodded briefly. "He took up where his father left off. It was a kind of obsession with him."

"You knew him well then?" I asked.

Childs looked alarmed. "Oh no. Not well at all. Just casually."

"So what happens to the contents of tombs like this?"

"What do you mean?" Childs shot a suspicious glance at me. Then he seemed to relax. "Oh, I see what you mean. Mostly it goes to national museums. You see, this site was worked on off and on over a long period of time. Archie's grandfather did some casual digging, I believe. Though in those days landowners could simply keep anything they fancied." He shrugged. "The way they thought, it was on their land so why should they hand it over to museums in London or Edinburgh. That was certainly the case before the Treasure Trove laws were passed."

"Treasure Trove?" I said. "That sounds exciting. But you said last night that there wouldn't be anything of real value in a tomb like this."

Childs hesitated. "Certainly nothing Neolithic. But later civilisations did come this way. The Celts and then the Norse, in particular. So occasionally other items have been found. Prior to the Treasure Trove Law of 1859 the Crown gave no compensation to finders, so there's hardly an old country house in Scotland that doesn't have a few antiquities."

"But nothing of much value?" I insisted.

Childs smiled blandly. "Oh, often of great value to academics and students--- stone artefacts, tools and so on. But rarely of real financial value."

"What about this beast Tom Drever mentioned?" I persisted.

Childs scowled, his thin face twisted. "Tom's dreaming. There was no beast in the tomb. You've seen the inside for yourself. Now, I better get you back." He strode rapidly away down the slope towards the house. By the time I caught up with him he had calmed down. He fished a pile of reference books out of his car. "Here," he said, his large watery eyes looking almost shyly at me. "Take these. This is your home-work. Contact me anytime, Terry, if you have any questions. And keep the books. I'll look you up and collect them next time I come south, if that's all right."

I had an uncomfortable feeling that I was being manoeuvred into something. "I'm a fast reader," I said. "I'll leave them with Tom. But I appreciated your guided tour." As he drove off he looked disappointed.

The rest of the day went badly. The only shirts I could find were so awful that I would certainly have to jettison them before I returned to Edinburgh. The candidates were hopeless too and the weather hadn't improved much either. Tom Drever telephoned to postpone our sail; the wind and rain had settled in for the night.

Before dinner I sat down with the books John Childs had loaned me. They included one of his own, a dullish technical analysis of Orkney Neolithic sites with pages of charts, maps and statistics. I flicked rapidly through that and turned to the others. These were more exciting, with accounts of sweeping Viking raids, large-scale migrations and settlements that took them from the North Sea to Russia, the Black Sea and the eastern Mediterranean and west to Greenland, perhaps even to America. "From the wrath of the Northmen, O Lord, deliver us" had been a common prayer in Europe a thousand years ago. But once the initial plundering phase was over the Norwegian Vikings who came to Orkney seemed to have settled down peacefully, farming and fishing, though they may have exterminated the locals in doing so. Opinions seemed to vary on that.

But they certainly brought their myths and legends with them, including a complete cosmology to explain the creation and the ultimate destruction of the world. The end would be a time of desperate desires and dreadful events that would bring a terrible holocaust of the gods.

The supreme God was Odin. He lived in Asgard where he had a great hall, Valhalla, from which he could see the whole of creation. Now who did that remind me of? Also Odin apparently had only one eye--- he had sacrificed the other one in return for great wisdom. I wondered guiltily how my fund management candidates were coming along. So Odin sat in Asgard and was brought news from the world by two ravens. Well, that didn't fit too well. Obsessed with power and knowledge, Odin would stop at nothing to gain control and domination. Yes, that sounded more like Grieder. He consulted with a wise but decapitated head that he kept for that purpose. Ho hum, I thought! That certainly gave a new meaning to head-hunting.

There were other Gods too, whose personal qualities were even less attractive. Like Frey, the God of sexual intercourse, who needless to say was quite a popular God. He had a sister, Freja, with whom he seems to have had a very close personal relationship. In fact Freja had a close personal relationship with practically everyone, including some dwarfs from whom she obtained a magnificent necklace in exchange for her favours. Her name apparently meant 'lady', but her behaviour didn't sound very ladylike."

Then there was Loki, who was a sexual freak, full of malice and yet a strangely complex figure. He was blood brother to Odin but was only half god, the other half being devil. Deliberately opting to be wicked, Loki was obsessed with evil for its own sake and had a cruel instinct for exploiting the weaknesses of others. Eventually he was destroyed by his desire to test his own capacity for wickedness to the ultimate.

Nice touch, I thought as I dined in the hotel. The meal was hearty rather than haute cuisine, but with superbly grilled sea trout as the main course who cares? I turned in early, closing the curtains firmly to keep the light at bay.

Next day had a better script. My exercises went well; the music was a Corelli Concerto Grosso; and one of the two candidates turned out to be ideal for the job. I had almost given up hope by then but it seemed that the Lennox good fairy was still looking out for me. The candidate was a young man who had grown up in the north of Scotland--- not Orkney, but then no-one is perfect. He had a good engineering degree and had been working as a management consultant on project management assignments, including developing a major hotel and leisure complex for wealthy investors in the Middle East. He was married with a young child and wanted to move to a quiet rural area to enjoy a better life-style. I fastened onto him like a hungry trout and in no time he was hooked.

Suddenly my visit to Orkney was a success and that evening I went sailing with Tom Drever with a pure heart and a clear conscience. Well, not exactly with a clear conscience. I had started to think about Patricia Raven again.

# CHAPTER 11

Next morning I was on the flight to Edinburgh and back in my flat by ten thirty. The abrupt change of scene left me feeling slightly bemused. But not as bemused as I had been on the previous night, when I had finally persuaded Tom Drever to go home. He made me promise to return later in the summer, for some serious sailing.

I sorted through the mail that waited for me. It was the mixture as before, a few bills and a special subscription offer for a magazine I wouldn't read in a dentist's waiting room under duress. There were also four personal letters in hand addressed envelopes. I hesitated about which one to open first. Then I chose the lilac-coloured, slightly perfumed one with the feminine handwriting. Don't ask me why. It was just a whim. The letter said simply; "Darling, I'm glad you're back. I missed you. Call me soon." There was no signature but I reckoned it wasn't from Hans Grieder or Anthony Raven.

The other letters were from my candidates for Odin Investments. All of them said that the job was exactly the kind of challenge they needed at this stage in their career. I punched the air in triumph and called Grieder's office to tell him I had a short-list and that I would be sending him written reports on the candidates.

Then I called Anthony Raven to give him the good news about the Scarisby assignment. What a harbinger of joy I was today! I was already working out the make of spinnaker I could afford and what to do with the rest of the fee. Raven's secretary sounded glad to hear from me but said that he was working at home today. She would have to call me back. Now when I say I'm working at home it usually means that I'm out sailing. I wondered what Raven did.

I was just starting work on my reports for Grieder when the telephone rang. It turned out to be Donald Lynch, telling me he planned to be in Edinburgh next day to meet his institutional investors, mostly insurance companies and fund managers, to explain what a terrific idea it was to invest in the Irving Group. "I don't suppose you made much sense of those accounts," he said. "Actually I can't understand how you get away with being so financially illiterate."

I ignored him. "I concentrate on broad strategic issues," I said airily, "and leave the detailed bean counting to people like you. Frankly, all I could see was a rather messy organisation. How are you going to persuade the institutions to support you?"

"Personal charm, reputation and charisma," he said cheerfully. Then he gave a hollow laugh. "Don't you realise? I'm the Group's saviour. Listen, I'm going to be busy all day performing miracles, presenting business plans and such. I know you don't usually work after five o'clock, but how about meeting me at the Cafe Talleyrand at seven for an early dinner? I'm paying." I agreed and hung up. In spite of the bravura style, Donald did not seem to be quite his usual assured self. And if he was still offering to pay for dinner he must be in serious trouble.

A few minutes later Raven's secretary rang me again. "I've been trying to contact you for ages, Mr Lennox," she said accusingly, in her polite Edinburgh accent. "Mr Raven would like to see you at his home as soon as possible." She gave me the address and I told her I was on my way. Frankly, the faster I got this assignment out of the way the happier I'd be. Quite apart from my doubts on the feasibility of the scheme, my thoughts about Patricia cast an uneasy shadow over the entire situation and what I had discovered about everyday life at Scarisby did nothing to comfort me. There was no doubt about it. Raven troubled me, and not just because he was Patricia's husband. Besides, I was looking forward to getting my hands on that cheque he had promised me.

The cab dropped me at the house in a leafy suburb on the south side of the city. At first sight the place seemed no different from a score or more of grand houses scattered about the area. I looked around for an entrance and spotted a large set of metal security gates set into the high stone walls. They were the type of gates that operate by remote control and they ran in solid steel tracks that would take a crowbar to prise up. On the wall was a call-box from where unwanted visitors could be identified. Anthony Raven obviously liked his privacy.

But today the gates stood open. To either side the high walls ran off for fifty yards or more before turning away out of sight. Beyond them I could see the tops of tall trees--- elms and horse chestnuts--- tossing and swaying in the endless breeze that chills this city. I walked up a wide gravelled drive that curved towards the front door. To my right was a bank of old-fashioned climbing briar roses and an array of carefully tended flower-beds and the perfume of the flowers hung heavily over me as I crunched along the path. To my left an expanse of lawn stretched away into the middle distance, curved around the side of the house and merged into a large stand of old trees. There was enough space for a polo field and for all I knew that was what Raven used it for.

The house itself was a typical Victorian pile on two floors, with a steep mansard roof, a pillared stone portico and a flight of stone steps that curved up to the imposing front door. At each side of the steps were shrubs in urns of a vaguely classic design. Except for the house being Victorian and belonged to

Raven, there was really little with which I could find fault. It all looked like serious money. I pressed a modern bell push and somewhere in the depth of the house heard a faint buzzing sound. After a brief pause the door opened and there in front of me stood something else that belonged to Raven. I don't know why I should have been surprised to see her. After all that was where she lived. But it came as a shock.

Patricia looked me coolly straight in the eyes, her hand poised against the door-frame. She didn't seem in the least surprised, though her tawny eyes widened ever so slightly and a quizzical smile flicked over her lips. "You must be Mr Lennox," she said calmly. "My--- husband is expecting you." There was just the hint of a hesitation in her voice. She was casually dressed, wearing a pair of designer jeans and a creamy silk white shirt with a broad black leather belt around her slim waist. Her long auburn hair was pulled tightly back and tied with a simple headband. She looked like about a million dollars.

Taking my cue from her, I smiled politely and followed her into the house. "I expect Anthony is in his conservatory," she said easily. "Do have a seat. I'll let him know you are here." She indicated a dark wooden side table flanked by a couple of well padded armchairs.

I watched her walk away down the long room. She didn't look back but in spite of that I enjoyed watching her. Then I began to look around. The room was very large and took up the entire height of the house, with a kind of mezzanine balcony that ran completely around it, accessed by a curved wooden staircase. Serried ranks of tall windows illuminated the room from two sides and there were glass panels high in the roof that gave even more light from above. Patricia disappeared from view through a half-glazed door beneath the staircase.

A moment later she reappeared and stood in the doorway. "Please go in. Anthony is playing with his pets." As I squeezed past close enough to smell her perfume, I looked at her questioningly and she said in a low voice, "Be careful, Terry." Then she turned away from me.

I walked into a short dimly-lit passageway and through a green painted metal door at the far end. Instantly I found myself in dazzling brightness, within a room which had an expanse of glass looking out into the grounds on three sides. As I got my bearings, I saw that the room was a mass of greenery, almost seeming to be an extension of the gardens outside. Exotic plants, rich, succulent and variegated, seemed to fill the room. Some of them grew freely in a profusion of clumps and extended tendrils and some were contained in special glass cases, like the one I had seen in Raven's office. Scattered through the foliage were literally hundreds of blossoms in a fantastic display of shapes and colours.

Raven was sitting at a low table doing something with a syringe to a tall odd-looking plant with large fleshy petals and the enlarged lower lip of the typical orchid. But unlike most of the plants, this one was entirely green. Petals were green, the leaves were green, even the stamens. It looked entirely unnatural and slightly obscene. Raven was wearing a short white jacket over his usual business shirt and dark trousers. "Paphiopedilum," he said without looking up at me. "Lady's Slipper as it is called by the great unwashed. You can see that the lower lip looks almost slipper-like. It's quite a common variety, really. But a true survivor; I have a soft spot for survivors. Do you like them, Lennox? Survivors, I mean." Without waiting for a reply, he went on. "No fuss or bother. Nothing exotic about Paphiopedilum. It will flourish in any cool shady place."

"Shady, eh? Sounds ideal for Edinburgh," I said casually. "But how does it come to be all green?"

Raven stood up. "Oh, just its survival technique. Orchids come in a remarkable variety of colours and shapes." He turned to a long tray of plants showing tiny delicate flowers. "These are

82

Pleiones. Very easy to grow and keep. No need to cosset them either." He moved across to one of the large glass cases and leaned casually against the wall. He shot a quick appraising look at me. "These are the little beauties you were admiring in my office. Phalaenopsis. Now they are quite a different proposition. They come from steamy tropical forests and they do need a lot of care." I recognised the delicate white blossoms and the roving tendrils. Raven went on with his lecture. "These are epiphytes. They cling to trees and take their sustenance wherever they can find it."

"Parasites?" I enquired.

Raven shook his head vigorously. "No, no! They're not parasitic. Not at all. They simply make use of the tree as an anchorage, as a secure base. But then they reach out their tendrils and cling on to anything that gives them a better position in life. Or an advantage of some sort." He smiled a humourless smile at me. "So like people, don't you think? But pretty little things. So I'm prepared to forgive them that little foible." He looked at me and smiled knowingly. "And though you might not think so to look at them, so pure and white, they are quite the most promiscuous of all the flowers. They breed happily with any other orchid they can find."

I decided to change the subject. "I wanted to give you the results of my meetings in Orkney." I watched him closely. "Scarisby is certainly a fascinating place."

"I'm pleased you enjoyed the visit," he remarked calmly.

"The bad news is that there is only one candidate who meets the specification. Do you want me to write reports on all the candidates. Or just that one?"

Raven peeled of the white jacket. "That's something I need to think about," he said shortly. "Let's go into my study. There's something I want to discuss with you." He led me back through the large hall and into a small book-lined room that opened off it. There was a traditional cast-iron fireplace in one corner and a circular table in the middle covered with papers and files. "Take a seat." He pointed towards a comfortable leather covered sofa and threw himself down into an armchair beside the empty fireplace.

He smiled at me charmingly, but his brown eyes were quite empty. "By all means send me your report on the candidate you liked. But there is no rush. No rush at all." He paused. "In fact it's beginning to look as if my client is having second thoughts about the entire project." He held up his hand before I could speak. "That would not of course affect the arrangement we made about fees," he went on. "The agreement will still stand. So please send me your invoice when you think it appropriate."

I pursed my lips. "I can't say I'm surprised, having seen the place. But isn't this a sudden change of heart?"

Raven shrugged. "These people are inclined to make snap decisions. Very irritating at times." He laughed lightly. "But I dare say you know all about difficult clients. After all, you do a lot of work for Hans Grieder, don't you?" He stretched out his legs and studied his polished shoes. "And that, in a way, is what I want to discuss with you."

I frowned questioningly at him. "What do you mean?"

He held up his hand again. "Please don't think I expect you to betray any professional confidences. I wouldn't dream of that. After all, we lawyers understand the importance of client relationships--- and ethics." He paused. "But now that we are in a client relationship of our own," he added blandly with a brief twisted smile, "I hope that I can raise an important matter with you. Of course I do stress that if for any reason you feel you can't help me, it will have absolutely bearing on the fee we have already agreed."

Big deal, I thought. I've already earned the fee. As if he had read my thoughts he went quickly on. "Which of course you have already earned, I am sure. So please regard what I am going to ask as being in the nature of a favour. But a favour that I will be willing to reciprocate, if there is ever anything I can do for you." He looked at me and smiled enigmatically.

"Just what is it you want, Mr Raven?"

Raven stood up and crossed to the fireplace. He lifted down a small seascape painting from the wall to reveal a circular wall safe. Then he adjusted the combination and swung open the solid steel door. Reaching in he took out a pale chamois leather pouch and brought it carefully over to the table, eased open the bag and slid out a package, neatly wrapped in dark red velvet cloth. He spread its contents out on the cloth.

Gleaming against the rich red of the velvet was a magnificent piece of jewellery; golden, heavily ornamented, large and roughly circular in shape. At first glance it seemed to be a single casting but on closer inspection I saw that its surface was covered with an elaborate pattern of fine inlaid wire and small particles of gold.

"Impressive?" Raven remarked casually.

I studied it in silence. "Is it gold?" I asked him.

"Oh yes. Of that there is no doubt." Raven glanced at me strangely. "But it's the decoration that really makes this piece interesting. That and its financial value of course." He smiled confidently at me.

"What exactly is it?"

"I'm told it's a Viking brooch," Raven said carefully. "Rather an old one, actually, as these things go. About a thousand years old in fact."

I studied the object again. The brooch consisted of a single pattern that wandered to and fro across the surface in an endless scroll. But the strange thing was that it traced an image in the form of a weird creature with a large troll-like head, two huge staring eyes and a savagely grinning mouth. The body was just as bizarre, unnaturally elongated and ribbon-like, writhing and twisting wildly back upon itself and contorted into shapes that no living animal had ever achieved.

But the most disturbing feature was the way in which the creature's long frond-like paws gripped the edges of its frame, almost as if the beast had an existence outside the brooch and was struggling to escape from the setting, its eyes bulging frantically with the effort. It was like something out of a very bad dream; like nothing I had ever seen--- or ever wanted to see.

Yet it seemed to strike an uneasy chord of recognition. It was something dredged up from the depths of a nightmarish collective unconscious, from some remote place filled with obsessions and disturbing desires; a place where things unknown, but not exactly unknowable, silently wait for a chance to escape. With an effort I took my eyes off the strange figure. "Is it very valuable?" was all I could find to say.

Raven inclined his head. "Ah, I see you are a man who appreciates money, as well as beauty. Yes, I'm told it is very valuable. Perhaps worth half a million pounds; perhaps more to an enthusiast, a collector of this kind of thing. Such a curious design, don't you think? I like it, I must say." He paused. "It's a creature derived from Norse art but its exact origins are obscure. I have heard that it is a corrupt version of some creature the Vikings encountered on their travels to Constantinople. It does look corrupt, does it not?" He smiled happily and settled back in his armchair. "At any event my principal thinks it would have a special appeal to a private collector with an interest in Norse culture."

Now I understood where the conversation was taking us. "Hans Grieder?" I looked questioningly at Raven. "He's not the sort of man you can chat to about hobbies. I doubt if he knows what small talk is and I most certainly don't have that sort of relationship with him, if that is what's in your mind."

Raven nodded. "I've heard he can be difficult," he said easily. "But I also understand that you are one of the few people he trusts." Before I could interrupt him, he continued. "You are well known to have worked for him on some very important appointments. And you are working for him currently--- as well as for me." He smiled, his brown eyes unfathomable. "A happy coincidence, don't you think?" He leaned forward, "Take my word for it, Mr Lennox. This is a collector's item. It is made for Grieder's collection--- absolutely made for it." He smiled at me again. "When he hears about it he will want to see it. And when he sees it he will certainly want to own it."

"How do you come to own it?" I asked cautiously.

"Sadly, Mr Lennox, it doesn't belong to me personally. It is the property of Island Developments, the client you have been working for. It was part of the estate that the trust acquired and I'm simply acting for the new owners."

"So this came from the McNaughton estate?"

Raven shot a quick look at me. "Ah! You heard about McNaughton." He nodded briefly. "Of course, you would be bound to hear about him. A colourful character I believe. And there are very few secrets in that part of the world." He laughed and leaned back in his chair again. "The object has been in the family for generations. It was apparently found by McNaughton's grandfather in excavations on the estate.

"Did that make it legally his?"

Raven smiled. "Positive proof of origin is difficult after so long a period. Nowadays anything buried reverts to the Crown and the finder is paid its actual value. But in those days, before compensation was paid, most landowners took the view that it was their property.

"Shouldn't you offer it to one of the museums?"

He shrugged. "That is a possible way forward which might offer some tax advantages for my client. But the owners are not domiciled in this country and they would like to see it in the possession of someone with a genuine cultural interest in the object. Preferably as part of a collection in which it would be seen to good advantage." Seen by whom, I wondered?

Raven went on, "Now I hear that your Mr Grieder is deeply immersed in the whole Norse tradition. After all, his group is actually named after the great god Odin!" Raven seemed vaguely amused at the idea. "I think he would be very interested to know about the object's existence. But to be frank with you, I have had no success in making contact with him. He is clearly a very difficult man to approach." Raven paused. "Not that I would blame him for a sceptical response. This seems an extraordinary object to have reappeared after such a period of time. But accidents of history do occur, perhaps fortunately for collectors like Grieder."

"Its provenance will be important. Do you know exactly where it was found?"

Raven nodded. "Oh yes. I've had it examined by an expert who was given access to all the family letters and papers. So we do have a good provenance."

"I did see some of the stone-age excavations on the estate but I was told there would have been little of value in them." I pointed to the brooch. "Surely this is of much more recent origin?"

Raven nodded again. "Yes, you are perfectly correct. One possibility is that the brooch was accidentally dropped there, or even deliberately buried at the stone-age site for safety by some passing Viking." His eyes hardened slightly. "I see you have been busy in Orkney," he said. Then he relaxed and smiled again. "I'm told by experts in the field that the Vikings sometimes used more ancient burial sites for their own purposes and that they actually dug in some of them, looking for hidden treasure. So the brooch may have been lost there, perhaps in some catastrophe, or hidden there for safety and never recovered. Who can say now?"

I took a deep breath. "What exactly do you want me to do?"

"I have some rather good photographs of the object." He said and returning to the open safe he took out a sheaf of standard 8x10 glossies. He tossed them down in front of me. "Photography is one of my other interests," he said carelessly.

I flicked through the pile of glossies and suddenly stopped short as I came to a close up of Patricia with the jewel round her slim neck. On her it looked even more fabulous. She was staring straight into the camera, giving her enigmatic Giaconda smile. I had seen a lot of that particular smile.

"As you can see, someone at some point has modified it to act as a necklace," Raven said. "Beautiful, don't you think? Now if I can persuade Grieder to look at these," he pointed to the pictures, "I believe he will want to see the real thing. Then my clients hope to be able to do a deal with him."

Most of the pictures were close-ups of the brooch. By any standards I could see that the creature was a superb work of art and it had also been superbly photographed by Raven. Now I knew what he did at home. The only flaw in the pictures was a very faint line that ran down the extreme right hand edge of each one--- barely visible and I assumed from some processing flaw. Unquestionably the object would be intriguing for anyone with an interest in the subject. Someone with a lot of spare cash.

I was having trouble taking my eyes off Patricia's image, lying there between us on the table and I hoped Raven hadn't noticed. I dragged my eyes away and switched my gaze to Raven. "You want me to discuss this with Grieder?" I asked him incredulously. "I don't think you know your man, Mr Raven. Grieder isn't a normal client."

"Perhaps not. But if you can help, we will all be most grateful," he said smoothly. "I am sure, Mr Lennox, that like me clients are your life blood. From time to time I expect the Trust to have other consultancy projects and obviously they would find it appealing to work with someone whom they know and can rely upon." I made it very clear to him that I could guarantee nothing, given my strange relationship with Grieder. But I did agree to do what I could to help. After all, Raven was a client too.

That seemed to satisfy him. He said he would contact the candidates I had spent three days and a lot of his money interviewing and tell them the Scarisby project had been put on hold. Then he called a taxi cab for me and I left with his photographs of the strange creature. Patricia didn't reappear. But now at least I had a picture of her. As the taxi drove me back into town I pulled out the glossy pictures and studied them again. Yes, it was a weird looking creature. But if it was as rare as Anthony Raven claimed, it was possible that Grieder might be interested.

Then I recalled what Tom Drever had said about a beast in the tomb at Scarisby. Could this be the beast he meant? But John Childs had denied any knowledge of such a thing. It was possible of course that Childs had never heard about the brooch. But he had been an acquaintance of McNaughton and he was an expert on local archaeology, so he might be expected to know if such a thing existed. Just what had Tom been hinting at? Was there some hidden connection between Scarisby and Edinburgh? Or was it all just drunken talk? I looked up the number of Tom's newspaper pal in my diary. Maybe he would have something to tell me.

I rang him as soon as I reached my flat. "Ray Morrison," said the flat Scottish tones at the other end of the line. I told him I was a friend of Tom Drever. "I'm very sorry to hear that," he said. "Is that your only problem?" I grinned. It sounded as if Morrison really did know Tom Drever rather well.

"I have been up visiting Tom---," I started to say.

"Right! So you're calling me from hospital--- or have they released you?"

I laughed. "Don't worry. I know Tom well enough to stay sober, more or less." I explained to Morrison why Tom had given me his name. "He said you might be able to tell me something about the break-in at police headquarters and how it might be connected with Orkney."

There was a long silence. Then, "Did he now? And what might your interest be in that?"

I explained why I had been in Orkney but without naming names. "It seems possible that something may be going on that could affect my assignment," I said carefully. No harm in being economical with the facts.

After a pause Morrison said, "I can't speak now. But I'll meet you later for a beer if you like. I'd like to hear more about this client of yours." He gave me the name of a pub in the old part of town and we agreed to meet about five o'clock . The rest of the day I spent working on the reports for Grieder. Then I made my way across town to meet Morrison.

The pub was an old fashioned establishment in a building that had been on the site for about three hundred years. Inside was dark and cool and even on a summer evening a fire was burning in the big open grate. The walls were lined with cosy little cubicles. Rough deal tables and chairs were scattered about the maze of small side-rooms and here and there customers were studiously engrossed in chess games and drinking beer. In a corner of a back room I found Ray Morrison.

He was a stockily built man running a bit to fat, with a strong square head, a round jowly face and short dark hair that was starting to grey at the ends. He looked up at me with a pair of sleepy looking brown eyes that didn't fool me for a minute. He was dressed in a pair of undistinguished grey trousers, a checked cotton shirt and a sweater that had seen better days, but not in the recent past. Beside him on the table lay a battered old brief-case. I bought him a beer and we started to talk.

He sipped his beer and gently floated a few questions at me about Tom Drever and how I came to know him. Once he realised we had been friends since university days he relaxed. "So Tom said I might tell you something about the break-in." He squinted at me. "Exactly what do you want to know?"

I mulled over his question, trying to clear my own mind. "There's something odd going on at a house on the Scarisby estate which happens to be central to my assignment. Something rather weird and sexual." I went on slowly. "Tom hinted that there might be a connection with the police headquarters break-in and said you knew the background to that affair." I smiled at him winningly. "That's about it."

Morrison rocked to and fro in his seat, looking into his beer glass. Then he looked up sharply. "I don't know for sure how it might connect with this place at Scarisby. But let me tell you a story. Then you can decide for yourself if there is a connection." He wandered over to the bar and came back with two more pints of beer. "You know about the break-in. Well, the

92

official story has been hard to keep up with, for it changes constantly. Which of course makes us journalists suspicious." He grinned at me. "The first version was that it didn't happen at all. Announcements about things that didn't happen always interest the press! Then we were told that it was Animal Liberation activists who had broken in looking for confidential files held on them by the police. The office was actually spray painted with AL slogans," Morrison added. "I saw the graffiti myself."

I must have looked sceptical for Morrison gave a hollow laugh. "No, I didn't buy it either." He slurped at his beer and wiped his mouth. "Though anything's possible in this crazy world." His brown eyes looked sadly at me, like a man who had seen it all. "What it did say was that someone had something to cover up. So we did a bit more digging." He frowned. "Then there was a leak that seemed to come from inside the police force itself to the effect that there were security implications involved. That's usually a good way to shut up the press. According to this version, a secret file on IRA activists in Scotland had been stolen. But officially all the authorities would admit was that unnamed documents had been removed."

He sat back and looked at me. "Now it seemed to make some sense--- if you can say anything about security makes sense. The rumour was that the break-in was MI5-sponsored; an attempt to discredit the local fuzz in the run up to a big inter-governmental conference." He pulled a disconsolate face at me. "There's a lot of competition for cash and resources between various arms of the security services these days, what with government cut-backs and the end of the Cold War. Anyway, it was a plausible story and we ran with it for a few days."

I sighed. "I can't see any possible connection with Scarisby."

Morrison stared at me over his glass. "No, nor can I. Not off hand. But the tale goes on! Things were quietening down and the story was going cold. Then suddenly there was a heavy handed police raid on the premises of an individual we knew a bit about--- a man with some rather strange contacts. That raid actually resulted in the recovery of some of the missing police files. But the man involved protested his innocence and the raid did have all the hall-marks of a frame-up of some kind." He gave a chuckle. "But nobody could work out who was doing what to whom. So now we in the press were really interested. There were articles in the local papers almost every day and speculation was rife for a while. Was it all murky security stuff? Or was something else going on? That was when we started to hear really interesting stories that definitely did come from inside the police. Now the story was that the documents that had been stolen in the break-in--- "

"But which had now been recovered?" I asked, to show that I had been paying attention.

Morrison nodded. "Well, some of which had been recovered. However it now appeared that the documents were a highly confidential internal file on the activities of certain criminals involved in property and mortgage frauds."

"So the break-in was connected with property fraud?"

"Indirectly," said Morrison slowly. "These particular fraudsters happened to be gay. The suggestion was that someone on the fringes of the gay community had broken in to get hold of the information."

"But why would they want to do that? I asked. "For blackmail? Or just to destroy the evidence?"

"That's what we don't know for sure. What was fairly clear was that there was a group within the police who were unhappy about the way those cases involving gay criminals had been handled at the prosecution stages. They apparently suspected a conspiracy of some kind, a cover-up involving gays in the prosecution service. possibly even in the judiciary."

"Phew! That is strong stuff. Procurators going easy on the accused because they were fellow gays?" I said incredulously. "Was there any evidence of that? What made these guys in the police think there was a cover-up?"

"Remember it was only a small group of disgruntled officers who prepared the report and strictly unofficially," Morrison pointed out. "But that's the obvious question. What make them think something was going on? Of course they might have been simply paranoid malcontents. It's not hard to believe there are police officers who are homophobic!" He shrugged. "It's not so unusual in our society generally, so why should the police be exempt? And of course, unofficial deals are done with criminals for all sorts of reasons. In exchange for information or assistance with other cases." He sighed morosely. "It wouldn't surprise me to learn that there are informers who receive special treatment from time to time, if they're unlucky enough to be picked up doing something naughty like drugs or breaking and entering. It's a murky world out there, I'm afraid. Worse than management consultancy! Or even journalism."

"So the cops could have been seeing gay conspiracies where none existed."

Morrison nodded. "Possibly. But just because your paranoid it doesn't mean there isn't a plot."

"What is clear however," I said thoughtfully, "is that someone did break in and steal the file. But who? Even more interesting, why? And who arranged for that police raid that drew attention to the break-in? Could blackmail have been the reason for the theft of the file in the first place?"

Morrison smiled and shrugged his shoulders again wearily. "Well, how can you tell? But stories have been circulating thick and fast, all unsubstantiated by evidence of course. The most invidious thing is that anyone with a grudge can start a rumour about virtually anyone in the legal world. It's open season for speculation. There are stories of compromising photographs involving prominent figures. So it would be a major scandal if that file was ever to be leaked, whether the original allegations were true or false."

"That break-in was bad news for some people," I muttered half to myself.

"Absolutely. The break-in drew attention to the existence of the report, even if its exact contents remained secret. But who was responsible?"

"Disgruntled members of the police?"

"Or perhaps someone else with a completely different motive," Morrison said. "Perhaps the same person who organised the abortive raid that recovered some of the papers. Because it was only after that the lid came completely off the story."

I shook my head. "It beats the hell out of me," I said wryly. Then I remembered more of Tom Drever's words. "Tell me how rent-boys come into this. And what do property frauds have to do with it?"

Morrison grimaced. "Think about it. The government withdrew benefits from the homeless young in 1988. Since then the only way some of the poor little buggers can raise the rent for the flop-houses they live in is by begging in the streets. Or by earning it in bed."

"Which could be with the rich and famous?" I said slowly.

Morrison nodded. "The gay scene cuts right across conventional social lines--- it's a kind of freemasonry. Remember that not all gay men have come out openly yet. Add the problem of AIDS and you can see at least the possibility of pressure being exerted and favours done for sexual reasons. Then bear in mind that some of the accommodation the boys occupy is owned by criminal elements. Often the property is purchased in the first place with cash or loans arranged by lawyers who are, let us say, not too fussy about who their clients are or about the origins of the money." He gave me a look of resignation. "That kind of property investment can be an ideal way of recycling illegal money like cash from drugs, for example. You won't be surprised to know that some of the kids who work as rent boys are hooked on drugs and have to feed the habit."

"What a mess," I said grimly. "Buy a property with dirty money or a phoney mortgage with the help of a co-operative lawyer. Then use it for male prostitution and drugs distribution, with a built in market and a supply of cheap labour!"

"And if you are really nasty and get hold of some embarrassing evidence about important people doing indiscreet things, well, you have it made!"

"But that's a dangerous game," I said. Suddenly the connection with Scarisby and its strange games room seemed clearer. It was a waste of time being coy and I knew he would be checking me out with Tom Drever. I told him all that we had seen in the house. "But why in Orkney?" I asked him.

"Why not?" Morrison answered. "It's far enough away to be discreet. Who did you say owns the place?"

I told him about the Island Developments Trust and Anthony Raven. "There has to be an angle we don't know about," Morrison said. "There has to be a connection. I'll see what I can find out. You say this Raven is a lawyer, eh?" He looked at me and grinned.

Yes, I thought, there must be a connection. And I think I know how to find out what the connection is.

# CHAPTER 12

I left Ray Morrison and walked across town to meet Donald Lynch. Cafe de Talleyrand was on the fringe of the New Town and the pub was deep in the heart of the old part of town. But Edinburgh has been built and rebuilt over the centuries and under its classical exterior there is a half-hidden medieval core with a network of secret alleys and steep narrow stone stairways. If you know your way around, the town has a strange Tardis-like quality that can transport you in minutes to places that seem quite remote on the map. You turn a corner, cross a road, walk down a flight of steps and emerge suddenly in a completely different part of town.

The restaurant was tucked away in a lane behind one of the main shopping streets. It looked very Gallic and outside it hung a sign in French telling people that it was forbidden to station their vehicles in the street. Inside were large mirrors, art nouveau posters for L'Opera and various brands of vermouth and pastis and the low ceiling and walls were painted a nicotine-yellow colour to simulate the effect of years of Gitanes smokers. With its black and white marble floor, well-stocked bar and clutter of small tables, the place might easily have been just off the Boulevard St Germaine.

Donald was already there, sprawling back in one of the plain wooden chairs. On the table in front of him was a bottle of wine and two glasses. His jacket hung casually on the chair-back but the rest of his outfit, white shirt and striped formal tie, looked immaculate, as if the day was about to start for him. In fact I knew that he must have been on the move since six am, with an early flight up from London and a string of difficult meetings, starting probably over breakfast. His incipient paunch thrust out against the waistcoat and his prematurely bald head gleamed in the candle light as he rocked back in his seat. He leaped to his feet when he saw me, his round jowly face split in a beaming smile and he grabbed my hand. "Thank God you've arrived," he said. "I've been giving this stuff time to breath. But it was reaching the point when it was going to be it or me.

I glanced at the label. It was a very expensive Hermitage "Hmmm. A nice little aperitif." If Donald was starting on a powerful red Rhone we were in for a heavy night. I wondered vaguely why all my friends were alcoholics, but decided not to pursue the question. Who knows where it might have led? I sat down and looked across at him. Donald was very good at what he did. In the firm where we had worked together earlier in our careers he had been the brightest and the best. He was still only in his mid-thirties, but after he was head-hunted into merchant banking and became one of the most formidable corporate finance specialist in the country I had assumed he was settled for life. Or what passes for life in the frenzied world of corporate acquisitions.

He had an outstanding record of orchestrating take-overs or organising defences against hostile bids with equal facility. In particular he had a brilliant track-record of putting together technical financial strategies that convinced wavering shareholders and also a reputation for ruthless efficiency in the murky rough and tumble of wrong footing and discrediting opponents. For when millions are at stake, anything goes and the normal rules are waived. Stories can circulate about organisations or individuals that damage their reputations and credibility in the eyes of institutional investors. So at the wrong time, someone's tax problems or personal foibles like drinking habits, unusual recreational activities or marital problems can be dug up and used to win the battle for the hearts and minds of shareholders. Well, the minds at least. Hearts don't usually come into take-over bids. I would have hated that kind of work. But Donald revelled in it, which made his decision to move to the Irving Group very strange.

We swapped our usual ritual insults and settled down to the meal. "Remember, Lennox," he said, "I'm paying for this personally. It's not an expenses job, so don't overdo it." I didn't believe him. I doubt if Donald had eaten at his own expense in a public place since his university dining hall. He proceeded to order fois gras with black truffles to start, followed by a rack of lamb and a mixture of seasonal vegetables. I settled for crudite, the establishment's version of cassoulet and a fresh rochette salad. The food was good, so we didn't say much about anything for a while.

When finally Donald reluctantly surrendered the pudding menu to our waitress he watched her remove it with the sad desperation of a mother seeing her first born carried away by flood-waters. We settled for cheese and coffee. I asked for decaffeinated, of course. The trouble is, if it's very good, the stuff tastes like the real thing. So how can you be sure it really is decaff? This has always been a worry for me. I mentioned the problem to Donald. "My God, Lennox," he said absently, shaking his head. "You really are pathetic."

I ignored him. Insults were Donald's way of asking for help. "So how is the Irving Group?" I said brightly.

Donald looked suspiciously around the room. Lowering his voice he said gloomily, "It's in a financial position that we accountants describe technically as totally screwed. But don't repeat that anywhere in this town, for God sake." He looked across at me. "You don't have shares in the group by any chance?" he asked. I shook my head. "Lucky you," he said with a groan. "They gave me a bundle of options to persuade me to join. It seemed to be a good idea at the time."

"What's the problem, Donald?" I couldn't believe he would have joined a company in serious trouble without knowing it. Although when you're being head-hunted, things can happen to your judgement. I imagine it's a bit like being seduced. Not that I would know.

He leaned back and gave a short humourless laugh. "The problem is I've been totally screwed."

I stared at him. "I don't get it, Donald. How could that have happened?" I ordered two glasses of calvados and started to pay more attention. I had a feeling this story would be educational.

"You saw the structure of the group, Terry. Well, I was brought in to rationalise it. Of course I knew the family were reluctant to allow an outsider into the business. But it was obvious that they had to do something drastic to reassure the markets. Once I was on board I looked at the problems in detail and gave them the bad news."

"So now they're reluctant to take the medicine, which is nastier than they expected?" I shrugged. "Well of course they are. But Donald, you must have know how it would be. You've seen it often enough before."

Donald grimaced. "Sure, I know what you mean. Blood is thicker than water and twice as nasty. I've done enough deals with family businesses to know that. What I didn't pick up was that the family were working on a completely different agenda to the one they discussed with me. I'm only now beginning to suss it out." I sipped the calvados and looked across at him. He went on. "The chairman has a son."

"Oh God," I sighed. "Donald, how could you? Why didn't you talk to me first?"

Donald shrugged. "Well, initially the son wasn't in the picture. I was told he had been running the electrical retail operation but had decided to go to Harvard to do the full-time MBA course. The chairman convinced me that the group had a serious succession problem as a result of his only son leaving the firm. The story was that the lad wanted to be an academic; teaching and writing books and all that crap. The proposal was for me to take over as Group Chief Executive in a year or so. Meanwhile I was to run the consumer credit company with a seat on the main board and the brief to develop a new strategic direction for the entire group. It seemed to make sense. And, as I said, the package is good."

"So what's the problem?" I asked quietly.

Donald took a deep breath. "This is definitely confidential, Terry. I've uncovered undisclosed losses in the group," he made a twisted face at me. "Very big undisclosed losses."

"How big?"

"Very big. In relation to turnover and shareholder's funds they are huge.

I blinked. When Donald Lynch said they were huge the situation must be serious. "But you were brought in to execute a recovery," I said. "OK. So the situation is worse than you expected. That isn't so unusual, is it?"

"The problem is the losses are in the consumer credit company--- mostly arising from slack credit control procedures in the retail side."

"Which arose while Mr Irving Junior was in charge?" I said instantly. "Oh dear!"

Donald smiled. "Precisely. Credit and insurance products account for most of the profits in a well run electrical retail business--- which this one most definitely was not. So suddenly Lynch is the bad news guy and the business I run is set to bring down the whole group. To make it worse, I'm blaming it on the dearly departed and much loved son of the chairman--- the little bastard!" He paused and looked at me. "It gets worse, Terry. I've come to the conclusion that the chairman and some of the family knew the position all along. They have set me up to carry the can."

I leaned back with a smile. "In that case it's easy," I said. "Blame it all on the Group Finance Director. He must be a clown anyway, to have allowed this to happen."

Donald laughed bitterly. "You're right, Terry. The Finance Director is a clown. He's also the chairman's brother-in-law."

"Hell," I said and thought for a second. "OK, so you were misled. What you do is resign on a point of principle. They're probably trading illegally by now anyway. Sue them for a settlement and walk away with a wadge of dough."

Donald looked glum. "Come on, Terry," he said. "People like me are not supposed to be misled. What do you think it's going to do to my reputation? To say nothing of my chances of another job in corporate finance."

I reflected on that. "Yeah, maybe you're right. That's the worst part of being infallible."

Donald drained his glass. "Very amusing," he said wryly.

"But Donald, why did they go to the trouble and expense of bringing you into the business?"

"Take your pick. As usual, it's either a conspiracy or a cock-up. I've come to the conclusion that secretly they had decided to demerge the original core businesses out of the group. Those are fuel distribution, plant hire and the bus and transportation operations. The things the family knows how to run, more or less." He laughed. "Ironically, that's not a bad strategy. But when they realised that Sonny had screwed up so catastrophically they knew they needed a fall guy. Then the lad can come back squeaky clean from bloody Harvard and take over from Daddy."

"And you are the ritual sacrifice?."

"Exactly! That's why the sky was the limit when they were negotiating with me." Donald grinned ruefully. "And I thought it was my bonny blue eyes and winning smile."

"So the end game is a demerged business they know how to run, a career for son and heir, and the sacrifice of a virgin to appease the gods of the City?"

Donald smiled feebly. "Well, I suppose I was the next best thing. Virgins are expensive these days." He glanced across at me. "However," he said brightly. "I have an idea that might save me from the knife. In fact I have several ideas. I'd like to try them out on you. Get your reaction." He grinned at me. "I mean, you're pretty much the typical man in the street," he said brazenly.

For someone who had just confessed to being conned by the board of a small family group I thought he was being a touch condescending. But I resisted the temptation to say so. Donald didn't need me to tell him how he'd been suckered--- and I knew how much it would be hurting. He went on cheerfully, "One scenario would be to let the group go down and pick it up the pieces cheaply in a management buy-out."

I grinned at him. "Without benefit of Irvings, I presume. A touch unscrupulous perhaps. But it wouldn't do your reputation as much harm as carrying the can for the whole thing."

He nodded casually. "Yes, it appeals to me too. The trouble is that I'd need serious leverage for a move like that."

"Which means support from the institutions," I said reflectively.

Donald nodded. "Yes. Or a partner or partners of sorts. And that would be a high risk strategy for me, personally. If the Irvings spread the blame around to include me, I might have trouble finding backers of the right quality." He shrugged. "But it's an option. The other approach of course is to go along with them for a while and convince them that I can save the whole group."

"You mean, do the job they hired you to do? That's a bit drastic."

He ignored my sarcasm. "Originally I thought it could be done. It's more difficult than I thought, given what I know now and it would require a major injection of new cash. A completely different capital structure."

I could see where he was going. "Take the group away from the existing shareholders? The family wouldn't wear that, surely?"

"If their private agenda was met, why not? Maybe I could dress it up well enough to get it past them. You know, with long dated convertible preference shares to keep the institutions happy until they decide to take the equity." He paused. "My problem is that I'm currently selling a completely different scenario to our present investors. With a strategy like that I'll have to come clean quite soon if I want to retain any credibility with the institutions."

"Tricky," I said.

Donald fiddled with his glass and nodded. "One way or another I need the support of a major investor. Someone in fund management for example who might be persuaded to take a stake in the group as a straight investment. Or a merchant bank willing to lend on the back of fixed interest convertibles. That could be quite attractive for someone."

He hesitated. "Or someone with interests in computing who would buy the electrical retail chain and use it to sell their own equipment and software direct to the public. Come to that, the Irving outlets could be set up to sell insurance products if they had the right IT networks and systems." Donald looked at me blandly. "Who do we know with that mix of activities?"

I stared at him blankly. "You're not thinking of approaching Odin Investments!" I said to him in amazement.

"No," said Donald calmly. "I was hoping you would do that for me." He had the grace to blush.

"You must be crazy!" I burst out. "You know Grieder! He wouldn't listen to me for a moment on a deal like that. And if you're not crazy now, you certainly would be after you had worked for him for six months. I can't think of any two people who are more incompatible."

"Maybe, but on the other hand I can put together a persuasive proposal and a water-tight business plan for him." He grinned. "You know that's what I'm good at. And if he won't listen to you, he won't listen to anyone. Just why I do not know. But the bastard seems to trust your judgement."

I drew a deep breath. Twice in one day was too much. "Donald, you don't know what you're asking me. I don't have anything like a normal client relationship with Grieder. And besides I've already--- " I suddenly stopped.

"Already what?" asked Donald.

"Oh, nothing," I said, thinking about the strange artefact I had agreed to persuade Grieder to buy. That was going to be tough enough. I groaned. "Oh, what the hell! If I'm going to be best buddies with Hans Grieder I may as well go for broke." I glared at Donald. "But don't expect too much." Then I groaned again in despair. "I don't believe I'm saying this. But do you have anything on paper I can show him?"

"Good God, no," Donald said dismissively. ""The situation is much too sensitive to have anything floating around in public. Besides," he added calmly, "you don't think I'd trust you to explain a deal like this to Grieder, do you? It's going to be quite complicated. I need to see him face to face. All you have to do is persuade him to see me."

I shook my head sadly. "Donald, you are an arrogant bastard. I don't know why I put up with you."

Donald beamed at me. "Because I'm buying dinner! Have another calvados!"

Several glasses later I left him to make his way towards the London sleeper. As we split up I extract the quid pro quo. "Listen Donald, I need some information on an investment trust called Island Developments. A lawyer called Raven tells me it's one of his clients and registered in Liechtenstein. I need everything you can find on it; activities, directors, shareholders. Use all the computer data sources in the world. Imagine it's a hostile bid. I want any dirt you can find, if there is anything." Donald nodded silently.

"And one other thing, Donald. Tell me what you can find about an outfit called Thai Entertainment Developments. I expect it's a public limited company." That had been one of the names on the board in Raven's office and there was something about it that didn't ring true. But if there was anything I should know, Donald would find it. The two of us swore eternal allegiance and went our different ways.

It was well after ten o'clock when I got back to my flat in the New Town but there was still someone else I needed to consult that evening, late as it was. But I knew he tended to keep erratic hours. If he was at home he would be in his study reading legal precedents for his next case or browsing through his library of books on early English porcelain. So I decided to call him. If there was no reply it would mean he was out cruising the local gay discos. Either way, it was too early for him to be in bed.

John Boyd had been a friend for years, in spite of the fact that we moved in different worlds. Our backgrounds could hardly have been more different. For a start, John had an impeccable pedigree of Eton, Balliol College, Edinburgh and the Faculty of Advocates. He was also the most intelligent man I had ever met. Just why he took to me I never did understand. Perhaps it was because we were so different. Also I think he had the naive idea that there was something exciting about the world of business and finance and that if he spoke to me often enough he would discover what it was.

For my part, once I had penetrated his austere facade I found a kind and thoughtful man; sometimes inadvertently arrogant, but essentially likeable. Somehow he had managed to liberate himself from the conventions that had governed his life from school to courtroom. Now, to the credit of stuffy old Edinburgh, he was able to be openly gay and also enjoy a brilliant career as an advocate. I was sure that John would be able to tell me the truth behind Morrison's story. But would he want to?

"John Boyd." His voice boomed down the line.

"Terry Lennox," I said quietly. "John, I need some information." I told him what I wanted to know.

There was a long silence. Then came the reply I expected. "Hmm hmm. Why exactly do you want to know about this, Terry?"

"I'm working for a client--- someone you probably know. There are aspects of the break-in story that worry me, John, things that may have an adverse effect on my assignment."

"Can you tell me who this client is?"

Right to the nub of the issue, as usual. "Anthony Raven, of Raven and Thompson. I take it you know him?"

"Oh dear," John said. "You do get yourself into some awful scrapes. Isn't he the one with the interesting wife?" He guffawed loudly. John always laughed at his own witticisms, in case no one else did.

"It's not that funny, John. I may be involved in a scandal of some kind and I need to know what is going on. John, I understand the sensitivities. But can you help me? I promise you anything you say will stay with me."

There was another long pause. "Come and have coffee with me tomorrow morning. About ten thirty?"

Before he hung up on me I added hastily, "One other thing, John. I'm trying to find a young man--- "

"Aren't we all, dear boy!" He went off into another bout of laughter.

"This is a fellow called Norman Orr. If he's in Edinburgh he'll probably be know to someone in the gay community. He'd have come down from Orkney in the past few months.

"So he'll be new on the scene? Shouldn't be difficult to detect." John guffawed again. "I assume your interest isn't personal?" He seemed to find the idea entertaining.

I waited for him to quieten down. "No, John. It isn't personal. This is a professional matter too. In fact it's the same professional matter."

"Hmm hmm," he said. "I'll see what I can do. How is the lovely Patricia, by the way?"

"Who?" I said and rung off.

# CHAPTER 13

Next morning I woke up with the wonderfully clear-headed illusion that things were falling into place. Grieder was the key to the different problems that Donald Lynch and Anthony Raven had dropped on me. All I had to do was raise the issues with him in the right way and at the right time. For reasons I didn't understand they both thought I could influence the great man. Was I was selling myself short?

The other issue that had been exercising me was what young Norman Orr could tell me about Scarisby and how it connected with the police break-in, if it did. But that was a less pressing problem and I wasn't being paid to solve it. I decided to forget about it meanwhile. My bright-eyed self-confidence lasted all the way into the kitchen, when I found I was out of coffee. Damn it, I should have realised--- I've had those clear-headed feelings before.

But I was sure of a good cup of coffee at John Boyd's. He always does things in style. I switched on the classical music channel. It was bad, very bad. The music was modern and hideous. I think it may have been written in the twentieth century. The composer might even have been still alive; it was as bad as that. I shuddered and reached over quickly to switch it off. The day was collapsing into chaos. I ploughed painfully through the floor exercises that my physio says are necessary to keep me walking upright. As the exercises became tougher my optimism faded.

Grieder would refuse to see me. Even if he did see me he would quite rightly tell me to go away if I tried to discuss anything other than the assignment he was paying for. After all, we were not even on first name terms after how many years? Why would he listen to me about some far-fetched business proposal from Donald Lynch that was well outside my brief? But at least Donald's proposal was business. How likely was he to listen to anything as personal as his collecting interests and Anthony Raven's Viking brooch? To date, my relationship with Grieder had been conducted with all the informality of a Byzantine coronation. As far as he was concerned I was strictly hired help. I groaned and staggered off to shower and dress.

Then I pulled myself together and decided to call his Brussels office. After all, I had to let him know my reports on the fund management candidates were ready. "One moment, Mr Lennox," his p.a. said briskly. "I know that Mr Grieder is anxious to see those reports." After a pause she spoke again. "Mr Grieder is on his way to London. He will be staying at our corporate flat this evening and would like to discuss the reports with you there. Will you please deliver them to him at 7pm." From her tone of voice it was clear this was not a question.

I was looking for a chance to talk to him, wasn't I? But being ordered about grated. "Just a moment," I said. "Let me see what I can arrange and I'll call you--- " She gave me no chance to finish.

"Mr Grieder will be expecting you at 7pm," she said remorselessly. "I will give you the address." I knew Grieder didn't like hotels and guessed that he would have a discreet hideaway somewhere in London. But I'd never been asked to go there before. Maybe my stock was rising. She gave me an address which I knew was in the vicinity of Great Portland Street.

"I'll see if I can make suitable travel arrangements," I said weakly. "It may be difficult to find accommodation in London at this late stage."

"Mr Grieder will be expecting you at 7pm this evening," she repeated. Then she rang off. As far as she was concerned I could spend the night in a cardboard box under a railway bridge.

I hung up and grimaced at myself in the mirror. "Masterly," I said. "Over the first hurdle. A face-to-face meeting with Grieder! I don't know how you do it, Lennox." I made a couple more telephone calls and booked an afternoon flight to Heathrow. Accommodation was a more difficult problem but eventually I organised a single room for one night at a London club where I had membership rights. Then it was definitely coffee time and I set off towards John Boyd's flat.

His place was only a couple of streets away, looking out into one of the charming tree-filled gardens that make the centre of Edinburgh such a civilised place. He opened the heavy front door and stood for a moment in the hallway, beaming at me. Tall, dark and distinguished he looked every inch the successful advocate; strong patrician features, small neat moustache and dark hair greying slightly at the temples. In spite of his normally mild manner he had a pair of coal-black eyes that seemed to look straight into the recesses of your mind. "Hello, hello," he boomed, ushering me up to a bright lofty drawing-room.

Everything about John Boyd would have fitted him ideally for life in the Age of Reason, maybe that was why I liked him so much and the decor of the room reflected the fact perfectly. Furnished in formal 18th century fashion to the smallest detail, the room was an image straight out of the classic Georgian period. The elegant drapes on the tall windows had carefully selected tie-cords which I knew he had agonised over for hours. The polished wood floors and the tall gilt mirrors, the white carved marble fireplace, the elaborate cornices and over-doors were all exactly right. There were some fine pieces of antique furniture, dotted here and there with a few choice items from John's collection of early blue and white ceramics.

Only the long low coffee table was out of period and this was laid out with John's best monogrammed china and the silver spoons with his family crest. Beside them stood a splendid Georgian silver sugar bowl and milk jug. John disappeared for an instant and returned bearing the matching coffee pot. I knew this was John's idea of an informal cup of coffee with an old friend! He placed the coffee pot carefully down on a tray and smiled broadly at me. "How nice to see you. Don't usually have visitors at this time of day." He splashed the hot dark coffee into a cup and the aroma wafted deliciously across to me. Perhaps life was worth living after all. "Now what was it you wanted to ask me about? Some young man who has caught your eye?" John went off into noisy guffaws of laughter. Then he subsided a little and, still sniggering, poured himself a cup of coffee. Despite his hilarity I thought I saw a slightly apprehensive look in his dark eyes.

John was establishment through and through, so discretion came naturally to him. He was gay of course, so he had a few internal contradictions to work out. But in our discussion I knew that there would be a real conflict of loyalty in his mind. Still, above all John was fair-minded and rigorously logical. For reasons best known to himself, he trusted my judgement, so I was confident that he would help me if he knew anything about Norman Orr and Scarisby.

"Norman Orr," I said. "Have you had any luck in finding him?"

"Tell me again what this is about?" John asked, absently stirring his coffee. "Do help yourself to sugar and cream, by the way. Terribly bad habits, I know. But----."

"I'm doing some work for Anthony Raven that touches on a property in Orkney," I said and paused, trying to give him as much of the truth as possible. "I believe the young man Orr may know something that would help me to understand the set-up there." I stared at John over my coffee cup. "There are things about Raven that I don't like. And I don't really enjoy working for clients I don't like. Although," I said with a short laugh, "that seems to be all I'm doing at the moment."

He grunted. "Not particularly surprised about Raven. Not my type either. But I understood you and the belle dame were on rather friendly terms?"

I shrugged. "She comes and goes."

John brayed with laughter, "I'm sure she does!"

"But that has nothing to do with the case. I'm sure Raven knows nothing about that. Why would he come to me for this assignment if he did?"

John looked at me thoughtfully and then smiled. "Why indeed? But Anthony Raven is a very complicated fellow. It wouldn't surprise me if he knows a great deal more about the beautiful Patricia's activities than you think. Still," he went on quickly. "what does any of this have to do with the ill-fated break-in at police headquarters?"

"I'm not sure," I said slowly. "Some friends of mine in the newspaper world seem to think there is a connection between the break-in and a plot involving figures in the legal world."

John snorted. "Newspaper world!" He poured out more coffee for me in silence. "I've heard the stories," he said contemptuously. "Preferential treatment for gay criminals in exchange for who-knows-what." He glanced across at me. "As far as I am aware there's no such thing as a "magic circle" of gay lawyers, if that's what you're getting at. Of course there are gay men in the legal hierarchy as you well know." He smiled thinly. "And some of the criminals they deal with will be gay as well. Undoubtedly there are sometimes deals done in exchange for information. But that applies across the board, not just with gays."

"But you don't deny that there may be, let us say, informal social contacts between gays on opposite sides of the law," I said.

"Of course it can happen," he said "After all, illicit sexual contacts are not exactly unknown in the straight world, are they?" He glanced at me challengingly.

Touché, I thought.

"But I'm told that the break-in was simply a crude attempt to attract attention to an unofficial, unauthorised investigation that would not have stood up to serious scrutiny. It almost certainly has no basis in fact."

"Almost certainly?" I asked.

"No evidence of any improper actions on the part of law officers has emerged," he said firmly.

I nodded. "So no evidence? Only the suspicions of a few homophobic policemen?"

"No evidence," John repeated. "Unsubstantiated rumours and innuendo."

I realised that I would get nothing more from him on that tack. "Why do you dislike Anthony Raven?" I said.

John twisted his mouth into a wry smile. "He's a strange fellow with, let us say, very odd habits? And also some peculiar business associates--- not counting yourself, of course." He was delighted with the riposte and went off into another braying bout of laughter.

I drank my coffee in silence and considered what John was saying to me. There was obviously a message in a bottle. But it was clear that he had told me as much as he could without breaching other loyalties. Still I could make no sense of it as yet. "What about Norman Orr?" I asked.

John reached for a pen and jotted down an address and telephone number on one of his cards. He pushed it towards me. "I understand he is staying with friends at that address. If you want to speak to him I suggest you wait a day or two to let me prepare the way. I gather he's not keen to talk to strangers at the moment. But I'll let you know if he wants to speak to you."

The address was in the Stockbridge area of the city, a slightly faded district to the north of the New Town that had recently become more fashionable. I didn't know the actual street but depending on its location it would either be on the way up or still on the way down. John showed me out to the top of his wide front doorsteps and we stood for a moment. He placed his hand on my arm. "By the way, my advice to you is to forget all about that break-in," he said gruffly. "And do watch how you go, dear boy." I knew he wasn't worried about me falling down his steps.

I went back to collect my reports on the candidates for Grieder's fund management position. Then I had a really bright idea. I pulled Donald Lynch's career history off the word processor and looked it over. Then I added the details of his role at the Irving Group and made a few changes of emphasis to highlight his investment experience. I supplemented that with a rather imaginative view about his personal objectives and his enthusiasm for a major strategic role at Odin Investments. And voila! I had a fourth candidate! At the very least it would give me a way to introduce Donald's name to Grieder. Well, it worked for the Greeks at Troy.

Then I looked through the pile of photographs of the

117

brooch and laid aside one of Patricia. Heaven knows why. Carefully I slid the rest into a large protective envelope. Exactly how I was going to bring them to Grieder's attention I did not know. But as someone once said, I'd think of that tomorrow.

CHAPTER 14

The trip to London went smoothly enough, though the best part was the cream tea they give you to take your mind off the fact that they have you strapped into a metal box travelling at 400 mph at 30,000 feet. Then I took a claustrophobic tube ride to Green Park Underground Station and emerged almost gratefully into the noise, heat and fumes of a steamy Piccadilly.

At the Club's discreet entrance near Hyde Park Corner the porter directed me to my room. It was tucked away somewhere on an upper floor at the rear of the building, but what can you expect as an out-of-towner with only reciprocal rights? This club had some distinguished army antecedents and the bedroom reminded me strongly of barrack rooms I had lived in during my military service. There was the single iron bedstead neatly made up with clean sheets and blankets, and beside it what could easily have been a regulation wardrobe and bedside cabinet 'officers for the use of'. Against one wall there was a wash-basin and a mirror that seemed to be reflecting bleakly on better days, probably with Gordon at Khartoum. Outside, across a dark passageway were the toilet facilities and a bath that looked as if it might have been floated down the Nile in the same campaign. This was standard single officer accommodation from garrisons all over the empire. Now, if only I'd been accompanied by a memsahib!

It didn't take me long to exhaust the delights of the bedroom, so I made my way back down the grand staircase and into the stylish Victorian grandeur of the public rooms. There I killed an hour or so in the Members Bar, nursing a gin and tonic and rehearsing how I was going to persuade Grieder not to throw me out of his flat. Then it was time to go over the top.

The taxicab dropped me outside a tall brownstone block of flats, tucked away in an inconspicuous cul-de-sac off Devonshire Street. At first sight there was little to distinguish it from hundreds of similar blocks in London. In front there was a short flight of steps and an anonymous looking front door. Beside the door there was an answer phone and a row of buzzers. I studied them. Unusually, none of the flats seemed to be occupied. The ground floor was the only one with any indication on the label. It said simply "Caretaker". I checked the address again. There was no doubt about it. This was where Grieder was supposed to be staying. I pressed the buzzer.

About a millisecond later the door sprung open and a man stood in front of me and now I knew I was in the right place. Only Grieder would have staff as well trained as that. I took another look at him. The building might look hum-drum but there was nothing ordinary about its caretaker. For a start, he was very, very big, towering several inches over me. He was also very, very wide. So much so that he seemed to fill the doorway. Odder still, he was wearing a modern loose fitting and expensive looking lightweight suit in a creamy off-white colour, a pair of Armani sunglasses and an even more expensive looking suntan.

His hair was iron-grey and cropped short against a solid square head that nestled securely into massive shoulders without any need for an intervening neck. His ears, nose and mouth all seemed too small for his face and gave the disconcerting appearance of having been removed at some stage and reassembled rather carelessly. It crossed my mind that Grieder might have had him made up from spare parts. The loosely cut jacket swung open and I caught a glimpse of a dark leather holster clipped to his belt. "Yes?" he said.

I fought down the temptation to say I was from the Young Conservatives. In any case I decided that the National Front was probably more in his line. "Mr Lennox," I said firmly. "To see Mr Grieder." The giant lead me into hallway and up a flight of stairs to what must originally have been the first floor flat. Now it had been turned into a kind of reception. An efficient young secretary at a desk checked my name on her computer screen, murmured a few quiet words into an internal telephone and invited me to step outside and take the lift to the top floor. The very large man went with me all the way.

The lift was one of those vaguely European structures, all cables, open metalwork grills and sliding doors. We squeezed together into the flimsy interior. I peered at the little brass plate that gave the lift maker's name and its weight bearing limits. Then I tapped it with my finger. "I expect we'll be all right," I said cheerily.

His eyes flicked in my direction for an instant. "Yes," he said, grudgingly. I decided to save the rest of my repartee for Grieder. The lift struggled up to the top floor, past a succession of deserted-looking apartments. It began to dawn on me that Grieder owned the entire block of flats and kept them empty except for his security people and his private flat at the top of the building.

As I stepped off the lift I was greeted by a smaller and more dapper version of the big security man. His suit was a snug fit and as far as I could see he wasn't carrying any weapons. He actually smiled at me. "I'm one of Mr Grieder's administrative assistants, Mr Lennox. Please follow me. Mr Grieder is expecting you." I glanced at my watch as I entered the apartment. It was 7pm precisely. Well done, Lennox, I thought. Grieder will be impressed.

I followed the acolyte down a long corridor, past several

doors and into a large drawing-room, still brightly lit by summer sun through a long expanse of windows. We were in a penthouse perched high up on top of the building. Glancing about I saw that the room was nothing special, just a standard middle-class 1920's London flat with low ceilings, an unobtrusive fireplace, and plasterwork and walls painted in a colour I mentally christened as "bank manager beige".

What was special was the collection of strange pagan-looking objects that lay dotted about on side-tables and shelves and in glass-fronted cases. Mostly they seemed to be made of stone or bronze, with a smattering of wood and what looked like ivory or bone and all were decorated with strange motifs carved or incised on their surfaces. Some had sets of abstract symbols arranged in regular columns, while others were shaped into more or less lifelike reproductions of human or animal heads.

Grieder sat in a winged armchair with his back to a window, his face little more than a dark shadow against the light. The assistant withdrew unobtrusively to a far corner of the room. Without a word, Grieder motioned me to take a seat directly in front of him. I found myself squinting painfully into the sunlight and my first reaction was one of irritation. Control yourself, I thought. You're here to use the Lennox charm. I smiled and said, "Good evening Mr Grieder," in his general direction." Then I moved my seat firmly around so that I was positioned to his left side.

Swiftly he swivelled about in his seat, raising one hand to cover his defective eye. "Really, Mr Lennox," he said stiffly, "I would prefer you to be seated where I can see you clearly." How interesting, I thought. It isn't just a power play. The guy really has a problem. For a moment I began to think of him as human. I moved my chair around until I could see his face clearly.

He sat tense and impassive, his one icy-blue eye cold and penetrating, his face tanned and finely drawn. In spite of all his strange ways it was impossible not to sense the authority of his presence. "I understand that you have three candidates to discuss with me. Mr Lennox," he began. "I know that you have worked for me on previous occasions and so you will be aware of my requirements. But I want you to realise how essential it is that I have the highest possible quality of person for this appointment. We must ensure a coherent investment strategy for the financial services group. I insist on the very best for Odin Investments, Mr Lennox. I hope you realise that. I do not want to be disappointed again." He sighed. "I do not need to tell you, Mr Lennox, how difficult it is to find men of quality and commitment."

No, I thought, you do not need to tell me. But I'm sure you're going to! He spent the next ten minutes reciting his mantra. When he had finished I stared at him severely. I'd discovered that he wasn't used to people staring at him severely and it seemed to knock him out of his stride. "In fairness, Mr Grieder," I said, "I do not think you can say that my previous assignments have caused you any disappointment." Oh God, am I really saying this, I thought. For some reason, when I was with Grieder I found myself lapsing into the same pompous language as himself.

He drew himself up a little and his face stiffened. A twitch appeared in the corner of his mouth. Then he relaxed slightly and ran a hand over his immaculately groomed fair hair. He made the faintest inclination of his head in my direction. "In fairness, as you say, Mr Lennox, that is the case," he said stiffly. "Which is why I asked you to handle this assignment. I have decided that for this appointment we need something more than mere technical competence in fund management."

Now there's a change from the specification, I thought. Originally what he had wanted was a sound technician who wouldn't make any mistakes. But now, look out, here comes Donald Lynch! Maybe the luck of the Lennoxs was about to work again. "--- or even man-management skills of the highest order, important as these will be in integrating the two businesses," he continued relentlessly. "No, what I need is the capacity for strategic thinking. Leadership skills and initiative---"

"Imagination?" I suggested.

Grieder leaned forward towards me, his face working, his single eye widening, "Imagination, Mr Lennox. Exactly!" he said intensely. "Imagination! That is what is lacking in this organisation. I'm surrounded by people who will only follow instructions. They fail to see opportunities for change! I cannot be expected to anticipate every problem in an organisation of this size and complexity! We are a world business now." He nodded approvingly at me. "Imagination and initiative is exactly what I need. Astute of you to see that, Mr Lennox."

I smiled and looked modest, at the same time trying to give him the impression that between us we might just have come up with a radical new concept that would revolutionise the world of business. He stared at me with what might have been renewed respect. "Tell me, Mr Lennox," he said anxiously. "Do you have anyone of that type on your short-list?"

Funny you should say that, I thought, restraining an impulse to giggle. Gravitas, Lennox, remember the gravitas. I went through the backgrounds of my three original candidates, all of whom met the original specification but who no longer seemed quite to fit his latest idea. I went over their experience in the various investment markets; UK and foreign equities, fixed interest and property. Then their exposure to management, administration, accounting and asset allocation responsibility, all gained at board level in some of the best investment houses in the country.

Grieder looked only faintly impressed but non-committal. I continued. "There is another candidate; a fourth possibility who has come to my attention very recently," I said. Was I being economical with the truth? Well, lying in my teeth, really. "He would certainly represent an imaginative appointment. But I have to say an expensive one."

Grieder waved aside my caveat, "Expense is not the issue, Mr Lennox. Quality is what matters. I have made it clear to you that we need the very best person."

I started to do a quick mental calculation of my fee as a percentage of Donald's likely starting salary. Fortunately he doesn't come cheap. I dragged myself back to the immediate matter and gave Grieder a detailed account of Donald's background; his financial experience at board level when still in his twenties, his time as an acquisition and disposals specialist and his brilliant consultancy career in corporate finance. Finally I described his time in merchant banking, organising take-overs and reconstructions. "At present he is on the board of a well known public group, responsible for overall business strategy in a recovery situation."

Grieder looked impressed. "But would he be interested in an appointment such as we have in mind?" he asked cautiously.

"He would have to be convinced that the role was right for him, of course. But he is looking forward to meeting you," I said. Well, that was true. "As you can see, he would contribute something a bit different to the situation. A strategic view, as you said, rather than simply technical fund management experience. He would certainly be an imaginative appointment."

Grieder nodded seriously. "I can see that." He brightened up. "Yes, he sounds the sort of young man I should meet. Please arrange for me to see him, Mr Lennox."

"Of course." Then I decided to cover myself. "I have to say that you may find him, well, quite strong minded." That was putting it mildly. Donald was an arrogant bastard. But then so are you, I thought to myself.

But Grieder was determined to ignore my objections.

125

"Someone with a record of such success is bound to have well developed views. The secret of management is flexibility, Mr Lennox. Flexibility and a willingness to listen to advice. I certainly don't want to be surrounded by 'yes men'. I have always made that a basic principle of my approach. You must not expect everyone to agree with you on every occasion, Mr Lennox."

I looked at him with what I hoped was an expression of rapt interest. I love it when my clients start persuading me that I'm right. But what had happened to Grieder? I'd never known him to be this agreeable. Still, I had long ago diagnosed him as manic depressive. Maybe I was catching him on the upswing for once? We agreed to put the other candidates on hold pending Grieder's meeting with Donald. Then I decided to take advantage of his expansive mood. "Mr Grieder, forgive me for commenting. But am I right in thinking that most of the objects in this room are of Norse origin?

He stared at me in astonishment. He looked like a man whose cat had just asked him for an opinion on European monetary union. "Why, yes, Mr Lennox! But what makes you ask me a question like that?"

I fumbled in my briefcase, diffidently pulling out the envelope with Raven's photographs. "Well," I said, "I would welcome your views on something I have here. It has been suggested that this object may be of similar origin." He drew himself up stiffly. I sensed his mood waver and for a second I thought I had overplayed my hand. Ignoring the cold gaze I spread the photographs on the table beside him. Almost in spite of himself his hand went out towards them. He picked up one of the glossies and glanced at it. Then he frowned and turned towards the light, holding the photograph close to his good eye. He glanced at me suspiciously and frowned again.

One by one he carefully studied each of the glossy images. I couldn't help noticing that several times he went back to a shot of Patricia with the ornament about her neck. Then he looked at me enquiringly. "This object, Mr Lennox. Does it still exist and do you know where it is?"

"It does exist and it's in Edinburgh."

He shot a suspicious glance at me. "Do you mean that it belong to you?"

I smiled and said that unfortunately it did not. He looked relieved. I think that would have been too much for him to handle, even in his current upswing phase. "So," he said, "to whom does it belong?"

"A friend of mine. Well, to be honest, not really a friend. It belongs to a client."

He nodded absently, toying with the glossy photograph of Patricia Raven. "You say to be honest, Mr Lennox? Does this mean you are not usually honest?" Then he actually smiled at me!

Hallelujah! I think Grieder has just made a joke! What is going on? I must have looked astonished but he was too engrossed in the photographs to be aware of me. The images seemed to fascinate him. "That object, Mr Grieder," I persisted. "Is it something that might be of Norse origins?"

He ignored my question. "Who is the woman in this picture?" he asked, holding it up to me. "Who is the model?"

I explained that Anthony Raven was my client. "The model is his wife, Patricia Raven."

"His wife? Ah," Grieder said softly, almost to himself. "She is very beautiful."

Suddenly he stood up straight. "You ask me about the

object in the photograph, Mr Lennox. It has the appearance of being of Norse origin. The image is certainly that of a mythical animal widely used in Viking art of the Borre period. This appears to have been manufactured in gold and if its origins could be verified it would be of great interest to a collector such as myself." He turned and stared at me, his single eye hard and cold again. "I take it that is the reason for showing it to me. But its provenance would have to be verified."

"Anthony Raven would be able to tell you much more." I suggested.

Grieder paced rapidly up and down the room for a few moments. Then he paused and picked up the photograph of Patricia again. He gave an almost imperceptible shake of his head. "Extraordinary." He spoke very softly. Then he turned sharply to me. "Mr Lennox, how well do you know Mr and Mrs Raven?" I explained that I wasn't exactly a family friend. Well, not exactly.

"I am prepared to meet them," he announced firmly. "Tomorrow is a possibility. But I'm very busy from lunch onwards. Mr Lennox, I would be grateful if you will ask them to meet me in London tomorrow morning. It is short notice I realise. But I would like you to try nevertheless." He gestured to the assistant who had been sitting quietly in a corner. "Take Mr Lennox to a telephone." He glanced back at me. "I assume you know how to contact Mr Raven?" I nodded and rose to go. "And Mr Lennox," he added, "since this is not a business matter I would prefer to meet them on some neutral ground. After all, I do not want to treat them as if they were trades people."

Not like me, you mean, I thought. I had an idea. "If Mr and Mrs Raven are available, you could meet them for coffee at my club in Piccadilly. I should be happy to introduce you to them."

Grieder's face was impassive. "Certainly, if you think that

is appropriate. Please go ahead. But you will explain to Raven that my interest is still very provisional at this stage. Tell him I want to see the object. And ask him to bring his lovely wife and model," he added, as if in afterthought.

The suave assistant showed me into a neighbouring room with a telephone extension. I punched in Raven's home number, realising that this was the very first time I had ever used it. Patricia had always preferred to call me, whenever it suited her. The ringing tones sounded. There was a click and I heard her voice on the line, low and calm, repeating the number without giving her name. Nothing ever given away, I reflected ruefully. "Patricia," I said quietly.

There was a stunned silence. Then she whispered fiercely, "What are you doing calling me here at this hour? Are you mad?" "

Before she had time to hang up I cut in, "This is purely business, Mrs Raven. I want to speak to your husband." I had never called her Mrs Raven before. Somehow it sounded like an insult and perhaps that was how I meant it.

She recovered her poise. "I see," she said smoothly. "One moment, I'll call him for you. I think he's in the conservatory." Playing with his promiscuous little pets, I thought as I listened to the empty hum on the line that connected me to Edinburgh and yet didn't.

Then I heard Raven's voice, firm and confident. I brought him up to date with developments. Without any hesitation he answered. "I know the Club. Tell Mr Grieder we'll be there by ten thirty at the latest. There's an early morning flight and we will be on it. I can fit some other business into the afternoon." He paused. "And Lennox, thank you. I'm most impressed. I knew your reputation as a man of action was fully justified." He rang off before I could think of a witty reply.

As I hung up I heard a faint click on the line. Strange, I thought and stood for a moment gazing out of the window. Had Grieder been listening to the conversation? It was possible. He didn't trust anyone and he didn't take unnecessary risks. So he must have heard Patricia's initial reaction to my voice. What would he deduce from that? Only that I was much closer to Raven or at least his wife, than I had admitted. Did that matter? I shrugged my shoulders. Not to me, I decided.

CHAPTER 15

The bedroom was hot and airless and I spent a restless night on the iron bedstead. London in summer is not my favourite place. But come morning I sallied out, bathed and dressed, to enjoy the more civilised public rooms of the Club. Just before ten o'clock a large Mercedes drew up at the front door and Grieder emerged, accompanied by the dapper assistant I had seen the night before. He handed Grieder a briefcase and stood patiently while Grieder lectured him on some topic with which, judging from his attitude, he seemed pretty familiar. Then the assistant vanished back into the car and was whisked off into Piccadilly's heavy traffic.

I met Grieder in the entrance hall and showed him up the Club's grand marble staircase. As we passed the giant painting of Captain Oates struggling out into the snow storm Grieder paused to admire it. "A very gallant gentleman indeed, Mr Lennox," he said seriously.

"Yes," I said solemnly. "I believe it's a member of the Club looking for a taxi on a bad winter night."

"Oh no," Grieder replied. "It is an incident from Antarctic exploration--- " He stopped and smiled knowingly at me. "I see," he said. "You were making a joke, Mr Lennox." Then he looked at me with a slight air of puzzlement. "I was not aware that you were a military man."

I decided that it wasn't the time for the Lennox family history and instead led him into the Ladies Sitting Room, which at that time of day was deserted. We claimed a group of seats by one of the big windows looking out onto Green Park and Grieder gazed about with obvious satisfaction. "This seems to be a very suitable place for our discussion." He nodded his head. "I am most impressed that you are a member here." At that moment one of the staff brought Anthony Raven and Patricia into the room.

One of the odd things about Patricia Raven was that when she was away from me I always forgot how beautiful she was. Perhaps it was a defence mechanism. But each time I saw her I remembered again and it hit me like a truck. This time she looked positively ravishing and yet somehow simple and unaffected. Her make-up was light and natural, her long auburn hair was tied back in a loose pony-tail and she was wearing a plain linen morning dress in a rich butter-yellow colour, carefully chosen to set off her tanned complexion and the tawny brown of her oval eyes. The dress, belted at the waist, outlined her slim athletic body as she moved gracefully towards us. The only jewellery she wore was her wedding ring and a modest gold bracelet. Apart, that is, from the magnificent golden image of the Gripping Beast clasped around her slender neck. The effect was devastating.

I glanced at Grieder. He was instantly entranced. I had never seen him like that--- and it was clear to me that Raven knew exactly the effect Patricia was having. He was watching Grieder, his dark eyes cold and the smile that flickered across his face was strangely knowing. Maybe with a wife like Patricia you get used to men looking at her like that. Well, he didn't seem to care, so why should I? But I knew I wasn't enjoying any of this.

Grieder shot to his feet as they approached and greeted

them with a rare smile. He stood there, tall and elegant, his fair hair gleaming in the morning sun. Ignoring Raven, he focussed totally on Patricia, his good eye, blue and clear, blazing with a strange intensity. He reached out and took her hand with a stylish and faintly old-world bow. "I am enchanted, Mrs Raven," he murmured. Patricia looked as if she was charmed too. But this was a Grieder I hadn't seen before. Somehow I had the feeling that no-one ever had. This had the makings of a morning of revelations.

I made the introductions, although by now they came as an anticlimax. Patricia was either genuinely intrigued by Grieder or else she was a great actress. Now there was a thought! Was I seeing a Patricia Raven that I hadn't known existed? And just how many Patricias were there? I watched as she turned on her charm, knowing for once that it was not aimed at me.

But it was the spectacle of Grieder coming to life that surprised me most. Or was I simply seeing Grieder in acquisition mode, with something in his sights that he wanted? Yet to begin with, he showed no interest in the golden artefact. Instead he concentrated on being gracious to me. "I was complimenting Mr Lennox on his choice of venue for our meeting." He spoke to Raven but still smiling in the direction of Patricia. "I had no idea that he had such distinguished military connections. In my country of course we all must carry out military duties," he remarked. "But then we are famous for our discipline. I am myself a major in our army reserve," he added proudly.

Raven was trying hard to look impressed. "How interesting Mr Grieder," he remarked vaguely. "Don't you find that quite a distraction from your business commitments?" Then hastily he went on. "But I am so pleased to have this opportunity to meet you. I know how busy you are."

Grieder shrugged off the remark and turned an icy stare in his direction. "It was good of you to have come at such short notice," he said shortly. "I confess that when I saw the photographs of the object your lovely wife is wearing I was intrigued." He gave a cool smile. "As, I suppose, you expected me to be."

"I certainly hoped you would be interested," Raven said smoothly. "I had heard of your interest in Norse culture, of course, and so when my client came into possession of the figure I thought you might be one of the few private collectors to whom it would be worth showing it." He smiled confidently at Grieder. "But I'm afraid you are so well guarded that it was impossible to contact you directly. That is why I seized the opportunity when I realised we shared Mr Lennox as a valued advisor."

Well, it's time to get my invoices out, I thought. Clients don't usually sit around swapping compliments about me, at least not to my face.

"May I see the necklace," Grieder spoke directly to Patricia and instantly it was as if Raven and I had ceased to exist. Obediently she unfastened the catch behind her neck and spread the figure out before him. The weird creature lay there, clutching the edges of the metal frame, its popping eyes staring at us.

Grieder carefully picked it up and held it close to his good eye to study it. "Yes," he whispered, half to himself. "This is excellent Borre." He licked his lips and shot a glance at Raven. I had never seen Grieder so animated. "If this is genuine, it is extremely valuable Mr Raven. I do not think you should allow your wife to wear it in public. Not without proper security." Raven looked amused but stayed silent, although I sensed a frisson of resentment mounting behind his bland facade. Grieder went on. "You say this is the property of a client. Who is the owner and how did it come into their possession? And what exactly is your interest in me?" he asked bluntly.

Raven inclined his head slightly. "My client wants to sell,

always provided a suitable price can be agreed. I understand that it is made of gold and probably of early Norse manufacture. Although you would of course want to reassure yourself of that." He gave Grieder a cool smile that hovered just this side of insolence. "I'm certain you have access to experts of all kinds."

Grieder stared at him. I could see that he was trying to assess Raven but his face revealed no sign of his conclusions. Patricia caught my gaze and raised one elegant secret eyebrow. I was starting to enjoy the spectacle of two men I didn't like sparring with each other. Raven went over the history of the McNaughton family and explained how the brooch had come into the ownership of the Islands Development Trust. 'When the last family member passed away' was how he described Archie McNaughton's death.

"This Trust is registered in Liechtenstein?" Grieder broke in. "Isn't that a little--- obscure?"

Raven gave a casual wave of his hand. "But perfectly legal, I can assure you Mr Grieder. All perfectly legal," he said. "Clients sometimes prefer to minimise their taxation liabilities. You will certainly understand that."

Steady, Anthony old chum, I thought. You're over-playing your hand. To my surprise Grieder didn't react to Raven's gibe. He only smiled fleetingly. "I assume there is a good provenance for the object, Mr Raven?"

Anthony Raven pulled an envelope from his inside pocket and removed a type-written document. He passed it across to Grieder, who studied it carefully. He leaned back in his chair and looked thoughtfully at the creature on the necklace. Suddenly his mood seemed to change again and he flashed another of his rare smiles at Patricia. "Very well! Let us agree that at this stage I am interested. Perhaps we should take the matter further."

135

As he spoke he handed the document casually to me. Instantly something flashed into Raven's eyes. Was it resentment? Or perhaps alarm? Almost imperceptibly he started forward. For a moment I thought he would reach out and snatch the paper out of my hand. But recovering his poise he sank back in his chair. I glanced at the document. It was an affidavit verifying that the object had been excavated by McNaughton's grandfather from the chambered tomb at Scarisby. What intrigued me most was the fact that it was signed by John Childs. On a separate page he had listed his credentials, academic appointments and publications. Childs was obviously an expert in the field. Yet he had denied any knowledge of the ornament.

Grieder seemed to be reading my mind. "I have heard of the man Childs by reputation," he said. "He is well-known as a researcher in the field of Norse history. But I should of course like to have the object examined by my own experts." He handed the necklace back to Patricia and smiled at her. "It looks so well on you, Mrs Raven that I am reluctant to part you from it, even temporarily." He paused. "At some stage it would give me a great deal of pleasure if you and your husband could visit me at my home in Switzerland." He turned to Raven. "Why not bring the object with you?"

Patricia glanced at Raven. "I--- ," she started to say. But before she could reply Anthony cut in. "Of course," he said quickly. "We shall be delighted." Beneath the urbane tones I could hear the note of triumph.

Grieder looked at his watch and rose to his feet. "Now I fear I must excuse myself, as I have some business to deal with." He took Patricia by the hand again. "Pleasure must wait. But I shall look forward to our next meeting. One of my assistants will be in touch with you to arrange your travel to Asgard--- that is the name of my home." He stared deep into her eyes. "I do hope you will enjoy it there." He gave another low bow, shook hands briefly with Raven and then he was gone.

Anthony Raven smiled a smile of relief. "Well done, Lennox. I knew you could persuade him. You have him eating out of our hands." He turned to Patricia, his dark eyes impenetrable again. "How very persuasive Lennox can be, don't you agree darling?" Before she could say anything, he reached out and reclaimed the Gripping Beast from her and slipped it into a small velvet bag. He opened his brief-case and tucked the bag away securely into an inner compartment. Then he slid the affidavit back into his pocket and gave Patricia a mirthless grin. "You know, I think Grieder has taken a fancy to you my dear." He looked at me appraisingly. "And now I too must go. I have other business to deal with."

I went out with them to the front steps of the club. Raven stood waiting to hail a passing taxi-cab. "Staying in London long?" he asked me casually. I told him I would be back in Edinburgh that evening. "Good, good," he said. "Nothing like your own bed, is there?" Before I could think of a snappy response he continued, "I'll give you a call tomorrow or the day after. There's something more you may be able to help me with." A taxi drew up and he gave the driver an address in the City. With an airy wave he disappeared, leaving me with his wife.

Patricia stood silently watching his cab weaving its way thought the traffic. She seemed to be in a kind of trance. Eventually, breaking the silence, I said "What did you think of Grieder?"

She turned to me. There was something desperate in her eyes; something I hadn't seen before. "What a terrible man," she whispered. "The whole thing is too awful, Terry." She reached down cautiously and gently took my hand. "I going back to Edinburgh this evening too. Can I come to see you? Anthony is staying in London overnight." Her eyes glistened as she looked up at me. For a second it would have been easy to imagine that she was close to tears.

Why was I feeling so bad about her suggestion? It wouldn't have been the first time she had taken advantage of his absence. "I'm sorry," I lied frantically, not knowing exactly why. "I have an old pal arriving from Orkney. I simply couldn't get away to see you tonight. And three would be a crowd, wouldn't it?" I added lightly.

Her eyes shot open and a strange look appeared on her face that silenced me. Her mouth twitched in a kind of grim half smile. Then she recovered and in a low voice she said quietly, "Terry, please don't ever let me go!" Under her usual control I sensed a note of real anguish. "You have no idea what you mean to me."

All the false dawns were forgotten in a flash and I almost took her in my arms there and then, on the steps of the Club. Perhaps it might all have ended differently if I had done. But then what I laughingly call reason prevailed. There was something wrong about this whole episode. So it might be better if I stayed away from my client's wife until I figured out what it was that was bothering me.

I gave her a modest kiss on the cheek. "I promise to call you as soon as I'm free," I said. Then I watched her making her way down the crowded pavement. She turned round once and looked back at me. She looked glorious and I decided that I must be mad to have turned her down. But then she vanished.

I sighed, went back to collect my bag and made the one o'clock shuttle easily, half expecting to see her on the flight. But any hope of destiny coming to my aid was dashed. I ate my snack lunch on the aircraft morosely looking out at the thick white carpet of clouds that seemed to cover the entire country and thinking about the virtuous evening that lay before me. That didn't get me anywhere much. So I started to think about John Childs. He had known about the object all along; in fact he was an expert on the thing. So why had he lied to me? Well, why not? Maybe he habitually told lies. Maybe he thought it was

138

none of my damned business; which it wasn't, come to that. Equally, he wouldn't have wanted Tom Drever of all people to know he was acting for Raven and the trustees of Island Developments. Then there was Raven and the connection between him and McNaughton. I dozed off thinking about it.

When I arrived at the flat the place seemed lonelier than usual. To cheer myself up I started to calculate the fees I had earned and decided that I could afford to take the rest of the day off. There was nothing pressing to do other than to tell Donald Lynch to contact Grieder's office and to break the news to him that he was short-listed for the fund management job. He'd love that! But after all, he'd wanted an opportunity to sell Grieder on his plans for the Irving Group and this was the best I could do. Life is imperfect, after all.

I threw some kit into a bag and headed for the gym. A healthy mind in a healthy body! Maybe a work out would relieve my frustrations. A couple of hours later I tottered back exhausted. There was some veal in the refrigerator and I cooked myself saltimbocca alla romana, drank half a bottle of Recioto Amarone and topped it off with a large malt whisky. Then I cleared away the dishes and fell into the sleep of the virtuous, if not the just.

# CHAPTER 16

The next morning was not good. I woke with a bad combination of stiff muscles and a heavy head, the result of mixing virtue with indulgence. Coffee, I thought and made for the kitchen. As I waited for the blessed liquor to drip through I consoled myself with the thought that virtue and indulgence were temporary states and the effects of both would wear off. But in view of my condition I decided to give the morning exercises a miss. I put on some music and showered and dressed leisurely, to the measured notes of one of Bach's fugues from The Forty-eight, his tribute to the art of compromise. Maybe that's why I liked it so much.

I pottered round the flat, trying to do nothing in particular and succeeding brilliantly. I knew I should be contacting Donald but the thought of swapping insults so early in the day was too much for me. I considered going for a sail. The sky above the grey roof-tops opposite looked clear and bright and the wind seemed manageable. But when I checked the tide tables I found the moorings would be dried out before I could get off and back.

I sat for a while staring out of the window and thinking about Patricia Raven. When she had left me yesterday she had seemed extraordinarily vulnerable, almost desperate. But why? Not for me, presumably. Or did she think I was slipping away and simply wanted to give a jerk on my leash? That would certainly be in character. But I sensed there was something else, some genuine fear? But of what?

Reluctantly, I forced myself to think about something I understood. I started to telephone my fund management candidates. They were all in meetings of course but their secretaries knew me well by now and promised that their bosses would call me back. That was good enough for me. No-one worth a place on a shortlist would disobey their secretary. Then just before eleven o'clock my telephone rang.

I reached out, mentally rehearsing a plausible story to keep them on hold until Grieder had met Donald Lynch and decided that he was a touch too imaginative for Odin Investments. Anthony Raven's voice came as a surprise. "Good morning Lennox," he said lightly. He sounded in high spirits. "Wanted to thank you again for your help. I did mention to you yesterday that there was something else I wanted you to do for me." He went on. "It's the Orkney project. The board of Island Developments would like to discuss your candidates with you." Your candidates, I thought? They had been his candidates when we started out. But he continued rapidly. "In fact, they would like to review the whole project with you." He gave a short laugh. "Your fame is spreading, it seems. Can you get over to Brussels day after tomorrow? I realise it's short notice, but--- ."

I thought rapidly. Brussels is a dreary place but at least you can eat well there. And for the money they were paying me they seemed to be getting very little. I reckoned that I owed them a meeting at least.

"Obviously, this will mean more of your time, Lennox," Raven went on. "So I suggest you add a couple more days to your bill at the same fee rate. I suppose you haven't prepared an invoice yet?"

I told him that fees were my last consideration. He laughed ironically. "Yes," he said, "Yes, I'm sure they are. We lawyers are much the same! Now, to make things easier for you," he said, "I've asked my secretary to make your travel and accommodation reservations for Brussels." I was about to object when he added, "I generally use the Hilton in the Boulevard de Waterloo. So she's organising you a room there for tomorrow night. I hope that is acceptable.

I decided it was very acceptable. I knew an excellent restaurant just off the Grand Place, within walking distance of the Hilton. But Raven wasn't finished yet. "Lennox, there is yet another favour I'd like to ask of you. While you're in Brussels I wonder if you would mind delivering some documents for me to another client. His place is not far from the hotel. I'm preparing the papers for him now and it would be a great help if you could simply hand them in to him."

I shrugged. It seemed I was becoming a Raven family retainer. A thought occurred to me. "Where are you now," I asked, curiously.

"I'm in my office in Edinburgh." There was a moment's hesitation. "I decided against staying in London after all and was lucky to get on a sleeper at the last minute. Not as good as one's own bed of course. But time seems to be pressing at the moment. Our friend Grieder wants us to fly out to his place today! He's actually laying on his private plane to take us to Bern and a car to the airport. All the trimmings, eh? He must be serious." He gave another ironic laugh. "Although to tell you the truth, I fancy the real reason he's anxious to see us again is more to do with Patricia than with the necklace!"

I told him stuffily that Grieder had no track record as a ladies man and that I was certain his motives were honourable, if not actually boring. He seemed to find that very funny and as he rang off he was laughing.

I went back to staring out of the window. I didn't like Anthony Raven. Of course, strictly speaking he had plenty of reasons to dislike me too, assuming he knew the truth about Patricia and myself. But who could tell what was going on behind that polished mask? Still, in my gut I knew there was something strange going on, something that I didn't understand. It was clear however that Grieder must be very interested to have invited them to his hallowed Asgard. Well, Grieder could take care of himself. So what was worrying me? I decided that I needed more information about Norse artefacts.

I called a woman I knew slightly at the National Museum. Norse history was not her field, she said. But she put me on to a colleague, an archaeologist who knew the period. I told him I had questions about the object and when he heard that I had photographs he agreed to see me later that day. Then I laid out the remains of the proscuitto ham from last night's meal and added a couple of slices of melon and some French bread. I eyed the remains of the Amerone thoughtfully but decided against it. I ate lunch and then headed up town to the museum.

I was shown into a small office that was probably used by the staff for meeting cranks and eccentrics like me who stagger in off the streets with questions about their pet subject. A few minutes later a tall heavy set man with a brush of fair hair, thick lensed spectacles and a brooding expression came in. He sat down morosely opposite me, obviously fearing the worst.

When I showed him the photograph he seemed to brighten up. "Do you have this object?" he asked. I explained that it belonged to a friend of mine. "It looks as if it could be interesting," he said slowly. "Have you actually seen it?" I told him that I had and he asked me to describe it to him. He nodded enthusiastically as I spoke and examined the photograph carefully through a small magnifying glass. He glanced up at me. "It looks as if this is gold. Is that the case, do you know?"

I shrugged. "I was told it was gold and it looked like gold to me. Is there anything you can tell me about it? I mean, is it really an old piece?"

"I should have to examine it before I could be sure of that," he said cautiously. "This funny little fellow," he tapped the photograph, "is certainly a well-known figure from ninth century decorative art in Scandinavia. Ugly devil, isn't he?" he added. "It's based on the familiar Gripping Beast motif, quite common in Norse and to some extent Celtic art." He studied the photograph again. "Yes, that's right. This image was a major force in the northern countries at that time. Though no-one seems to know exactly what the creature means or even where it came from. Can you describe to me the appearance of the brooch?"

I thought back to the necklace I had seen. "It appeared to be a solid casting, but it was heavily ornamented with fine wire and small globules of gold. Is it possible that something as fine as that could be produced as early as the ninth century, in that part of the world?"

"Oh yes!" he said eagerly I must have pressed the right button for he proceeded to give me a twenty minute lecture on Norse jewellery manufacturing techniques, the crux of which was that casting of small pieces by specialist craftsmen was commonplace in the main Scandinavian markets and towns. "Mostly they were made in bronze, mass produced as ornaments for cloak fastenings and the like. But they could and did make objects of great beauty in silver or even gold, often embellished with filigree work and granulation," He tapped on the photograph. "As we seem to see here."

"So this could be as old as the ninth century?" I insisted.

He grimaced. "Well, it could be. Or it could be a later copy. I can't say from a photograph. To be frank, it would be difficult even with the object before me. What is crucial with most works of art is the provenance of the object. Do you have any idea of its origins?"

I nodded. "I believe so," I said thoughtfully, thinking of

John Childs. "But is it possible for something like this to be counterfeited well enough to fool an expert?"

He leaned back in his seat. "Remember there is a difference between a copy and a fake," he said enigmatically. I looked at him enquiringly. "A copy is only a fake if someone pretends it's something that it isn't. But the short answer to your question is 'yes'. Most things can be counterfeited by an expert. There are ways of testing materials, of course. But if gold is used--- " He shrugged his shoulders, "well, it will test as gold, naturally enough. It can be difficult to tell old gold from new gold. Usually the best way to identify an object is from certain stylistic elements that an expert will recognise as being right for the period. Images or patterns. Or the methods of manufacture."

"Like the motif?"

"Exactly. The style says it's from the Borre period of Norse art."

"Or a good copy?" I said.

"Sure. That's why the provenance is so essential."

"But fakes do occur?" I persisted.

"Oh yes. Fakes or copies, call them what you will. But if you have a skilled craftsman, with the right materials and technical equipment; a melting furnace and so on--- and of course the knowledge of the correct stylistic design for the period---." He paused. "Well, it's possible to fool most people."

"Even an expert like you?"

He laughed. "Sometimes the experts are easier to fool than an amateur. You see, they know what to look for! So when they see it, they're naturally convinced that the object is alright. You probably know about the Tiara of Saitapharnes," he said casually.

That one had definitely escaped me. I shook my head. "Um--- no," I said. He looked surprised. Obviously in his circle it was as familiar as the Hanson demerger programme.

"Oh, it was a famous incident. The Louvre--- ," He paused and glanced at me doubtfully. "The Louvre in Paris?" I smiled encouragingly and he went on, reassured. "Well, at enormous cost their experts bought the fabulous golden tiara of Siatapharnes, the famous Sythian king. Fourth century Crimea?"

"Oh, that Siatapharnes," I said cheerfully.

"Yes," he said slowly and looked closely at me for a moment. Then he continued. "Years later they discover that the tiara had actually been made in 1904 by a goldsmith in Odessa, which was a centre for that sort of thing." He smiled . "So it can happen to the best of us--- if you have an audacious forger with enough skill and knowledge and a buyer with more money than caution. And a good provenance for the object, of course."

I made my way thoughtfully back to the flat and heard the telephone ringing as I entered. It was John Boyd, telling me that Norman Orr would meet me in Stockbridge next morning at about ten o'clock.

# CHAPTER 17

When I found the right street it turned out to be neither on the way up nor on the way down. Instead it seemed to be locked into a shabby 1950ish gentility. A line of neat rather taciturn doorways, each with a set of clean stone steps and a heavy wooden front door painted in regulation New Town colours, curved away into the middle distance in a sombre classical facade. Above them were serried ranks of windows gazing blankly out onto the grey cobbled street.

The door I wanted had lost its original brass bell-pull with the carefully engraved nameplates, probably melted down to make shell casings in the last war, and it had not yet acquired a modern answer phone system. But John had warned me that Orr was staying in a flat at the very top of the building. I pushed open the door and started to climb. The public stair was dark and the stone steps worn and uneven.

But things brightened up as I approached the top floor, where the light from a domed glass cupola streamed in. There were only two flats on the top floor. On one door was a metal name-plate with the name of a married couple. I guessed Norman Orr had to be staying at the other one. This had a red painted door and a piece of cardboard that listed five residents, with a variety of hand written additions and deletions recording the ebb and flow of the inhabitants. None of them was called Orr but undaunted I pressed the door bell and waited.

Vague noises sounded from within. Suddenly the door was dramatically flung open and a tall, statuesque brunette wearing a three-quarter length evening dress in purple and black stood poised before me, hand on hip. This wasn't exactly what I had expected. At a glance I took in the shapely legs, the high heels, the stylish hair-do, the strong attractive features and the bold dark eyes. Now, as it happens I have a slight penchant for tall statuesque brunettes and finding one here, dressed to kill at ten in the morning, triggered a whole set of conflicting emotions.

This was not your typical Edinburgh housewife, at least not at this time of day. Had I stumbled accidentally into the lair of a working girl? Possibly I had misunderstood John's directions. Or was this some product of his school-boy sense of humour? "Hello," the figure said meaningfully in a low throaty voice, looking me up and down. "Is there something I can do for you? I hope." The look was unmistakeably challenging and strangely familiar and in spite of myself I felt a flicker of interest. Well, if I'm honest more than a flicker. Then I recognised the delivery. It was Mae West!

Before I could find a suitably suave opening line a strong male voice sounded from somewhere in the interior of the flat. "Oh Dave, get out of the way." The glamorous brunette made a little moue in my direction and with a shrug and a resigned lift of the eyebrows stepped back from the doorway. A big young man in his early thirties appeared. He was athletically built, with a gorgeous tan, closely cropped fair hair and a neat masculine moustache. He was wearing the standard gay uniform of blue jeans, boots and a checked plaid shirt. "Yes?" he said abruptly.

"Dave?" I said to him. "Did you say, Dave?"

"Oh, he's such a slut!" He waved his hands in the air dismissively. "Don't tell me he made a pass at you?" As I was recovering my wits he went on. "Dave is staying for a day or so

148

while he does his drag act at one of the clubs in town. Bloody queen!" He stared at me and then gave a derisive laugh. "Did he fool you?"

"Well--- ," I started to say weakly.

He cut me off. "Anyway, who are you?" I told him I was a friend of John Boyd's. "Right," he said and led me into a small sitting room at the front of the flat. "Have a seat and tell me what you want."

"Is your name Norman Orr?" I asked him.

"Why do you want to know?"

I controlled my irritation and briefly explained my interest in Scarisby and Orr. "You're not from that bastard Davis, are you?" He stared fiercely at me. Then he relaxed slightly. "No, you don't look like one of his thugs. But you're not a newspaper reporter either, are you? Norman has had enough trouble with this thing. He's still upset about--- everything. He doesn't want to be bothered with all that crap."

"Who is Davis? And what the hell are you--- Orr's self-appointed guardian?"

"Yes, you might say that," he said arrogantly. "Look, Norman has had a rough time. You may find it hard to understand. But he has lost someone very dear to him."

I shook my head. "No, I don't find that hard to understand in the least. And I'm glad the lad has friends looking out for him. All I'm trying to do is find out a little more about some aspects of this thing that affects me too."

"Such as what?"

"Such as what led to his friend McNaughton's death. I

149

can promise you that anything he tells me will be strictly between us."

The big young man was silent for a moment. "John Boyd says you're OK. And he isn't usually wrong about people," he said grudgingly.

I smiled engagingly, "I taught him everything he knows."

"I doubt that," he said, with the hint of a smile. "Wait here." Then he disappeared into a room at the rear of the flat. A few minutes later he returned with a smaller, slimmer, gentle looking young man, fresh complexioned, with a round head and a boyish face, neat pleasant features and a cap of straight dark hair. He sat almost diffidently in a chair opposite me.

"Norman Orr?" I asked.

He shook his head. "No. But I'm a friend of his."

I laughed. "I should have known! I'm glad he has so many friends. But I really would like to see Norman Orr."

"Tell him what you told me," the butch gay said to me brusquely.

Patiently, I repeated my story. Then the small one said mildly, "You say John Boyd is a friend of yours?

I nodded. "Yes. He told me you would be expecting me. Look, is something wrong? Because if this is a bad time, I can go away."

He paid no attention to my question. "Mr Lennox, do you have anything to do with a man called Anthony Raven?"

I thought quickly. Maybe this was not the moment to be entirely open with them. I leaned forward towards him confidentially. "No. That is to say, not exactly. But I'd be very interested to find out more about Raven. Can you or Norman tell me anything about him?"

The two young men exchanged ironic glances. The mild-mannered young man smiled gently at me. "There are quite a few of our friends who could tell you about Anthony Raven."

I was beginning to find this interesting. "But what about Norman Orr?" I said. "Do I get to see him?"

He nodded. "Yes, I think so," he said quietly. "But you should understand, Mr Lennox, that Norman has been under a lot of pressure recently. He happens to know---- well, certain stuff about some influential people. And they want to keep him from talking about them."

"Things about Archie McNaughton's death?"

"Yes that certainly--- and other things too."

The butch young man broke in. "Norman has his own ideas about Archie McNaughton's death and they don't fit the official line. Archie didn't commit suicide. That's for sure. But that isn't exactly why Norman is being hassled."

His friend added quietly, "We don't know the whole story, I'm afraid. To tell you the truth I'm not sure Norman does either. But there are people in this town who think he knows enough to make him uncomfortable to have around. How it all fits together--- well, we just don't know."

"Look," I said, "I don't know enough about this business to know what I want to know, if that makes any sense to you. But I have the feeling I'm involved in something that isn't quite right and that Raven is involved in it. But whatever is going on may have serious implications for me and for my business clients. I can't go into all the ramifications now. But it's important for me to know how Anthony Raven connects with McNaughton. I was told that Norman Orr might help me and I'd like to meet him. If you can help me, fine! If not, I'll deal with the problem some other way." I stood up as if to leave the flat.

They exchanged hurried glances. Suddenly the smaller one rose and put out his hand. "I think you are OK. My name is Brian. And this," he indicated his butch friend, "is Bob. The reason we're being so careful is that some of the people looking for Norman are pretty nasty. We just want to keep him, and ourselves, out of any more trouble."

"This man Davis you mentioned, is he one of the people who are causing trouble?"

Brian nodded gloomily. "Davis is always trouble. But if you want to see Norman, Bob here will take you to meet him. He's not far away."

"Is all this necessary? I asked. "If you're having trouble with this guy Davis why not tell the police. Ask them for help?"

He smiled sadly at me. "You don't know how these things work for gay men, do you? Or how much influence certain people have around here. But I'll let Norman tell you about that. We're simply trying to look after him, Mr Lennox. We like to take care of our own. So go with Bob. He'll introduce you to Norman."

Bob lead me out of the flat and down the stairs. As we went, I passed Dave in the passageway. He flashed his eyes at me. But this time it had no effect. I was glad about that. Out on the street, Bob strode ahead of me. "The place is a couple of blocks away," he said over his shoulder. "Listen, I'm sorry if I was a bit rude back there. It's just that we've been getting so much hassle recently. It was so bad he had to lay low with some friends in the country for a couple of weeks. We thought we had shaken off Davis. So when you showed up,--- " he glanced sideways at me.

"When I showed up you were pissed off?"

He grinned at me. "Absolutely!" He stopped and indicated a short flight of steps up to the entrance of a slightly seedy looking cafe. "In here." The place was all stripped pine tables and benches, with at one end a small counter on which there was a cash-register, a couple of steaming coffee jugs and some trays of wholemeal muffins and slices of carrot cake. The walls were covered with hand written posters advertising worthy causes like experimental theatre, meetings about anti-global warming and gay/lesbian support groups. It was the kind of place for people who knit their own yoghurt. In fact there were a few likely prospects sitting there, drinking coffee out of hand made mugs and reading the Guardian.

As we entered, a young man stood up and waved to Bob. We went across to his table. He was tall and strongly built, probably in his late twenties, with a pleasantly open face, large brown eyes and a shock of curly brown hair. He was wearing a pair of countrified blue cords and a Fair Isle patterned sweater that had clearly taken a battering from a few northern winters. It didn't take much to figure out that I was looking at the elusive Norman Orr.

His handshake was strong and he looked me steadily in the eye when Bob did the introductions. I took to him immediately--- especially when he went off in search of coffee. He came back with two mugs and took a seat opposite me. "I gather you are interested in Archie's death," he said to me directly. "I'm glad some one is."

I hesitated. "To be honest, I don't really believe your friend's death has a bearing on my problems. But I'd be interested in anything you can tell me about Scarisby." I told him frankly about my involvement with Raven and my trip to Orkney, but without mentioning what Tom Drever and I had found in the private rooms.

153

I saw a look of alarm come suddenly into his brown eyes when Raven's name was mentioned. "You're working for Raven?" he said stiffly, shooting a worried glance at Bob.

I held up my hand. "Not really. I'm doing a job for a client of his, but that's almost finished. There are still some loose ends however; things I don't like. Things that worry me. Moreover I have an important meeting with the client coming up when I will be giving him my advice. So I'd like to understand exactly what the hell is going on." I grimaced at him. "If I get it wrong, it won't do my reputation any good. And in my business you're only as good as your last job."

Orr nodded. He seemed to accept my explanation. "It's just than Anthony Raven always seems to be bad news for me. Some people connected with him are giving me a hard time," he said. "They want to make sure I don't speak out of turn about--- certain things." he hesitated.

"The parties at Scarisby?"

"That had nothing to do with Archie," he said hotly.

"They took place in his house," I said gently. "Do you mean he didn't know about them?"

Norman Orr sank back and stared into his half empty coffee mug. "No, you're right, of course." he said reluctantly. "Archie did agreed to all that. Why, I could never understand." Then he looked up at me helplessly. "But he always made sure that we, he and I, were away when the parties took place. He was never involved in them, I can assure you of that! So I think Raven had some hold over him. Archie wouldn't have agreed otherwise. He was too--- well, decent." He shook his head sadly. "Archie was the nicest man I ever knew. No, he must have been forced into it somehow."

"Norman," I said quietly. "Forced into what? What was Raven doing there?"

Bob intervened. "I can tell you that. God knows, it's simple enough. Raven provided young guys to meet wealthy older men there. Mostly married men with special tastes, if you know what I mean."

"I'm not sure I do," I said. Then I remembered the equipment in the rooms at Scarisby and flinched. "Well, maybe I do," I added hurriedly, before either of them offered to complete my education. "You're saying Anthony Raven was involved in that kind of thing?"

They both smiled wryly. Then Bob nodded his head vigorously. "Anthony Raven is the primo in that scene. He and a man called Tim Davis who does most of Raven's dirty work. It's Davis who recruits the boys and makes sure they keep quiet afterwards. He's a real thug. A nasty piece of work--- and he has some even nastier friends."

"How do you know all this?" I said. "And where do they find the young men? Tell me how it works."

Bob looked grim. "Davis runs a series of lodging houses for Raven. Places where kids with no income can find a bed. If you're desperate enough--- for money or excitement or even some kind of relationship, I suppose, it's easy to be drawn into something like the parties at Scarisby. Most of the men who provide the money are well off and influential. So it seems glamorous to the boys. And once they're in it's easy to keep them in--- as long as they are useful. Davis uses a combination of threats and cash or favours of some kind; jobs and the like."

"Fear, greed and excitement. The best three reasons for doing anything." I looked at Norman Orr. "But if all this is so well known, why are you being pressurised by this man Davis. Why is it so important for you in particular to keep quiet?"

Orr grimaced. "Because with Archie dead I'm the only one, other than Raven, who can name names. The only one who could identify some of the men who used Scarisby. I suppose they're worried in case I talk." He gave a contemptuous laugh. "If only they knew! Why would I do anything to damage Archie's name?"

I thought for a second. "Surely any of the young men can identify their clients?"

Orr shook his head. "Unlikely. Each one was taken to Scarisby just once. So unless they formed some kind of permanent attachment with someone they met there they probably didn't know real names."

"How did they get up to Orkney? And to that house?"

"Mostly by car and ferry, if what I've heard is true. Usually Davis drove them up and in the summer they were taken across on a fast motor launch that Raven keeps there. That was a special treat!"

It all sounded bizarre. But it was beginning to have a horrible smack of reality. "Tell me," I said, " why would a man like Raven be involved with something like that?"

"From what I hear," said Bob casually, "I'd say Raven is a complete moral pervert. He's simply corrupt."

"I'm told that Raven gets his kicks from corrupting other people," said Orr. "I'm sure that's what he tried to do with Archie. With the other men, the ones who used the place, I think he probably wants to have a hold over them. Something he can use to control them. All Raven cares about is power and control." He shrugged. "I don't know what these men do for him in return. But some of them are important; powerful and influential."

I mulled over what they had told me. "Norman, you say you and McNaughton always stayed away from the house when these affairs were being staged. How come you know who was present?"

He flushed. "Well, Archie always knew. He always knew who was coming. To be honest, he thought it was amusing to have those kinds of people beholden to him in some way. And he'd tell me, sometimes. When he'd had a drink or two. Not that he ever drank too much," he added quickly.

"But did you ever see any of them?"

"But everyone knows about it," Bob burst out angrily. "I mean everyone knows the kind of man Raven is!" Norman nodded agreement and Bob went on wildly. "I mean, any man who would make use of his wife like that is definitely not normal. However you define normal!"

I stared at him. " What are you talking about now?"

He pulled a face. "Oh, Raven uses her to pull some of the young men for his parties--- offering them his wife to get them involved."

"But I thought--- I mean, you said the boys were gay?"

Bob smiled pityingly at me. "Some of them don't mind either way." I must have looked sceptical and he exclaimed angrily, "For God's sake! Some of them are bi-sexual! Just like Raven!"

"Hey. Stop, I can't handle this," I heard myself say. By now I was reeling. Suddenly I felt sick. It wasn't possible! What I was hearing had to be false; lies or idle gossip between these strange young men. It was simply not possible. Patricia, cool, distant, Patricia involved in something as crude and disgusting as this? I shook my head desperately. No, I couldn't accept any of it. They had to be wrong. It was all hearsay; a product of the fantasy world in which they lived. I could just about accept the idea that Raven had done some pimping for important clients who could do him favours, gay married men with strange tastes. That would explain Scarisby. But Patricia? No, that was beyond belief.

I turned to Norman Orr. "You say you think Raven had some hold over your friend. Have you any idea what that could have been?"

He shook his head. "Not really. Most of the time they moved in different worlds. Although they were at university together. I believe they did law about the same time and may even have shared a flat in Edinburgh. But Archie never spoke about it." He paused. "And of course Raven handled Archie's estate after, after what happened." His voice quavered and he stopped, looking down at his coffee.

At last, a fact I could check on! "Tell me about Archie McNaughton's death," I asked him.

Orr looked bleakly at me. "They say he shot himself. But I know he didn't." The young man shook his head. "Archie rang me to say he was coming home that night. He said he was looking forward to seeing me." Orr's voice trembled slightly. "There was no way he would have taken his own life," he went on strongly. "He was happy--- happier than he had been for years. He told me that often." The young man's voice shook again. He cleared his throat and stared at me. "He said it to me that night on the telephone. So I know he didn't kill himself."

He looked doggedly at me. "Archie must have been murdered to keep him from exposing something he was investigating. Something financial, I think." He looked at me helplessly. "I don't know what. But he had a lot of enemies. There were papers missing from his briefcase that were never found. I'm sure he was killed because he was making himself a nuisance to someone."

That fitted with Tom Drever's theory. But the idea of Patricia having any part in this nightmare still gnawed horribly at me. I turned to Bob. "What makes you think Raven is gay, or even bi-sexual come to that?

He lounged back in his seat. "That part is easy. Because I know that he hangs around gay pubs and picks up young men. Do you think that makes him gay?" he said with a laugh.

"You've seen this yourself?" I asked. "Or is that something else you've heard too."

He shook his head. "No," he said scornfully. "I don't go to places like that. But I've been told about it by a lot of the guys."

"And what about Davis? Is there any proof he works for Raven?"

He reddened. "Well, he fronts up these properties for someone. And half the gay world knows that Raven is involved. But he's too smart to get his hands dirty. You don't think he's going to come round collecting rents personally, do you? That's why he needs Davis and his muscle to keep discipline."

"And yet you say Raven personally involves the boys in sexual activities? Does that seem likely? Why would he take that risk?"

Bob sprang to his feet. "Everybody knows it's true!" He shouted angrily. "What are you trying to say?" He gestured to Orr. "Norman knows what went on at the house in Orkney!"

I nodded quietly. He was right, of course. It was the Scarisby connection that made it all too convincing. "What about you, Norman? What do you plan to do now?"

"I just want to get away from here, if I can find a job. I've been applying to a few places a long way away," he smiled ruefully. "That seems to be the most popular thing I can do."

It didn't seem they could tell me much more, so I paid for the coffees and we left. I shook hands with them on the pavement outside and wished them well. "Regards to Dave, too," I said. Bob looked pained as he strode away down the street with Norman in his wake.

Back at my flat I thought over what they had told me. If it was even partly true then Raven was a monster; a control freak with a flair for corrupting others, including Patricia if I was to believe what the young men told me. But I couldn't accept that. The story was probably a product of their over-heated imaginations, built up out of spite and jealousy. But if there was a secret connection between Raven and McNaughton it almost certainly involved the use of Scarisby for extramural entertainments of some kind. Could it be part of something wider, the so-called magic circle? Obviously it might be. But then there was the brooch and the Grieder connection. There seemed to be no obvious connection with the gay scene there. As for Patricia, what they claimed was out of the question.

If McNaughton and Raven had been acquaintances in the past I knew exactly how to find out. In the part of town that was vandalised by the University in the 1960's there's a hideous slab-sided monstrosity they call the University Library. Looking a bit like a Stalinist railway station, it is one of those modern buildings that have a better view from inside looking out than outside looking at it. I walked across town and into what had once been a charming 18th century square of houses before our cultural leaders demolished them to erect a rectangular concrete block covered in grimy glass.

I flashed an out-of-date membership card at the warder and must have looked respectable enough to get by. I suppose compared to the students I was. But that doesn't say a lot. A nice lady told me I would find what I was looking for in the Special Collections Department. That had a slightly racy ring about it and my hopes were raised for a moment. But it turned out to be a pretty dull collection of old catalogues and prospectuses. But it did house the General Council Register, which has a record of everyone who has graduated from Edinburgh over the past few hundred years. My name was in there somewhere but it was Raven's name I was looking for.

I found him in the Law Department list. Then I dug further. With a deadly thud of inevitability I found the name of Archie McNaughton. They had been students in the same year. So Raven had known McNaughton since university days. Perhaps even, as Norman Orr suggested, had shared a flat with him. Then Raven had acted as McNaughton's executor for the Scarisby estate after his death. The connection might make the use of Scarisby for their gay parties more understandable. But did it tell me anything about McNaughton's death? Well, at least it was a fact. And facts had been pretty hard to come by so far.

As soon as I reached my flat I called Ray Morrison. He was at his desk and sounded glad to hear from me. "You've called at just the right time," he said cheerfully. "I'm trying to write an item on the effect of the European Union on Scots law."

I blinked. "I think you have the wrong man," I said. "I don't know a thing about Scots law."

"I know," he said. "Neither do I. That's why I'm so glad you interrupted me. Now what can I do for you?"

"I wanted to ask you if you had come across a man called Davis."

"Tim Davis?" he asked. "Hey, you do get around, Lennox."

"So you do know him?"

"Not personally." He laughed, "Tim Davis isn't quite my cup of tea. For a start he's a butch gay! But you remember what I told you the other day about that abortive police raid? Well, Davis is the guy--- the one whose shop was raided by the police. But they decided that he had been set up by someone else unknown and the evidence wasn't strong enough to hoist him. Davis is what you might call a minor entrepreneur! Involved in a raft of small businesses--- some more or less legal. But a lot of his activities are, well, on the cusp to put it mildly. Anyway, there was the tip-off I told you about and the police found some of the incriminating documents at his place. But they couldn't connect them to him directly and it began to look as if the papers had been a plant by someone who wanted to incriminate Davis. The whole thing got too complicated for the police and it turned into a bit of a cul-de-sac."

"Except that it helped to keep the story of the break-in alive," I reminded him.

"Yes, there was that." Morrison said thoughtfully. "Are you on to something, Lennox? Remember I'm supposed to be making my living at this game. So if you have a story--- ."

"Don't worry," I said. "You'll be the first to know if there is anything printable." I hesitated. "Do you know this man Davis well enough to set up a meeting for me?"

Morrison sounded cautious. "As I said, I don't know him that well. But I might be able to contact him. What should I say you want? He won't see you just for the hell of it. And better watch your step. Davis isn't a man to mess about with."

I thought rapidly. "Tell him I'm writing a book about great miscarriages of justice and I want to hear his experiences with the law."

162

Morrison chuckled. "I like it! I'll see what I can do to help. I'll call you as soon as I get a lead. But remember, watch your step with Davis."

I explained to Morrison that I would be away on a business trip for a day or so. Then I started to prepare for Brussels. Whatever the truth about Raven, I was still working for him. Or at least for Island Developments. By the time I finished packing, the tickets and the details of my trip had arrived from Raven's secretary.

They included a large brown envelope addressed to a M. van Heulen in the Petit Sablon, with strict instructions to deliver it promptly at nine-thirty the following morning. 'M.van Heulen needs these papers urgently.' was written in large letters on the envelope and the word "promptly" was underlined twice. I was beginning to resent other people's secretaries telling me what to do. If it hadn't been for the money--- . Oh well!

There was also a note from Raven telling me I was expected at the offices of Island Developments near the Place Stephanie immediately after lunch. Now that was more civilised, giving me time for a leisurely lunch somewhere around the Grand Place. Would the expenses stretch to Maison du Cyne? I decide reluctantly that this time I'd have to make do with something less glamorous.

CHAPTER 18

My flight was late arriving at Zaventem so I took the airport train into the Gare Centrale and from there, with the time difference working against me I decided to go directly to my hotel. The taxi driver I found was obviously not a Belgian and the language he spoke had only a passing resemblance to French, even allowing for a Walloon accent. Judging by the way he drove, my best guess was that he was a Serbian war criminal on the run. Luckily the Hilton sounds the same in any language and within a very few minutes he had hurtled up the Rue de la Regence, whirled round in front of the monumental Palais de Justice and dropped me triumphantly in front of the hotel on the Boulevard de Waterloo.

I checked in, collected my room key from the concierge's desk and made my way to my room. Raven's secretary had done well by me. The bedroom was spacious and equipped with every TV channel in Europe, a glamorous tiled bathroom big enough for a small family to live in and a king-sized bed that you needed a compass to find your way around on. I threw myself down on the bed and started to think about Patricia. I'd been doing a lot of that since I heard Norman Orr's story. What they had said about her was too ugly to be true; scurrilous lies, dreamed up in the strange twilight zone in which those young men lived. I could accept that Raven was involved with something nasty in the wood-shed. But Patricia? No, never her

164

and certainly what they had suggested was unthinkable.

By the time I had convinced myself of Patricia's virtue, it was too late to venture out to eat. I called Room Service and ordered a steak and one of those beers with the funny flavours that the Belgians make so well. Who else would think of making beer like that? Then I settled down to a spot of desultory channel hopping in the hope of finding a programme worth watching. After a while I gave up and climbed into the north-east corner of the huge bed. For a long time I lay listening to the traffic streaming past on the Boulevard and watching the reflection of their headlights flickering across the ceiling. I think I fell asleep wondering about Patricia.

I woke late, after eight o'clock, and ordered coffee and croissants to be sent to my room. Inevitably the knock sounded just as I was coming out of the shower. With a curse, I wrapped one of the Hilton's dressing robes around me and still wet and dripping, sprang across the room to open the door. Standing there in the corridor holding my breakfast tray was Patricia Raven. "Bon jour," she said. "Avec les compliments de la maison."

I took the tray from her with one hand and drew her into the room with the other. I had no idea where she had come from and at that precise moment I didn't care. As the door slammed shut behind her she slid into my arms and kissed me. By some miracle the tray found its way safely onto a side table as she pressed herself against me. I forgot all about Norman Orr's stories. Then I forgot all about breakfast as I felt her firm strong body melt into mine, burning through the thin robe. She started to loosen the tie of dressing robe, still with her lips locked against mine, her eyes closed. I drew back my head for a moment and gasped, "Patricia, what are you doing here?"

Barely removing her mouth from my lips and tugging at the robe she murmured "I'm trying to undress you, silly. I should have thought that was quite evident. Has it been that long?"

After that there didn't seem to be much opportunity for conversation. Somehow we made it to the big king-sized bed and over the next hour or so I think we pretty much covered every point in the compass. Finally, we lay tangled together, exhausted and wet with our mingled perspiration. I propped myself up on one elbow--- that was about as much as I could manage at that stage--- and looked down at her. Her hair was a mess and her face looked strangely naked with the make-up smeared and her lipstick gone. The tawny eyes stared steadily back at me in silence. I shook my head in wonder. "Where in the world did you spring from? And how did you persuade them to let you come up to my room?"

With a strange smile she said, "I told them I was your wife." Then she paused. "Wouldn't it be nice if it was true," she whispered quietly, almost to herself.

"And they believed you?" I said in amazement. "You could have been a hired assassin!"

Her eyes widened for an instant. Then she smiled a crooked smile at me. "They were expecting me," she said. "I called last night to tell them that my plans had been changed and that I would be joining you for breakfast." She had the grace to blush. "Actually, I said it was our anniversary and you had been so upset that I couldn't come on this trip with you that I wanted to give you a pleasant surprise.

I took a deep breath and kissed her. "That," I said, "you most certainly did!" I leaned across towards the bedside table and looked at my watch. "Jesus Christ!"

"Something wrong, darling?" Patricia's voice sounded indistinct as her mouth travelling warmly down my body.

"It's after ten o'clock. And I'm late for a very important date."

She didn't seem to care. Instead she burrowed closer to me and I heard her mutter something that sounded like, "Bless your fuzzy ears and whiskers." Pretty soon I didn't care either. I'd always been told that if you're going to be late for a meeting, be good and late.

About eleven o'clock I rolled away from her and found the telephone book. "I must call this guy and apologise." I found van Heulen's name and rang him. I glanced at my watch again as I listened to the odd continental bleeping noise of the connection being made. Only an hour and a half late. Maybe he had given up on me. Then there was a click followed by a long silence.

"Monsieur van Heulen?" I said eventually.

A man's voice answered in French. "Oui." He sounded tense and suspicious and his accent was so curiously nasal that for a moment I could barely understand him. I apologised and explained that my previous meeting was running late and I doubted if I could get to him until later in the day. There was a short silence. "Ca ne fait rien," he said shortly. "Je vous verrai plus tard."

His French accent still sounded strange to me and it rang a very faint bell. I decided that with a name like van Heulen he was likely to be Flemish. I switched into English, "Or perhaps I can have someone from the hotel deliver the papers to you?"

"No, that will not be convenient," he said quickly, still in his oddly accented French. "It is necessary for me to give you a receipt to take back to Mr Raven."

"OK. Why don't I look in on my way to the airport later today? I'm due to leave this evening."

"Ca va." But he sounded disappointed. "A bientot, Mr Lennox."

167

I hung up. Something about the conversation struck me as odd. For someone who needed the papers so urgently he was surprisingly relaxed about my change of plans. Also, it was pretty unusual in Belgium to find someone called van Heulen who would speak French without having their arm twisted. Yet he hadn't answered me in English when I gave him the chance. For some reason he had preferred to use his atrociously accented French.

By this time Patricia had found another of the hotel's dressing robes and was curled up in an arm chair near the window, listening to my conversation with van Heulen. I walked across to her and cupped her chin in my hand. She looked up at me solemnly. "This is another fine mess you've got me into," I said with a grin.

An expression I couldn't read flickered across her elegant face. "I've never wanted to get you into any kind of trouble, Terry. You are the only good thing that has happened to me in years. I only hope that one day you will understand. But the Gods are just, it seems."

"And of our pleasant vices make instruments with which to plague us?" I said, puzzled. Her change of mood threw me for a moment. "I thought you were in Switzerland. How did you get back here? And how did you know where to find me?"

Her lip curled slightly. "That awful man Grieder gave me a lift in his private plane at some ungodly hour of the morning." She tossed back her long auburn hair and in an instant her seriousness seemed to melt away. "I'm not going to tell you anything else," she said firmly.

"Come on," I insisted. "What was Asgard like? And what happened about the brooch?"

Patricia seemed to give a faint shudder. "Please don't

talk about that horrible creature. Anthony left it with Grieder for his tame experts to examine." Her almond eyes glanced at me cautiously. Then suddenly she said almost playfully "I don't want to talk about it, darling. Perhaps when your older and wiser."

I leaned down and kissed her. "Well, I do feel a lot older," I said. "Thanks to you." But it was clear that she didn't intend to tell me anything more and I didn't have time to play games with her. It was almost time to vacate the room so I called the desk, explained that we were running late and ordered a light lunch from the room service menu. We ate it together in picnic mode, still in our bath robes. In spite of my questions, all she would tell me was that she was flying to Edinburgh alone later in the day.

I left her soaking in the tub of the Hilton's glamorous bathroom. Her hair was tied up and she lay back in the water, her beautiful high-cheek boned face just above the deep perfumed suds of a bubble bath. Tiny beads of sweat trickling down her from her temples and collected in a fine film above her full lips. I sat on the edge of the bath for a moment and dipped my hand into the hot water, running it smoothly up across the slickness of her body. Her eyes looked up at me, doe-like and melting. She looked the most desirable thing I had ever seen. I bent forward and kissed her damp mouth. "Thank you for coming," I said quietly.

She smiled her small enigmatic twisted smile at me. "Take care, Terry." I checked out and explained to the concierge that Madame would be leaving shortly. He didn't even bat an eyelid. And this was Brussels, not Paris!

From the hotel the walk up the broad Avenue Louise to the Place Stephanie was an easy one. I dodged across through the traffic and between the street-cars that clanged along the Boulevard and strolled past the comfortable looking brasseries that lined the streets. After a few hundred yards I came to the wide expanse where the Avenue meets the almost equally imposing Chaussee de Charleroi in a tangle of traffic lights and tramlines. After five minutes risking my life crossing the no-mans-land of the Place Stephanie I found the offices of Island Developments in an unobtrusive doorway of a standard three-storied 1950's grey stone building that was trying hard to look like something from the turn of the century. I pushed through a pair of anachronistic modern glass doors and found myself in a poorly-lit hallway.

Overhead a set of Imperial-looking electric candelabra was giving out a feeble glow and even on a bright summer day very little light penetrated from outside. I peered at the ranks of brass plates screwed to one wall. For a building of this size there seemed to be a lot of them but I found Island Developments. However, there was no indication of which floor they were on. I glanced around but I could see no sign of a call button or buzzer system.

At the rear of the hall there was a smaller glass door. It was locked but beside it was a small button and the label "Concierge". I pressed the buzzer and waited. After a few minutes a figure, fat and dishevelled, appeared and gesticulated at me through the glass. He was waving his hands around in a manner that was clearly intended to indicate that the place was closed and that he most definitely didn't see any good reason to open it and certainly not for me.

I lapsed into continental custom and waved back at him enthusiastically in a way that I hoped would let him see that I had an urgent need to speak to him and had no intention of going away without doing so. For good measure I grinned at him furiously, to reassure him that I was harmless. Reluctantly, he opened the inner door and squinted suspiciously at me. "Oui monsieur?" he asked cautiously.

I told him in my best French that I had a meeting with the Chief Executive of Island Developments. He shook his head. "Not here," he said in halting English. So much for my French accent, I thought ruefully.

I taped the plaque on the wall. "But this notice says they have an office here," I insisted, "I have an appointment with them here."

He shook his head again. From his expression it was clear he'd decided he was dealing with some kind of an idiot. "No," he said, slowly and distinctly. "Not here. Only an address for---," he paused, searching his mind for the right word. Then he brightened up. "for letters," he ended triumphantly. Then he shut the door on me.

I hammered furiously on the glass and he turned back even more reluctantly. Before I could utter a word he launched into a mixture of French and English. "There are no bureaux here, monsieur. No offices in this building. It is simply an address for the post." He nodded to himself thoughtfully. "Yes, that's it! An address for the post."

I stared at him. "What do you do with the letters for Island Developments?" I asked him in French.

He shrugged. "There are never letters for them, monsieur. Not in the three years I have been here. Now monsieur will excuse me?" He smiled politely and shut the door firmly in my face again.

I studied the hallway for some other clue. But there was nothing, so I examined the notice-board again. Island Developments was listed there with a head office in Liechtenstein. This was the right address. It was certainly the one that Raven's secretary had given me. There didn't seem to be much more I could do except call Raven's office in Edinburgh to find out what was going on. Then I remembered van Heulen. I still had to deliver his papers to him. He'd let me use his phone to call Raven's secretary. I made my way back across the Boulevard de Waterloo, towards the old part of town.

The Petit Sablon is a quiet corner of Brussels, only a step away from the bustling Grand Sablon but a world away in style from its shops, cafes and boutiques. Little more than a patch of grass on the Rue Royale with houses straggling untidily around it on three sides, its 19th century buildings had mostly been split up and converted for use as offices by lawyers, doctors and architects. It looked eminently respectable and a little dull, with the faded grandeur that inspires confidence in a certain type of client. Somehow I couldn't see Raven as that type of client.

All I had to do was find van Heulen's address, deliver the papers, use his telephone and take back the receipt he had been so determined to give me. I strolled round until I came to the correct street number. It was an unobtrusive entrance with a heavy varnished wooden door, lots of brass fittings including a letter box and a small rectangle of etched glass protected by solid-looking metal bars. There was no name on the door. I pressed the bell-push and heard the sound of a buzzer from within. Nothing happened for several minutes. I tried again. Still nothing. This trip was starting to feel like a complete waste of time. Apart, that is, from Patricia's visit.

I gripped the chunky door knob and turned it. The door swung easily open and I stepped into the dim interior. Inside was a small office area, gloomy, old fashioned and cramped. In one corner was a solid wooden desk. A small coffee table with two chairs pretty well filled up the rest of the space. On the counter was a telephone and a cash register of the kind that disappeared from the UK in about 1970. The walls were bare apart from a few dusty posters for out-of-date fine art and jewellery exhibitions. "Hello," I called out in French. "Monsieur van Heulen?"

There was no reply. The silence was absolute. At the far side of the room was another door. I set down my travelling bag and crossed to the inner door, knocked loudly and pushed it open. It led into a workshop of some kind, a long room with neon

172

strip lights hanging low over a group of benches. Around the walls were a series of racks holding tools, small and neat and mostly not like any tools I had seen before. Hanging from hooks were coils of wire that looked like gold and silver and pinned to an old-fashioned baize notice-board was a dusty collection of drawings and photographs. In the centre of the room, battered, stained and burned stood a particularly heavy work-bench and on it was the one piece of equipment I had no trouble recognising. It was a small electrical furnace and it was obviously well used. But there was no sign of its user.

I flicked through some of the drawings on the notice-board and realised with a start that the images on them were sketches and detailed drawings for pieces of jewellery. Some were actual photographs of finished items. Raven's connection with van Heulen was starting to become clear. Thoughtfully I went back out to the outer office and reached across the desk for van Heulen's telephone.

Then I saw him. He was lying neatly stretched out of sight on the floor behind the desk. Even in the half light I could tell from the pallor on the face that, if this was van Heulen, he wouldn't object to me using his telephone. He looked very dead. And if I had any doubt about it, the bullet hole in the middle of his forehead would have convinced me.

Kneeling down, I felt his wrist. It was cold and there was no sign of a pulse, there or at the side of his neck. I guessed he had been dead for several hours. I examined the area around the body. There was no sign of a gun. I sat back on my heels and considered the situation. Did I want to become embroiled in a Belgian police investigation? On the other hand I could hardly go back to Raven and tell him that I had found his business associate dead---murdered most probably--- and hadn't reported the death. To say nothing of the risk of being seen by someone as I left the premises and perhaps even arrested at the airport. I picked up the telephone and asked for the police.

CHAPTER 19

The Inspector was small, dark, intense and efficient and all things considered remarkably understanding. Once he had established who I was and why I was there he asked me politely if I knew the deceased. I said that I assumed it was Monsieur van Heulen but had no way of knowing for sure. Then he asked me to take a seat. While he waited for a forensic team to arrive he studied the body and went through the dead man's pockets. He fished out a wallet and examined an identity card.

"You are correct, Mr Lennox," he said looking up at me. "This is van Heulen. You say that you spoke to him on the telephone earlier today? About eleven o'clock?" He frowned and shook his head. "I should guess this man has been dead for at least six hours." He beamed at me. "Perhaps you are mistaken about the time of the conversation?"

I told him that I was not mistaken about the time. "I had an appointment to meet him at nine-thirty this morning but I was," I hesitated, " unavoidably delayed. So I rang to apologise and to agree a later time. I definitely spoke to him then. At least," I added carefully, "I spoke to someone." I glanced at the little Inspector. "I had no way of knowing who it was. Could it have been the killer?"

He grimaced at me. "At eleven o'clock? That is unlikely,

Mr Lennox, very unlikely." He looked at me amiably. "After all, would you remain at the scene of a murder longer than necessary if you were guilty?"

I found the remark vaguely reassuring, though I was uncertain exactly why. I thought for a moment. "Only if I was, for example, looking for something important?"

"There is no indication of theft or even of a search. And I think you would have to be, what is your expression? A very cool customer he must be to wait so long, with his victim's body beside him? With the murder weapon in his possession." He looked pensively at me. "Or he would have to know the victim's routine very well, which might help to narrow down the possibilities." He smiled at me again. "This telephone conversation, did you have any witnesses to it?"

I shook my head. "I called from my room in the Hilton. They will have a record of the call." I hesitated. "There was someone with me in my room--- a lady," I paused. "I'd rather not have her involved in this if possible. You see, she happens to be married to someone else."

"Come Mr Lennox," he said firmly. "This is not Paris. Here we are not so understanding about such matters. I'm afraid I shall require the name of this witness."

Oh shit, I thought. Summoning up a carefree smile I gave him Patricia's full name and address. "Will you please be as discreet as possible if you have reason to contact her?" I asked him winningly. "You know how it is?"

He nodded blandly. "Yes, monsieur. I do know how it is." Then he stared at me. "I assume she will vouch for you during the time since about six am this morning? The approximate time of death?"

"Not exactly," I admitted. "You see, she came to my

175

room at about eight o'clock this morning. Before that I was asleep in my room and I suppose the hotel staff will vouch for the fact that I did not leave the building."

"And this lady, was she also staying in the hotel?"

"No. She told me that she arrived in Brussels on an early flight this morning." I was starting to feel distinctly uneasy. "Look Inspector, I had never seen this man van Heulen before today. I know nothing about him. I came here to deliver some papers for a client in Edinburgh--- ."

The Inspector held up his hand to stop me. "Exactly, Mr Lennox. And these papers, where are they?"

I found the envelop and gave it to the Inspector. He turned it over in his hands and studied it carefully. "You have no idea what this contains," he asked.

I shook my head. "Only that they are papers I was asked to deliver. The time of my appointment is written there." I pointed to the instructions from Raven's secretary.

He nodded. "So I see. But I think we should open this now, Mr Lennox." He carefully peeled back the flap and slid out several foolscap pages. He frowned and shuffled quickly through them. Then he held them up in front of me, one by one, turning each of them over so that I could see it.

"What do you think this means, Mr Lennox? Do you have any explanation?"

I stared in astonishment. They were all sheets of Raven and Thompson's note paper. But each one was completely blank. I shook my head dumbly. I felt like saying, "Beats the hell out of me." But I didn't. For a start I wasn't quite certain how it would translate into French.

"It seems that you have been sent on a fool's errand, as I think you say in English," he said to me. "Could it be that your client is this Mr Raven?" He pointed to the name on the note paper. "The husband of the lady who visited you this morning?"

None of this was making any sense to me and I told him so. But then when you're on a fool's errand, nothing is supposed to make sense.

"It does not make much sense to me either, Mr Lennox," he said solemnly. "Not yet. But perhaps I know more about van Heulen than you seem to do. We know him as a very good maker of jewellery. He specialises in one-off expensive pieces and sometimes we know he makes copies of famous pieces, quite legitimately, for the big stores and even for museums and exhibitions. Sometimes, interestingly, we suspect that he does very special jobs, where the origin of the piece becomes, shall we say, more obscure."

"You mean he makes fake jewellery," I said. The thought of Hans Grieder buying a fake suddenly hit me like a truck. I needed to get to Grieder quickly, before too much damage was done. After what seemed like hours the Inspector agreed to take my statement and let me go. I was relieved. But disappointed that he didn't tell me not to leave town, like they do in the movies. I suppose he knew I was innocent. Well, at least not guilty of murder. After all, no one is entirely innocent.

Before I left van Heulen's work-shop he allowed me to make a phone call. But not to Raven's office. Now it was to Grieder. He was still in town and his secretary said he could see me if I came right away.

# CHAPTER 20

Fortunately Brussels is a small town and within fifteen minutes I was standing outside the tower block that housed the European headquarters of Odin Investments, gazing up at thirty storeys of post-modernism that totally dominated the surrounding buildings, as Grieder had intended it to do. Inside, a vast reception area rolled away in a sea of white marble that stretched off into the middle distance, breaking here and there around little islands of expensive leather seating and heavy black desks. Groups of well-groomed young women dispensed information in low tones into telephones and gave brightly smiling directions to men in suits. Through the ceiling-high external walls of tinted glass I watched the traffic on the Avenue drifting past like silent images on a large screen.

One of the well-groomed young ladies took my name and checked it on her computer screen. Then she told me that Mr Grieder was expecting me. She seemed to find that a little puzzling but did her best to conceal the fact. She gave me a visitor's badge and directed me towards what she called the Executive Elevator. There a large young man in a blazer and grey trousers checked my badge against his list of names and pressed a button. A door in the marble-clad wall slid open to reveal a very ritzy elevator with a deep-pile carpet and dark walnut panelling. I stepped inside and looked about for clues. "Which floor?" I asked him.

"This only goes one place," he told me. "The thirtieth floor; Executive Suite. Only Mr Grieder and the board are allowed on that floor." He looked at me doubtfully. "And certain approved guests," he added.

"I don't see a control."

"There isn't one," he said laconically. "It can only be operated from the thirtieth floor. They know you're here."

At that moment I heard a faint buzz and the door gently closed in front of me. The elevator drifted upwards at what seemed to be a leisurely, almost dreamlike pace. But in a very few seconds I was aware of being stationary again. Smoothly the elevator door slid open and in front of me stood a very glossy young woman who managed without any effort to look important. I think it was the spectacles and the discreetly expensive dress.

"This way please," she murmured quietly. "Mr Grieder is in conference but he will be with you shortly." She drifted silently away down a corridor over a carpet with a pile deep enough to lose a shoe in. As we walked we passed half a dozen offices, all with their doors wide open and each with a clone of my guide, serenely doing things with computer screens and telephones.

This floor reeked of power and status. But most impressive of all was the eerie, almost religious silence. Vague sotto-vocce murmurs emerged from the depths of the offices as we passed. Nowhere was there anything as vulgar as the sound of a ringing telephone. Maybe the carpets soak it all up, I thought. What happens if you drop any small change? Or stand around too long in the same spot? It was an alarming notion. With an effort I concentrated on what I wanted to say to Grieder. I caught up with the glossy young woman. "Are you Mr Grieder's p.a.?" I asked her.

"One of them," she replied vaguely. "Please have a seat here." We were in a big open area with glass walls on three sides, looking out on an unobstructed view across the city to the surrounding woods and the countryside beyond. She indicated one of the islands of luxurious-looking seating and vanished into another corridor.

I walked across and peered down at tiny figures of cars and people going about their business on the avenues and boulevards below. The parks, the patches of trees and the roofs of the houses and offices looked like Legoland, miniaturised and Lilliputian. From up here you could see half the city and I knew that with his computers and his teams of financial analysts beavering away on the lower floors, Grieder could just as easily monitor half the world. Or at least the part that Odin controlled.

"Good afternoon, Mr Lennox." His voice took me by surprise and I swung round sharply. Grieder was surrounded by a group of brisk looking young executive types. He went on, "I see you are enjoying our view--- I am afraid that I too rarely have the time to enjoy it. Now I understand that you have something important to say to me, Mr Lennox. Perhaps you will sit here and tell me what is concerning you. Coffee?" He nodded to one of his staff, who leaped for a telephone.

We faced each other across a wide table. He looked at me enquiringly. "I'm pleased to have found you here, Mr Grieder," I said.

He gave a slightly pained smile. "This is where I work, Mr Lennox. Now if you will be so kind, I have a great deal to attend to. Please come to the point."

I decided to ignore him. "I understand that you have been at your home in Switzerland, Mr Grieder. With Mr and Mrs Raven." Before he could reply I went on quickly. "How did the discussions go?"

The lean handsome face tightened. "That is a matter that need not concern you, Mr Lennox. I am grateful to you for effecting a useful introduction." He paused. "Very grateful. A most propitious introduction," he added grudgingly. "But I must make it clear to you that I do not expect you to play any further part in the matter."

I nodded understandingly. "Of course not. However, I have by chance become aware of something I think you should know." I told him what I had learned about van Heulen and his line of business and what had happened to him. "I think you will see that this raises questions about the authenticity of the object you were shown by Anthony Raven."

Grieder took my news remarkably calmly. He gazed at me unmoved. "You were sent to that place by Mr Raven to see this van Heulen?" he asked me quietly. A faint smile seemed to flicker across his features. Or it might have been a silent grimace. Then after a moment he nodded briskly. "It was correct of you to tell me this so promptly, Mr Lennox. There is clearly some possibility for misunderstanding, at the very least. It will be most helpful to have this information." The coffee arrived and a minion poured out a steaming cup of black continental coffee for me. I could almost smell the caffeine. But after the day I had been having I decided I needed it. Besides, it was served in a real china cup and saucer and who can resist that?

Grieder gave me a faint fleeting smile. "Now on the more immediate matter of Mr Lynch? Your candidate? I have decided I should see him. Will you ask him to contact my office to arrange a meeting. He seems to be a very enterprising young man."

I sipped my coffee and looked at him cautiously over the rim of the cup. Yes, Donald certainly was an enterprising young man. Grieder didn't know yet just how enterprising, though it seemed as if he was going to find out. But it was odd that the possibility of the ornament being a fake didn't seem to trouble

Grieder over much. That I didn't understand. Still, I told him I would follow up with Donald Lynch as soon as I arrived home.

One of the acolytes had been hovering discreetly at a polite distance. Now he drifted closer. "Mr Grieder," he whispered, "the North American review meeting is waiting." Grieder nodded briefly and fixed me with his cold gaze. "Now, if there is nothing else---?"

As I rose to leave I asked him casually if the Ravens had travelled back with him. I saw the familiar tightening of the lines around his mouth. "Mr Raven left me at Bern Airport. I understood that he was going to Zurich and on to the Far East on business. Mrs Raven did travel with me as far as Brussels on her way home. Though why that should concern you--- "

I interrupted him blandly "You must have had a very early start this morning."

For a second he seemed nonplussed. "I make it my habit to arrive at this office by seven thirty each morning," he said stiffly. "Regardless of where I have spent the previous day. It is a matter of routine and discipline, Mr Lennox. It is not a problem for me, Mr Lennox, I can assure you. It is all a matter of discipline," he repeated, glaring at me. I nodded silently and turned to go. But he stopped me. "One moment, Mr Lennox. May I ask how you knew that I would be in this office today?"

I waved a hand lightly and kept walking away. "Just luck, Mr Grieder," I said cheerfully. "The Lennox luck is famous on two continents." Looking back, I could see from the look on his handsome damaged face that he didn't understand. And that was fine by me.

CHAPTER 21


The journey home was long and complicated but it gave me time to analyse exactly what I knew about Anthony Raven and his assignment. His little assignment that had pitched me into real problems! I cursed myself for ever agreeing to work for him. What had made me change my mind? Well, partly I knew it had been Patricia, appearing unexpectedly as she did. Although, if I was quite honest, the generous fee had helped.

Could the death of van Heulen be a mere coincidence? Perhaps the accidental result of a burglary gone wrong? On that reading the confusion over the Island Developments address could be no more than a misunderstanding. But a misunderstanding on the part of whom? And how did I explain the blank note paper that was so important that it must be delivered at nine-thirty promptly? I shook my head at my image in the darkened aircraft window. No, there were too many coincidences there and I don't believe in coincidence at the best of times. Especially when they are linked to murder. So Raven had deliberately set me up, either as a suspect for van Heulen's murder or possibly even as another victim.

If it hadn't been for Patricia's seemingly capricious appearance at the Hilton I might have walked right into the killer. In which case I would probably have joined van Heulen at nine thirty promptly. Just a minute, I thought. Patricia Raven had been in Brussels for more than an hour before she showed up at the Hilton. Could she have called on van Heulen and--- ? I shook my head again. No, I was becoming paranoid. That was out of the question. Maybe the whole thing was no more than a series of strange unconnected mishaps.

But that weird artefact was the key. If it was a fake, as now seemed likely, there was one person who would know for sure. I needed to speak to John Childs. He was the key to that part of the puzzle so soon as I reached my flat I called Tom Drever. I was put thought to him almost at once. "Terry," he boomed, "I've been trying to speak to you all bloody day."

"Tom," I interrupted. "I need to ask you about John Childs, the little fellow who showed me the chambered cairn at Scarisby?"

There was a silence at the other end of the line. "Terry, you must have a highland grannie. That's one reason I was calling you. Childs has had an accident. Fell from the cliffs at Scarisby the other day. Killed himself. Well, it's a long way down as you know and the sea's pretty wild most days. So even if he survived the fall--- ."

I was silenced for a moment. Childs dead too! Scarisby was proving to be an unlucky place; and Anthony Raven a very unlucky client. "Do you know exactly when it happened, Tom?" I asked.

"Not for certain. A lobster fisherman found his body at the foot of the cliffs early yesterday morning. It looks as if he had been in the sea for a day or so and he was last seen alive a couple of days before that. I suppose he must have been doing something at that damned tomb and slipped. You know how tricky it can be there."

Now it was all beginning to fit together. John Childs was dead; the man who had produced the provenance for the object was dead. And if the brooch was a fake, van Heulen, its maker, was also dead. It was too all neat and my doubts vanished. I

But on the other hand how could Raven have anything to do with the death of Childs? Or van Heulen's death, come to that. I tracked events back carefully. Three days ago, when Childs fell from the cliff, Raven was in London with me and Hans Grieder. The very next morning he had called me from Edinburgh to say he was leaving for Asgard with Patricia. They had both stayed there until this morning, as Grieder had confirmed to me.

Was it possible for Raven to have travelled from London to Orkney, killed Childs and returned to Edinburgh by ten thirty the following morning? "Tom, there's something very strange going on. Something much stranger than you think. Can you use your contacts to find out if Anthony Raven has been in Orkney in the past few days--- in particular during the afternoon or evening of the day Childs died."

"What are you getting at, Terry?"

"I'm not sure, yet. But it's beginning to look as if Childs was involved with Raven in some scheme. I'm sure there's a cover-up of some kind going on. But I don't know all the angles yet. Maybe it's the sexual stuff we know about. Maybe someone's been blackmailing someone else. I just don't know for sure. But it involves the ornament, the Beast that Childs said he knew nothing about. Anthony Raven is certainly into some very strange activities. And Tom, I've found Norman Orr." I gave him the story the two young men had told to me. "Have you heard anything about this man Davis? He's one of the many unknown factors in this. But if he is tied in with Raven---."

"Never heard of him, Terry old son. But Ray Morrison will help you, if anyone can. He has the right connections and you can trust him. Listen, Terry, I'm coming down to Edinburgh soon. Is it all right if I stay with you?"

185

My heart sank at the prospect of a succession of drunken evenings as Tom renewed his acquaintanceship with his old haunts. "Sure," I said faintly. "Tell you what, I'll leave my spare keys with a friend, in case you turn up while I'm away." I gave him John Boyd's address. "If I am away, do make yourself at home. I'll leave a bed for you and I expect you'll find the whisky on your own."

"Don't worry about that," he said cheerfully, "I never travel without my own supply."

Then I had another thought. "Tom, it's possible that Archie McNaughton is involved in all this. The artefact was found on his property, after all. So his death might have nothing to do with politics or financial interests. I know your theory Tom. But you may just have got it wrong this time. If I'm correct, you could have another chapter to write for that book of yours."

I could tell by the silence that the idea didn't appeal to Tom. But he promised to check on Raven's movements for me. I knew that if he had even set foot in the islands Tom Drever would find out. I hung up and called British Airways. A nice young lady answered my call. "Is it possible to travel from London to Orkney, leaving central London about mid-day?" I asked her.

After a couple of minutes she came back to me. "Yes, sir. You can travel on the two pm flight via Aberdeen or on the three o'clock via Edinburgh. Both flights will get you to Orkney in the early evening."

I thanked her. That answered my question. Raven could have got up there in time to push Childs off a cliff that night. I knew the early morning flight to Edinburgh arrived at about ten o'clock. There was just time for Raven to have travelled up and back in time to call me and still keep his rendezvous with Grieder. Tight, but he could have done it. And if he had he must have left some trace somewhere. Tom would find out. I stuffed my spare keys into an envelope ready to drop them off at John's flat in the morning. Then I crashed out on my bed. It had been quite a day, one way and another.

# CHAPTER 22

I woke slowly, swimming up out of some deep black hole with a strange ringing sound in my ears. Gradually the room took shape and I realised it was my own bedroom. Well, that was vaguely comforting. But the ringing continued and eventually it penetrated my befuddled brain that I was hearing the sound of my telephone.

With a groan I rolled over and picked up the receiver. "Good morning, Vietnam," screamed the voice. It was a passable impersonation of Robin Williams but I recognised Donald Lynch. I squinted at my watch. "Donald, you crazy bastard!" I mumbled at him. "Do you know what time it is?"

"It's seven thirty am and time for reveille," he said. "And what is it with you, Lennox? Are you becoming some sort of a time freak? It's the same every time I speak to you. All you ever want to know is the bloody time. In case you're interested it's two thirty am in Boston and just before midnight in San Francisco," he said. "That's midnight last night," he added.

I listened to him patiently, groping for my dressing gown. With Donald as hyper as that you simply had to wait for him to come down. "Why are you bothering me at this ungodly hour of the day, Donald?"

"It's early bird time, Lennox. I've been trying to catch you for days, you worm. I've got some information for you about your man Raven. You remember asking me to check on the Thai Entertainment Developments Corporation and Islands Development Trust?"

"Yeah. Well?" I muttered ungraciously.

"You do chose some very odd bed fellows, Terry old son. Sometimes I worry about you."

By this time I had surfaced fully. "Tell me what you have, Donald. It could be important. Things are getting to a critical stage."

"Now pay attention to me," Donald said slowly. "Go and switch on your fax machine. I don't know why you can't get on the Internet like a normal human being but if you must use archaic technology at least learn to switch the bloody thing on. Have you got that?" He paused and then went on slowly and carefully, as if he was talking to an idiot. "Then go into the kitchen and make a cup of coffee. Or have a brandy or whatever it is that you take in the morning to get started. I'll call you back in half an hour to explain the fax to you. You probably won't understand it. And by the way, the time is now seven thirty-five am in the UK, or two thirty five in Boston, or--- ."

I hung up on him and pulling on the dressing gown went to do as I was told. Some days it just doesn't pay to swim against the tide. The smell of fresh coffee was beginning to fill the air when the fax machine whirred into life and four sheets of paper slid out of it. I poured myself a cup and savoured the bite of the real McCoy--- this was no time for decaffeinated.

As I was sheaving through Donald's fax the telephone rang again. "Right," he said briskly. "Are you sitting comfortably? Now look at Page 1--- that's often a good place to start with a complex financial analysis." He broke off. "You do realise I usually charge good money for this kind of thing? You'll see that Islands Development Trust, registered in Liechtenstein, has only one principal asset, the Scarisby estate in Orkney."

"I knew that, Donald. They're my damned client, after all."

"Yes, but the interesting thing about the Trust is that there are three trustees who essentially control the Trust. Their names are Anthony Raven, Patricia Raven and someone called John Childs. The other interesting thing is that they're also the beneficiaries of the Trust. I seem to recall that Raven was supposed to be an advisor to this client?"

Now it was beginning to hang together. Raven and Childs were the real owners of the ornament, genuine or fake. With Childs dead it became Raven's property. I had been sent to Brussels on, what had the little Belgian policeman called it? A fool's errand? But why would Raven take the risk of me finding out about van Heulen and the Trust's phoney address? Of course, I thought slowly, if it hadn't been for Patricia appearing I would have walked right into the murderer. In which case I wouldn't have gone to the false address of Islands Development and I'd be none the wiser. As well as dead. There was no doubt that Raven had expected me to die with the jeweller.

But why was he so keen to get rid of me? Come to that, why did he try so hard to involve me in the first place? Van Heulen's death I could understand. That was necessary to cover his tracks. The jeweller would always be a potential danger to him, especially with Grieder lined up as a buyer and half-a million pounds at stake. The same went for Childs, whose reputation gave the object its real credibility and who of course also had a claim on part of the proceeds. But why would Raven want to kill me? There was only one answer. He knew about Patricia and he hated me.

"Are you still there, Lennox? You haven't fallen asleep

again?" Donald asked politely.

"No. No," I said vaguely. "I was thinking."

"Yes," he said sympathetically. "I know how tricky that can be for you. Anyway, if you look at the other pages you'll see an interesting story about the Thai Entertainment Development Group."

I glanced through the papers. Donald had drawn a chart of the organisation for me and in the centre was a box labelled P.I.B Inc, a company registered in the Cayman Islands. From it tentacles reached out to half-a-dozen other boxes, one of which was the Thai company I had seen on the board at Raven's office. Donald had listed its main activities and they made interesting reading. Mostly it was property development and the operation of clubs and discos, with a sideline in prostitution and gay sex bars. It seemed to be a wholly-owned subsidiary of P.I.B. "Donald, what is this P.I.B. animal?"

"It's the Property Investment Bank, based in the Caymans." He went on breezily, "The whole set up is a maze of cross holdings. You see the European Property Development Group? It's based in Amsterdam and it has the same mix of activities as most of the organisation; hotels and casinos. Then there's a Jersey-based investment company whose principal activity is funding international property development. At the bottom of the page there's the real giveaway, a US corporation based in Nevada and set up to run gambling casinos." Donald was in full flight now. "As you probably know, gambling and prostitution are legal in Nevada--- by the way, do you know where the word Nevada comes from? It's Spanish for snow!" I heard him laugh. "I think you can take it that drugs and drug money play a part in this somewhere. If not, someone is missing a terrific opportunity."

"You mean it's set up for laundering illegal cash?"

"The Thai/Amsterdam axis would indicate drugs and there will almost certainly be a mob connection in Nevada. The various businesses are all cash-rich, so they're ideal for re-cycling dirty money into legitimate profits. Property development and property management can also be a handy way to re-invest illegal cash into front activities. You'll notice that your chum Raven is Managing Director of the European wing and acts for the Thai business in this country, raising finance and handling surplus cash for them. He's been a very naughty boy for a Scottish solicitor. Or else he's incredibly naive. As you know, a solicitor in a small private practice is ideally placed to channel dirty money back into the legitimate financial system."

What Donald was telling me made complete sense. Lawyers continually move cash around for clients, holding the proceeds of property sales in temporary accounts or depositing mortgage advances pending final purchase agreements. So institutions like banks and building societies are unlikely to question where the cash is really coming from. Whatever Anthony Raven might be, and it was beginning to look as if he was quite a lot, naive did not seem a good word to describe him.

I thanked Donald. "All you have to do now, Donald, is contact Hans Grieder. In spite of everything I could say about you he wants to meet you. Just remember you're supposed to be a candidate for that fund management job. So don't get too carried away."

"Wonderful," he said cheerfully. "And don't worry. I'll be the soul of discretion. An hour with him and I'll have him eating out of my hand."

"Sounds pretty unpleasant, if you ask me," I said. "But whatever turns you on."

He laughed. As I was about to hang up, he suddenly sounded serious. "Listen, Terry. Thanks for setting up the meeting with Grieder. I really need that connection. The Irvings are revolting--- well, they always were. But Terry, watch your step with Raven and especially those pals of his from Nevada. People like that can be very nasty when large sums of money are involved. They're even worse than corporate lawyers!"

I sat for a while thinking about Anthony Raven. He was a liar and a fraud, a dangerous criminal and quite possibly a killer. To say nothing of being a sexual pervert who preyed on vulnerable young men and who might have used his own wife for God knows what. Which brought me face to face with the question I had been trying hard to avoid. How much did Patricia know about all this? The picture was coming together fast, although what a Norse ornament had to do with international money laundering I couldn't quite see. Or for that matter how Scarisby connected.

But if what I suspected was true, Patricia must know more than she had ever hinted. How could I find out? I knew how difficult that was likely to be, because in spite of everything she had always been curiously loyal to Raven. In her fashion, I thought wryly. Then I had an idea. And being a bear of little brain it was a very simple idea. I'd ask her.

I rang her home number and stood listening to the sounds on the line, visualising her and the big house. After a few seconds I heard her voice repeating the telephone number. She sounded listless. "Good morning madam," I said. "I'm doing a survey on behalf of the Hilton Hotel. Can you tell me if you have ever been disappointed by room service in any of our establishments.?"

I could tell from the low laugh that she was alone. "Not disappointed, exactly. But they do take a long time to come sometimes," she said solemnly.

"In that case I'm authorised to offer you at a special discounted rate one of our gourmet dinners at Chez Terry. Tonight at seven thirty? Well, it's free actually. Can you make it?"

"What a wonderful idea," she said softly. "How very civilised! I'm "à seule" at the moment. You-know-who is still away in Bangkok. So I won't have to rush off. Did you have a successful day after you left me in Brussels?"

"Not really. It was all downhill after that," I said blandly. How much did she know about van Heulen?

I hung up and glanced out of the window at the blue sky. From the cloud movement there seemed to be a light breeze from the west and the local paper told me the tides were right. I called a taxi and in five minutes I was on my way to the harbour with my sailing gear. I needed to do some clear thinking and there is no better place to blow the irrelevances out of your head than out there with the wind and the tides

Half-an-hour later I had rigged my boat and was gliding past the harbour entrance, aided by a strong tidal flow out of the basin. With the ebb underway I reckoned there was only time for a quick sail up towards the two great bridges that span the Forth estuary. I put the helm over and she heeled quickly, turned like a dream into the wind and took off on a reach up the river. I glanced longingly back at the mass of Inchkeith island with its lighthouse and wished there had been time to sail right around it. But from bitter experience I had learned that on a falling tide it was essential to get the difficult part of the trip over first. Then you could run back with the river, the tide and hopefully the wind all on your side.

I held her close hauled and braced myself against the angled cockpit as she sliced through the blue-grey water, a steady cold curve of spray leaping up and swirling white along the surface of lee deck. The jib and the main sail thrummed in the wind, taut as drum skins. I felt the grime of Anthony Raven washing away from me as I steered into clear water between Cramond Isle and the long stretch of reef lying to the east end of little Inchmickery. I knew these rocks could damage even a wooden boat like mine and a plastic hull would be ripped open like an envelope. But at least you could see these rocks clearly at low water. Further out the red and white markings on the Oxcar Light marked shallow sandbanks, less dramatic, but just as dangerous and lurking unseen ready to trap the unwary.

I shivered in the keen wind. Having sailed in waters around the world, I decided long ago that the Forth estuary was the most uncomfortable I knew. Its short choppy run of North Sea waves never allowed you to settle and the endless wind, whatever its direction, seemed to come from the Baltic. But at least it was fairly safe, apart from requiring a nice judgement about when to cut and run to reach your mooring before it dried out. There was certainly nothing as deadly as the Pentland Firth had to offer in bad weather.

As the boat drove upstream towards the bridges I went over the facts again. It was time to separate what I knew about Raven from what I suspected. I knew he owned a house in Orkney where strange parties were held. I knew he had lied to me about this. Well, he would, wouldn't he? I knew he was almost certainly involved in processing illegal cash for dubious overseas clients and I also knew he was almost certainly not the first partner in a small law firm to do so. He had lied to me about the Trust and sent me on a wild-goose chase to Brussels. Come to that, he had sent me on a wild-goose chase to Orkney as well. Now it was obviously that the Trust had never intended to make an appointment. It was all a scheme to gain access to Hans Grieder. I hauled in the sheets a touch and steered still closer into the wind, feeling the boat leap under me with an exhilarating burst of speed. What else did I know for sure? I knew that Raven had known McNaughton since their university days. So why had he sent me to the very place where I was most likely to find out about his activities? I grinned into the wind. Raven obviously thought I was an idiot. Or else he simply enjoyed the sheer thrill and risk of sailing too close to the wind.

What did I suspect? Well, he was almost certainly trying to sell a faked version of the ornament to Grieder and he was probably involved in some way in the deaths of the jeweller van Heulen and John Childs. Perhaps even in McNaughton's death too, though I had no evidence of that.

And that was the real problem. So far, I hadn't a shred of evidence that would stand up to scrutiny. Certainly nothing strong enough to take to the police, least of all if Raven really had some kind of pull within the legal establishment. Then there was the story of Raven's involvement with the rent-boys, which depended entirely on the statements of Norman Orr and his friends. How credible would they seem, even if they agreed to testify? Which, given the pressure they were under from this man Davis was not likely. That brought me back to my starting point; the business of the break-in and the rumours of a "magic circle" and influence in high places. But again there was no evidence.

So what could I do? I might confront Raven with my suspicions and see how he explained away events in Brussels. That would probably scare him off from Hans Grieder and of course it might give me some harmless pleasure. But that apart, it wasn't likely to be a rewarding experience. God knows, Grieder was big enough to look after himself. Though I still felt responsible for introducing him to Raven and a fake Norse artefact.

The truth was there was little or nothing I could do legally. But at another level I knew that the question I wanted answered was quite different. What kind of man had Patricia Raven married? What was the beast that gripped Anthony Raven? And Patricia, come to that? That was something I didn't know for sure. But I had a feeling I was beginning to find out and the more I learned the less I liked.

Refreshed and clear-headed, I turned for home and a smooth run back to harbour entrance. I had a guest coming to dinner who could tell me more about Raven than anyone in the world. The problem was how to penetrate that hard glaze of well-mannered ambiguity?

## CHAPTER 23

While I was sailing I had decided on a menu for my meal with Patricia. On the way back to the flat I stopped off and to buy some fresh tuna and enough smoked trout to make a starter course. Since the animal welfare people started becoming vocal it was difficult to find a butcher brave enough to sell veal. Instead, I bought enough sliced roast pork to inflame the population of a large synagogue. That would have to do in place of veal. Then some very fresh crusty Italian bread and I was all set.

Back home, my first step was to stick the best part of a bottle of good Polish vodka in the deep-freeze. Then I looked out one of my best white wines, a powerful and mature Savennieres and stood it in the fridge to chill. For what I had in mind only the best would do. I toyed with the idea of making a batch of lethal dry martinis but decided that would be overkill. Not combined with iced vodka! I wanted her to stay awake, at least for a while.

Working quickly I opened a tin of anchovies and chopped a few of them up with the tuna, sloshed on some top grade olive oil and pureed the mixture through a fine sieve. Then I frothed up an egg yolk and mixed this with the fish, added some lemon juice and another cup or so of the olive oil, beat the whole thing into a thick sauce, thinned it down with double cream and voila, I had the sauce for vitello tonnato. Or in this case, pork tonnato. I layered the slices of meat in a glamorous dish, sprinkled them lightly with coarse salt, spread the tuna mixture generously over the meat and finally scattered a handful of washed capers over the dish before sliding it into the fridge beside the wine. Then I showered the salt water of the Forth estuary out of my hair and started to dress for the rest of the evening's entertainment.

The door bell rang exactly on time and she stood there like a vision from some fashion magazine. She wore a long black silk skirt tightly belted at her slim waist and a satin evening jacket, ivory coloured with a subtle chinoiserie pattern embroidered through it in almost the same colour. Her long auburn hair fell loosely over her shoulders, her almond shaped eyes surveyed me calmly and as always I was silenced for a moment by her sheer beauty.

"Aren't you going to ask me in?" she said half mockingly. I swallowed hard and took her in my arms. She pressed her body against me, slim and warm. I ran a hand down over her hips and across the front of her thighs and felt with a frisson of excitement the outline of a suspender-belt. She'd come prepared for more than a civilised dinner-party. I kissed her and she seemed to melt into me. It was a miracle that I didn't take her there, on the door-step.

I stepped back, gasping, and looked her over appraisingly. "So you're not from the Young Conservatives," I said. "What will the neighbours say?"

Quite quietly she said something very rude about the neighbours and slid past me into the flat. I inclined my head thoughtfully, closed the door and followed her in. The evening was off to a good start. And that was without the iced vodka. Dinner went well too. The vodka was bone-chillingly cold and the wine chilled but not to the point where its pungent flavour was destroyed.

My real problem was that I still had no clear idea of how to persuade Patricia to talk about her husband and his personal foibles, and my alcohol intake wasn't helping me to become more lucid. I had topped up her vodka glass three times. They were small glasses but even so the neat spirit packed a punch that the iciness masked. Still she sat there, poised and proper, complimenting me on the wine like a good little middle-class Edinburgh wife. "How unusually powerful for the Loire? And how clever of you to serve it with vitello tonnato."

The Savennieres was almost gone and the alcohol had still not removed any of the veneer. I glanced across at her appraisingly. My body weight was probably fifty percent greater than hers and I was feeling the effect. So she had to be feeling it too. How was I to loosen her tongue? "Patricia," I said, toying with my glass. "Tell me about life with Anthony."

Instantly I sensed a change in her mood.. The cool poise stiffened and I saw her fingers tighten round the stem of the glass. "He's my husband," she stared at me challengingly. "What else do you need to know."

I decided to duck that one. "Well, some strange things have been happening, Patricia. And I've heard even stranger stories. Frankly, I'm becoming worried that I'm involved in something criminal. I thought you might help me to understand what's going on. That would be a start at least."

She smiled her enigmatic smile. "Help you to understand," she murmured softly, half to herself. The tawny eyes hardened and gleamed a shade more yellow as she stared at me. She tossed back her wine and held the empty glass out to me. I topped up both our glasses with the last of the bottle. "What is it exactly that you want to know, Terry?" she said. Her voice suddenly sounded harsh. "What are these stories that bother you?"

I decided to go for broke. "Is there anything odd about

200

Anthony? Sexually, I mean?"

Patricia laughed bitterly. "I see! Is that all you want to know, Terry? Perhaps you'd like me to tell you what he does to me in bed. The things he makes me do?" She took a gulp of wine. "Is that what you want? Would that excite you, Terry?"

I realised this was going badly wrong. I stood up to clear away the dishes. "Let's have some coffee and a calvados." I said and walked round to her side of the table with the bottle in one hand and two brandy glasses in the other. As I approached, she slid easily from her seat and kneeled down in front of me. One arm went round my hips to hold me and I felt her fingers expertly unzip me. I stood in a dream as her warm mouth closed on me. A moment later I had lost interest in the coffee and any of the questions I wanted her to answer. Then she stopped and looked up at me, her eyes wide and innocent, "Do you think I could have the calvados in bed?" she whispered.

It was very exciting, as ever. But no, not as ever. Actually, it was very different from the other times; very different. For tonight it wasn't Patricia Raven in bed with me. This was a stranger and a stranger who was determined to make me into a stranger. I knew I was being used--- that she had cast me in some role and it was a role I didn't like. Yet I had to admit it was a role that excited me. In spite of everything it excited me. That was the worst part of it. The veneer had gone completely now. The mask had slipped at last. Or was this simply another mask?

Frankly, for a time I didn't care. She was like a mad woman and her madness infected me. "Let me tell you about Anthony," she panted repeatedly in my ear as I drove into her. I tried to cover her mouth with my hand and she bit into my flesh until the pain made me release her. Then she twisted round until she was kneeling in front of me on the bed, her haunches in the air. "You want to know what Anthony does? Well, Anthony likes to take me like this," she said, her voice half muffled against the mattress and trembling with what might have been excitement.

201

Or was it anger.

"He likes to tie me up sometimes and do things to me," she gasped. She stretched her arms out behind her back, her wrists together. "And he gives me to other men---- boys, really. While he watches! He likes to watch, Terry. Do you want to know if I enjoy it, Terry? Well, sometimes I do enjoy it! Does that shock you? So tie me up, Terry," she panted. "Tie me up and use me. Use me anyway you want! That's what Anthony does! That's what he likes, Terry. Is that what you wanted to know, Terry? Does it excite you to know that? What else do you want to do to me?" In spite of myself, I grabbed her by the wrists and forced her face down into the bed, thrusting into her body again and again.

Finally we rolled apart, sweating and panting. As I lay recovering, I knew, with something like despair, that whatever our relationship might have been, it had been changed forever. The heat of the last few minutes had transformed it into something very different; into something much harder. But unlike steel in a furnace, not any purer. I poured her a glass of the calvados and we lay silently together, our eyes not meeting. She pulled the crumpled sheet up over her breasts in a bizarre gesture of modesty and glanced sideways at me.

"Does that answer your questions?" she said coldly.

I tried to put my arms around her. "Darling, I want to understand," I said. But she shook me away angrily. "Patricia, I want to help if I can."

"You can't help. No-one can. And don't call me darling."

"All right," I said calmly. "Then tell me how you knew I was staying at the Hilton in Brussels.

She stared at me blankly. "You never give up, do you? All right, I'll tell you. I heard Anthony speaking on the telephone while we were at Asgard, to a man he knows; a criminal. The man who was supposed to kill you when you arrived at that address in the Petit Sablon. That's how I knew where you were staying. That's why I made sure you were late for the appointment."

I stared at her, thinking back to that morning in Brussels. I started to speak, "So you knew--- ".

She stared at me defiantly. "Yes, I knew. I saved your life, you bastard. You were going to be killed! Now I wonder if it was worth the effort."

"Who was the man I was supposed to meet?"

"He's called Duchene. I've seen him once or twice here in Edinburgh. He came to our house with Anthony's American business associates. Though I think Duchene is Canadian, maybe a French Canadian. He's very tall and lean, with thinning dark hair. Easy to spot once you've seen him."

"You're seriously saying he was supposed to kill me?"

Patricia laughed bitterly. "Oh yes, Anthony left him in no doubt about that. I saw Duchene in Brussels that day. He was in the foyer of the Hilton when I left."

More things fell into place with a clatter. The strange French accent and why he didn't want to speak English to me. A Canadian accent is almost unmistakable. Patricia was telling the truth. "Did he see you?" I asked.

"No. I'm sure he didn't. He would have been looking for you in any case." She glanced at me ruefully. "I don't imagine he expected to see Anthony's wife."

"So you did that for me," I said softly and laid my hand on her shoulder.

She gave another short laugh and gulped down her calvados, choking slightly on the fierce spirit. "Yes. I know how amazing that sounds. A rotten bitch like me?" She shook me off as I tried to take hold of her.

"But why," I asked her. "I mean, why would Anthony want to kill me?"

"Because he hates you."

"Because of you?"

She gave another cruel little laugh. "Yes, surprising as it may seem, I think he's jealous. Isn't that weird? In spite of everything he's actually jealous." She stopped and shook her head violently. "No, I won't talk about it. I can't tell you any more."

"Do you know anything about a man called McNaughton?" I went on relentlessly. "And what is the true story about the necklace?" She shook her head at me mutely. "Do you know when Anthony will be back?" I asked. There had to be a showdown with Raven, I thought grimly, and the sooner the better.

She shook her head again. "I have no idea when he's coming back. I don't even know where he is now. He said he was going on a trip to Thailand to deal with some problem that had cropped up." She shot a glance at me. "He handles the legal work for an American-owned hotel chain that has property interests there. But he's disappeared. I haven't known how to contact him now for days."

I stared at her in confusion. Apparently she didn't know everything about Raven's business activities. Yet she had to know some of it. But did any of this really matter? The bottom line was that she had saved my life that morning in Brussels.

"So Grieder has the necklace," I said slowly. "I suppose Anthony intends to collect on it, one way or another. Do you know what he plans to do next?"

Patricia shrugged and rolled away from me, reaching for her clothes. "I don't know anything about the Gripping Beast or whatever it's called. But that man Grieder gives me the creeps--- the way he looks at me." She shivered slightly. "I want to go home now," she said quietly, struggling into her dress. "There's no more I can tell you."

It was after midnight and the New Town was deserted as I walked her to where she had parked her car. The place had reverted to being a village again. The distant city sounds carried only faintly on the breeze and yellow lights glimmered fitfully through the dark trees in the private gardens, each a city block in size, that divide up the central part of the town. We didn't speak as we walked to the car. Suddenly there didn't seem much to say. Her car was a stylish white Lancia sports job; nothing run-of-the-mill would do for Patricia. She had left it discreetly at the top end of a steep narrow street that ran down the side of one of the gardens, far enough away from my flat to avoid drawing attention.

As we reached the car I tried to thank her for what she had done in Brussels. She smiled wanly at me as she stepped into the car. Then as she drove away she rolled down the window of the car. "Whatever happens, don't think too badly of me, Terry. I still need you, whatever you may think." She gave a hopeless little smile. "But I suppose you hate me. Now that you know."

Then the white Lancia raced away down the hill and I watched it out of sight and heard its tyres screech on the cobble stones as she threw it around the corner. I stood for a moment wondering how much I really did know about her. Then I started to walk slowly down the quiet street, in the shadow of the tall chestnut trees. After a few steps I sensed rather than heard a faint swishing sound that came from somewhere behind me. It was the sort of sound that water carts make as they move slowly along, spraying dusty streets in the heat of summer. But I hadn't heard that sound for years and certainly not in Edinburgh.

I glanced back and saw the large dark car gliding rapidly and silently towards me, its near-side wheels half way across the pavement. In a split second I realised that its lights were off. But as if my glance had been a signal, the engine roared into life and the headlights blazed out at me in a blinding flash. The car catapulted towards me. In that instant I threw myself sideways and felt a dull thud as the side of the car struck me a glancing blow on the hip. Then I crashed painfully against the metal railings of the gardens. Scrambling to my feet I saw that the car had slithered to a stop some twenty yards away down the hill.

Any thoughts I had about this being a drunken accident vanished as the car door opened. A man, tall, slim and dark-haired stepped out. He held in his hand something that gleamed metallically and he was pointing it in my direction. It was the French Canadian, Duchene! I mean, how many people are there who wanted to kill me? From some deep recess of my mind the old Vietnam training came back. I hit the deck, in the same movement rolling away behind a low stone bollard put there to stop law-abiding citizens from parking on the pavements. Or driving their cars at innocent pedestrians. There was a faint coughing noise that I recognised as the sound of a silenced automatic and almost immediately a high pitched clang as the bullet ricochet off the cast-iron railings beside my head.

When you find yourself under fire, I remembered my instructor saying, don't hang around worrying about it. Just get the hell out of the way. I knew the wide empty streets didn't offer much protection and before the man could get off another shot I had leapt up, hauled myself over the railings and tumbled awkwardly to the grass on the other side, feeling the sharp stab of pain in my side where the car had struck me.

Picking myself up I scrambled away into the darkness of the quiet gardens and the cover of the trees. Why is it that you can never find a policeman when you want one I thought, plunging deeper into the head-high bushes.

# CHAPTER 24

It was dark under the trees and I stopped to catch my breath. Looking back I could see a tall slim figure silhouetted against the street-lights for an instant as he levered himself easily over the railings. Shit, I thought, this guy is serious; I must really have upset Anthony Raven. But if you are going to be hunted, it's a good idea to be in terrain you know better than your hunter. However good Duchene might be, I was sure he didn't know my town as well as I did.

The New Town gardens are mostly rectangular with an irregular border of thick trees and mature shrubs fifteen to twenty yards wide. This one was no exception. The middle was an open area of parkland dotted with only occasional cover, small clumps of trees, and here and there a garden hut. If Duchene followed me it would be safer to stick to the perimeter and work my way around to a point nearer my flat, where I could climb back out into the street. The alternative was to go to ground and hope that he missed me in the darkness. Sooner or later he was bound to give up the game, I hoped.

On the other hand, I was out of his direct vision for as long as it took him to move through the first band of trees. Only fifteen or twenty yards, I thought uneasily. But he would be moving slowly and carefully, searching for me in a strange place. Uncertain of what I might do. I kicked off my shoes.

They'd be there when I needed them. In the meantime I would move faster and quieter without them. I took one deep breath and started to run.

The ground was bone dry underfoot and I hit a good pace quickly, skimming almost soundlessly over the short grass. I headed diagonally across the open part of the gardens towards the nearest cover of trees on the far side. It was about two or three hundred yards away and slightly downhill. With any luck it would take Duchene at least thirty seconds to clear the bushes on his side of the park. Until then he couldn't see me. It may not be enough, I thought, as I ran, but it's better than waiting like a rabbit in a snare. Besides, if I reached the other side safely I recalled that I would be within easy reach of John Boyd's flat.

I was half way across the open space and still going well. My breathing was easy and my legs felt strong. Thank God, or rather my physiotherapist, for the morning exercises. I swerved abruptly through a small group of trees clustered around a little pavilion, putting as much cover as possible between me and Duchene. As I did, the silence of the night was broken by another of those coughing noises. In the same instant a tree beside my head erupted into a blaze of white razor-sharp fragments and a fierce pain stabbed at the side of my eye. As I ran I could feel something warm and sticky flow down my face.

It had been a very long shot at that distance, I thought, especially with a handgun. But it meant he had sighted me rather faster than I had hoped. He was obviously good at this sort of thing. Checking my stride for a second I glanced back from behind the cover of the pavilion. He was loping steadily in my direction and closing fast. I looked around frantically for a weapon of some kind. Maybe some careless gardener had left a spade or a rake lying around. But there was nothing. You just can't rely on staff nowadays.

Quickly I got my bearings and sprinted the rest of the distance into the trees. As I ran I wiped the dripping blood away from my eyes. Tonight's dinner party hadn't been a complete success, I thought. At that moment I stood on a loose branch that had been left lying on the path, hurtled forward full length and slammed into the hard ground with a thud. Gasping and badly winded I rolled over as another shot tore up the earth beside my face, showering me with dirt. I scrambled painfully up and staggered the final few yards into the cover of the shrubs and trees. But I had lost vital seconds. Bloody gardeners, I thought savagely.

Now it was time for a policy decision. Keep on going and try to get over the railings before he had a chance to get a clear shot at me from close range? Not a good idea, I decided. I was beginning to realise that I hated Anthony Raven; and I wasn't too keen on the man they called Duchene either. But Duchene was the immediate problem.

I dropped down behind a thick rhododendron bush and rapidly considered my options. I had trouble believing this was really happening to me. I was being hunted by a killer in middle of the most civilised part of my own town! Now that the first burst of adrenalin had been consumed I was starting to feel scared. Get a grip, Lennox, I said to myself. Think. What's the point of being a management consultant if you can't organise a simple situation like this? But this was no place for a SWOT analysis. The threat was obvious enough and there were very few opportunities that I could see. The weakness was that he had the gun and I didn't. My only strength seemed to be local knowledge. So use it, you stupid bastard, I thought desperately. What do you know that he doesn't?

I guessed that by now he would be circling in the trees to cut me off from the street. Suddenly I remembered that in this corner of the gardens there was a kind of classical temple, a stone folly, with a high curved dome that in summer was almost entirely hidden by trees. Silently I worked my way in that direction, moving carefully to avoid the patches of light that here and there illuminated the dark turf, pausing from time to time to listen for any sound of Duchene. I reached the little folly and slipped gratefully into the shadows behind it. Reaching up I caught hold of the edge of the domed roof and pulled myself into the shelter of the leafy trees above. The safety of the street seemed tantalisingly close. But it was just too far to jump and the thought of landing on the cast-iron spikes of the railings and waiting like a stuck pig for the French Canadian to finish me off, did not appeal.

With patience and a touch of luck perhaps I could outwait him. I braced my feet on the stone ledge and spread myself against the dome of the temple, realising with surprise that the dome was made of some light plastic material. From within the structure I heard a quiet humming sound. Then I remembered that the temple was actually a local gas pumping sub-station, probably the only neo-classical gas pumping station in the world. It could only happen in Edinburgh. I just hope this guy doesn't hit something inflammable with his next shot, I thought slightly hysterically. It would be a pity to see classical Edinburgh going up in flames. I clung there for what seemed like an age with my face pressed against the dome, hidden in the shadows. Every ten or fifteen minutes a car would race past in the darkness or the rattle of a taxi cab's diesel engine sounded on the road outside. It was all achingly close and yet totally out of reach.

After about half an hour I raised my head cautiously and risked a glance around me. He must have given up by now. I tried to imagine what I would do in his place. Logically the best strategy for him was to move on to my flat and wait there until I returned. My legs felt stiff and cold and I was about to ease myself down to the ground when I heard a faint rustle in the undergrowth.

I held my breath. On the top of the dome was an elaborately decorated hollow finial. I raised my head very carefully far enough to squint through the lattice work. Then I froze. No more than six feet away, moving carefully towards me and half crouched in the darkness, the automatic extended in his

211

hand, was the tall dark figure of Duchene. As a patch of light fell across him I saw his swarthy face clearly for the first time, impassive, his eyes dark and wide-open like a hunting cat.

He circled the temple cautiously, checking out the likely hiding places in the shrubs nearby. Finally he stopped for what seemed like another age but was probably only a couple of minutes. He leaned back against the wall directly beneath me and looked about him in puzzlement, the gun hanging loose down by his side. For one second I considered jumping down to tackle him but quickly decided against heroics. I didn't know how good he was at close quarters and it had been twenty years since I had tested my unarmed combat training. Besides, it didn't seem a good idea to push my luck too far. It had been a pretty exhausting evening already, one way and another. So I hung there, frozen into immobility.

After a long time he seemed to come to a decision. He tucked the gun slowly into the back of his waistband, grasped the railings and half vaulted, half hauled himself nimbly up and over, landing neatly on the pavement outside. With relief I heard his footsteps disappear down the street. I checked my watch. It was now one o'clock. I waited another quarter of an hour and then followed him over the railings, heading in the opposite direction.

My own flat was clearly out of bounds for the rest of the night. I decided it would be wiser to pay a call on John Boyd and two minutes later I was ringing his door-bell. I knew he kept late hours and I stood looking nervously around me, praying that he was at home. Anxious minutes passed and then the heavy front door swung open. John stood looking at me sleepily. He was wearing a checked woollen dressing gown over a pair of warm pyjamas and the kind of comfortable slippers your mother gives you at Christmas. With his hair tousled and a puzzled expression he looked rather like Christopher Robin without a teddy bear. I pushed quickly past him into the hall. "You know you look like Christopher Robin?" I asked. "Without the teddy bear."

He seemed to be still half asleep and stood for a moment at the door looking about before he closed it, as if he half expected more maniacs to arrive. Finally he said. "Teddy's upstairs in bed."

That's what I want to talk to you about," I said with my best effort at insouciance. "Can you give me a bed for the night?" I went on. "I'm being chased by a man.

"My dear," John murmured gently. "Some people have all the luck!" He led me upstairs to a snug little sitting room where the remains of an open fire still burned. He glanced at me shrewdly. "You look terrible. Is that blood on your face?"

I touched the side of my head gingerly and nodded. "It's a long story," I said.

"You need a brandy," John said firmly. "There's a bathroom through there. Why don't you clean up and I'll pour you a drink. You'll find some sticking plaster in there too."

I came back and joined him by the fire, clutching a goblet of John's best brandy. I was starting to flag but the bite of the alcohol revived me a little. I told him the whole story, including what I now knew about Raven. "Tell me the truth, John. What do you really think about him? The time for hints and discreet warnings is over. The guy is trying to kill me. Twice I've been lucky, but--- ."

John stared at me in silence and I could see in his eyes exactly what was going through his mind. He weighed his conflicting loyalties. "Yes," he said slowly. "It does seem to be--- a rather serious situation." That was John's way of saying it was a catastrophe. I waited patiently, nursing my glass and staring at the fire.

Finally he made up his mind. "You asked me some time ago about a so-called "magic circle" and I told you it didn't exist. Well, strictly speaking it doesn't. There has never been any question of senior legal figures being suborned, not for illicit sex or by any other means. That simply wouldn't happen, in my opinion. But Raven is known to have been involved in recruiting young men for older homosexuals who for whatever reason are unwilling to let their preferences become generally known."

"You mean men who don't want their wives and families to know they are gay?" I said sharply.

John shifted uncomfortably. "Possibly. Sometimes they have other reasons. Perhaps simply a reluctance to face up to the facts."

"And Raven is the nice man who helps them out," I said caustically. "What a terrific guy. And what does he get out of it? Apart from the warm glow of helping mankind?"

John shrugged. "I'm suppose from time to time he has favours of some kind; inside information, preferential business deals, useful contacts; that sort of thing." He smiled half nervously at me. "You are in trade." He gave a braying laugh. But half-heartedly this time. "You'd know better than me what goes on in your grimy commercial world. I think essentially Raven is a man who loves power; control over people, especially influential people. " He hesitated. "There is a rumour that he is to be offered a seat on the board of one of the institutions."

I whistled. Once that had happened Raven would be part of the establishment--- an insider and virtually untouchable, given the way they look after their own. Especially their own mistakes. John went on slowly. "However, recently there have been stories circulating that he may be in financial trouble. If the stories are true, of course that would put paid to any such appointment."

"It would certainly knock any significant board appointment on the head," I said thoughtfully. "Maybe that explains why he needed money in a hurry--- and why he's trying to sell that golden ornament. Those parties at Scarisby could have been his way of buying insurance against anyone looking into his affairs too closely."

John nodded his agreement. "From what I've heard about him there's a lot to look into. But Terry, my advice is not to look for purely rational explanations with Raven. Yes, money means a lot to him. But it doesn't end there. My impression is that he loves control for its own sake. He enjoys playing games with people, exploiting their weaknesses, seeing just how far he can push them. No-one who knows him personally trusts him." He paused and looked at me seriously for a moment. "I'd say he is something quite rare in my experience. He's a truly corrupt individual. Or depraved, if you prefer that word."

I didn't like either word. But after what I had just done with Patricia, was I in any position to make moral judgements? "It would fit with what I've heard," I said slowly. "What do you know about the young men he uses for his games?"

John looked even more disapproving. "Most of them come out of Raven's cheap rental accommodation. He's rumoured to have quite a network of down-market flats around the city."

I shook my head. I was starting to unravel rapidly, as alcohol replaced the adrenalin in my system. "So it's true. What young Norman Orr said to me is true. Anthony Raven is gay, which means the rest may be true as well," I muttered half to myself.

"Gay?" John said coldly. "Well, I prefer to say he uses people. It doesn't matter to him what they feel, or who they are. It's just a nasty twisted game of hate with him."

He made me a bed on the sofa beside the fire and I toppled gratefully into it. For a long time I drifted in and out of sleep, thinking about Raven and Patricia. Obviously I was still in danger. But why, exactly? Because of Patricia? Or because of the Gripping Beast? Oblivion eventually arrived before I could decide.

# CHAPTER 25

I slipped out early next morning leaving a note for John thanking him for the bed and brandy and for a pair of shoes I had borrowed. In view of what he knew about the attack I also warned him that Tom Drever might turn up at some stage and demand the keys to my flat. I didn't want John to call out the militia. "Remember he's friendly, though he may not look it. But you'll have no problem recognising him," I wrote. "He's a big ugly guy with red hair and an Orkney accent."

With rather more caution than usual I walked round to my flat. As I passed the gardens where last night's chase had taken place I gazed at them in wonder. In the morning sunshine they looked exactly what they had been designed to be, a civilised haven away from the busy streets. Last night was starting to seem like a bad dream and it was hard to believe that just a few hours earlier I had been running for my life across these quiet gardens. I knew now that Raven had a long reach. Just why he hated me I still wasn't sure. But clearly he wasn't going to let me escape easily.

As I entered my flat the smell of stale alcohol and sex hit me. Quickly I opened every window I could find and started to clear up the shambles. The telephone rang, shattering the quiet. I stared for a moment, wondering how persistent Duchene was likely to be. Picking it up, I said apprehensively, "Lennox".

But Ray Morrison's voice answered me. "Good news," he said cheerfully. "I've spoken to Tim Davis and he says he'll meet you. You owe me a drink."

I hesitated. Then I remembered what I had asked Morrison to do for me. "Davis? Oh, yeah, right. That's great," I said, hoping I sounded more enthusiastic than I felt. Somehow now my idea of investigating Raven's activities didn't seem so appealing.

"But I should warn you," Morrison went on, "he's a pretty suspicious guy. He has a big chip on his shoulder about what happened to him after the break-in." He paused. "Or maybe he just has a big chip on his shoulder. Anyhow, he says he'll meet you this morning. At the top of the Calton Hill. You know the spot? I think he chose the place so that he can get a good view of you first. To make sure you're alone."

"Alone?" I said suspiciously. "Why does he want me to come alone?" It occurred to me abruptly that Davis was one of Raven's associates--- and after last night I had my doubts about meeting any more of them. "What does he think I want?"

"Well, he certainly didn't buy the story about you writing a book." Morrison paused. "My guess is that he's still smarting from the way he was set up for the police break-in."

"He doesn't think I'm police, does he?"

"No. He knows the way the fuzz operate. Anyhow, he says he'll meet you beside the pillars of the old monument on the hill this morning at ten."

The old monument was another of Edinburgh's neo-classical piles, this time at the top of the Calton Hill. It had been planned as a copy of the Parthenon in Greece and it was supposed to set the seal on the city as the Athens of the North.

218

But of course they ran out of money before the building could be completed. Then, being Edinburgh, the city refused to accept help from the rest of the country. So it was left unfinished. It stands there, looking reprovingly down on us as a reminder of folie de grandeur. It was christened Edinburgh's Disgrace and eventually acquired an odd cachet of its own. I suppose it does take a certain style to survive a disaster like that. But then that's what this town is good at. It was no more than a brisk fifteen minute walk from the flat, if I could manage anything brisk after last night. My muscles were stiffening up by the minute and I was aching in places even my physio didn't know about. "OK." I said. "How will I recognise Davis?"

"You shouldn't have any trouble. He'll be the chunky little guy in leathers riding a big shiny motor-cycle. And don't worry. He'll recognise you. I told him to look out for a big ugly guy with dark hair. Good luck." Morrison rang off.

At about nine-thirty I headed out across the New Town, cut through a handy modern shopping mall and used its high level walkway to reach the edge of the Calton Hill. Climbing up the narrow winding cobbled streets on the south side of the hill it seemed as if I had been transported into another world, with the noise of the traffic sounding only faintly from far below me. The first entrance to the hill I found was a set of damp overgrown steps that twisted upwards under a dark canopy of trees and shrubs. No, I thought, not today. A hundred yards or so further on I came to a set of big gates that opened onto a wide carriage drive that ran up around the side of the hill. I followed it and in a few minutes emerged into open ground near the top. Away to the north and east the great sweep of the Forth estuary and its scattered chain of islands lay in the sunshine.

Ahead of me, a broad grassy slope ran up towards a rather motley collection of buildings that were scattered about in no special order on the crest of the hill. The mix of styles was eclectic to say the least. There were the towering classical columns of the ill-fated monument and in the distance what looked like an elegant Georgian folly. Further away stood the slim castellated pillar of an old observatory and dominating the foreground was a sprawling vaguely Romanesque structure that even at a distance looked to have seen better days. I made my way up the driveway towards it.

The road widened to form a turning circle immediately outside an incongruously grand doorway which bore a sign saying cryptically, "The Edinburgh Experience." Ho hum, I thought. Now there's something I'm beginning to have views about. Maybe Davis would tell me more. I perched on a low stone pillar from where I could watch the old monument and settled down to think about how to handle him.

I had to admit that I found his choice of venue reassuring. The area was completely open, so that no-one could approach without being seen. At the same time there were several different ways off the hill in an emergency, three or four paths leading steeply down in various directions towards the city. Behind me was a wider road that probably connected with the dark steps I had avoided on my way up. There was no doubt that Davis had chosen the spot well. Which raised the question of why he had been so careful. What exactly did Davis have to fear? I glanced at my watch. It was still only a quarter to ten, the sun was shining and I relaxed a little. Time spent on reconnaissance is never entirely wasted.

Five minutes later I heard the deep burbling noise of a engine and a moment later a motorcycle came into view. It was big and bright red and it eased its way smoothly up the hill towards me with that air of quiet restraint that tells you something is running well within its reserves of power. Turning slowly past me, its helmeted and goggled rider gave me a close look as he passed. The machine was a Yamaha, a big bruiser of a bike with a 1200cc engine that would take a powerful man to control if ever it was cut loose. The rider stopped on the far side of the turning circle, as far away from me as possible. He swung himself out of the saddle, hoisted the massive machine up on its stand and stood for a moment surveying the area with his hands on his hips. Then he pulled off the helmet and ignoring me completely he walked away in the direction of the monument.

It was Davis all right. Morrison's description fitted him perfectly. He was small, no more than five feet six, but stockily built, with a powerfully developed torso and strong heavy thighs. Even with the awkward biker leathers and clumsy boots he moved easily, with just the hint of a swagger. He had the air of a man who was aware of his own physical strength and enjoyed the confidence this gave him. On such massive shoulders his head, round and heavily boned with close cropped dark hair, looked absurdly small. But I fancied that not too many people cared to point it out to him.

He reached the base of the old columns and stood looking around. From that vantage point he could see all the paths leading up the hill. Obviously a careful man, I thought, and a worried one too. I waited until exactly ten o'clock. Then I slid down from the pillar and wandered across the grass in his direction.

He watched me as I approached. He had a round pugnacious face and his eyes, small and dark, were set deep in the strongly boned forehead and prominent cheek-bones. A boxer's face I thought to myself. The eyes were cold and hostile. "Hi," I said to him cheerfully. "Tim Davis, I presume." I reached out a hand.

He ignored it. "Are you Lennox?"

I nodded. "Yes. Thanks for coming. I appreciate you meeting me."

Davis seemed to relax slightly. He unzipped his leather jacket and then almost as an after-thought stuck out his hand and grabbed mine. "No problem," he muttered. Ah, the Lennox charm still has powers to soothe the savage beast. His grip was strong and at close quarters I could see why. The upper body development was sensational and heavy muscles rippled through a thin white t-shirt under the leather jacket. I could only guess at the hours of weight training and the sweat and strain that had gone into building up that physique.

I decided that a bit of male bonding would do no harm at this stage. I looked at him admiringly. "Terrific pecs," I said. "You must work out a lot."

"A bit," he admitted grudgingly. "You?"

"Used to," I said. "Not any more. Too old."

He shook his head. "Nah, you've got to keep at it. So what can I do for you, Lennox?"

"I'm interested in a man called Anthony Raven."

Davis turned away and spat on the ground. "He's a bastard. What's your interest in him?" He looked back at me and I noticed for the first time that he wore a little gold ear ring. "You gay?" he asked me curiously.

"Ah, no," I said, perhaps too hastily. But I didn't want to take this male bonding thing too far. "You?"

"Sure," he nodded. "So why are you interested in Raven then?" he asked bluntly.

"Let's just say I've had business dealings with him that have been less than satisfactory. I was told that you help him with some of his interests. So I wondered what you could tell me about him."

Davis laughed scornfully. "Less than satisfactory," he mimicked. "You're telling me! He'd screw his own mother for half-a dollar. But you're damn right. I know a lot about Raven.

222

That's why the bastard tried to set me up with the fuzz. After all I've done for him. So he conned you as well, did he?"

I decided Davis might after all be a useful ally. "As a matter of fact, I think he tried to have me killed," I said quietly.

Davis whistled and looked at me with more admiration. "Hey, he must really like you. What did you do to deserve that? He only tried to have me sent down for about ten years, the way the fucking courts work here."

"You mean when he tried to blame the break-in at police headquarters on you? I heard about that. Do you have any idea who really did the job?" I asked him ingenuously.

Davis looked around uncomfortably. Then he seemed to make up his mind. He stared back at me, his piggy little eyes hot and angry. "Oh, I did the job all right," he said belligerently. "But I did it for him. Raven set the whole thing up. It was him who wanted that fucking report. He had inside information. It had to have been an inside job--- he told us exactly where to find the stuff and how to get into the building." He shrugged. "It was all fixed for me and a mate. Then once he had the stuff Raven turned me in. Or tried to! It was just luck that I didn't go down for it. Now he's disappeared, the bastard," Davis spat contemptuously at his feet, "and he still owes me a lot of cash. But he knows what'll happen to him when we meet up again. They tell me he's out of the country now. You any idea where he is?" He shot the question at me.

I shook my head. "I understand you look after some of his properties for him," I said. "Don't you have access to any of his cash? That's why I thought you might know how to contact him."

Davis spat again. "I used to have access to some of his cash. But he's sold everything off. Something seems to have gone wrong and it must be something serious." He sat on the edge of the monument and I squatted down beside him. "Besides," Davis admitted, "I was only a small part of the set-up. He was involved with some of the big money people as well--- I mean really big. Not the kind of stuff I handled for him."

"Big money?"

Davis nodded. "Sure. Overseas drug money mostly. And a lot of it, from what I heard. He was getting into the big league." He glowered at me. "I suppose he thought he didn't need me any longer and that HQ job was a good way to kill two birds. Get rid of me and get hold of that report at the same time. But now he has a problem--- I don't know what exactly. So he's emptied the flats and the kids are all gone. I think he's doing a runner." Davis stared at me angrily. "Or else he's already done one. But I'll find him, don't worry about that. And if you ask me I'm not the only person looking for him."

I eyed him carefully. Davis seemed genuine enough in his own way. "Listen," I said. "Have you ever heard of a man called Duchene? A Canadian?" Davis shook his head. Well, he had been small beer in Raven's eyes. Duchene and the Americans probably lived in another part of the forest. "Look Davis, maybe you can help me. I don't know where Raven is now. But I'm certain he'll turn up and when he does I want to be there just as much as you do. There are questions I want answers to."

"Oh, he'll turn up all right," Davis said promptly. "He won't leave that slag of a wife of his. He'll want to hang on to her in spite of everything." I didn't like the sneer in his voice.

"You know Patricia Raven?" I asked, half dreading his answer.

"You bet," he said with a crude laugh. "Raven used her in some of his parties. Though you'd think butter wouldn't melt in her mouth, to listen to her." He laughed again. "Oh yes, I know

Patricia Raven all right."

"Parties," I said weakly. The whole of Edinburgh seemed to know more about Patricia than I did. "I'm not with you."

Tim Davis stared at me. "If you know anything about Raven you must know about the boys--- the ones he pimps for his posh pals." He paused. "The ones I find for him," he stressed. "That was just one of the things I did for Raven. And all the thanks I got was to be fitted up," he said.

My head was swimming. This was Norman Orr's story all over again. "But," I said hoarsely. "I thought you were gay? The young men you're talking about--- ," The claims of Norman Orr and his friend came back to haunt me.

Davis stared at me. "Where have you been living," he asked me scornfully. "A lot of gay guys are bi. Raven likes to use Patricia to line them up for his other games. For the parties up north where he entertains his influential friends." He sneered again. "I reckon it gives him a big kick to know he can make her do anything he wants. He's a total control freak, you know."

"You know this for sure? You've seen this?" I said faintly, disgusted and yet still wanting to know the truth.

"Sure. I joined in sometimes. If I was in the mood for something different."

None of this made sense. None of it fitted. But it was starting to have a ghastly kind of reality. Everything I had learned about Raven made his story credible. Even Patricia's own words. I swallowed hard, fighting down the nausea that was close to overwhelming me. Then, trying desperately to sound casual, I said,. "So you think he'll come back for her--- for Patricia?"

Davis nodded. "Bound to. He won't let her go. In fact I'm

225

pretty sure she knows where Raven is hiding. I went to see her at the house but she had those security gates locked and wouldn't let me in. She gave me some crap about him being abroad. I've had some of my people keeping an eye on the house just in case he turns up. Been watching it myself most nights." He shook his head. "She's definitely up to something, that's for sure. Gave me the slip last night and went off somewhere. But I lost her in town in the traffic." He shook his head at me. "No, she's in touch with him, I'm sure of it. It was well after midnight before she came back. If you ask me he's in one of his properties. I know he didn't tell me about all of them. He's a crafty bastard." Last night, I thought. That seemed several lifetimes away. I decided not to explain Patricia's recent movements. "But don't worry," he said grimly "She won't keep me hanging around for ever. I can get into that house any time I want. And when I do she'll tell me where Raven is. I'll screw it out of her if I have to."

Now he was really starting to worry me. Davis wasn't the type to make idle threats and, whatever the truth about Patricia, I couldn't leave her to deal with Davis alone. I eyed him cautiously. I still remembered a few moves from my army combat training. But I was far from sure that I could handle him if it came to violence. True, he was smaller than me, but stronger and in much better shape. I decided to use my brains for a change. That's what I'm supposed to be good at. Although so far, I thought wryly, they hadn't been much help to me.

"Listen," I said. "If you really want to find Raven maybe we could work together." I thought furiously. "I'll let you know anything I hear. I could give you a hand to stake out the house. It'll be easier with two people."

He looked less than impressed. "Well, maybe," he said reluctantly. "We could use your car. It would be less conspicuous than this beast." He gestured towards the big Yamaha. "It's a wee bit conspicuous," he admitted. "

"I don't have a car," I said.

He looked at me with disbelief. "OK," he said slowly. "Then meet me outside Raven's house tonight at seven o'clock. We'll find a quiet spot to wait where you can watch her driveway. That will give me a break. I don't want the neighbours getting twitchy about me and calling the police. If you see her on the move, give me a ring on the mobile. Then I'll pick you up and we can follow her. But I warn you! I'm not going to wait long. If nothing shows, I'm going in after her."

"The mobile?" I asked. "Oh I see! I'm afraid I don't have a mobile phone."

"Christ," Davis said in amazement, "how do you live?" Before I could reply he went on hurriedly, "OK, I'll loan you one for the night. No problem." I gave him one of my business cards and he studied it carefully. "Management Consultant, eh. Well, I knew you must be good at something," he said with a short laugh. We walked in an awkward silence back to where he had left the motorcycle. There were still things I wanted to find out from Davis. But at least for now he seemed to accept that we were on the same side. "Drop you anywhere?" he asked me casually. "Does 0-70kh faster than anything else on the road." I looked at the massive frame of the big XJR and then at the steep narrow paths leading down from the hill.

"Ah, no thanks," I said. "It seems like a nice morning for a walk." Davis positioned the helmet comfortably and straddled the machine, kicking it into life. He shook his head at me. I think he was laughing under the helmet. Then in a sudden screech of burning rubber and a shower of dirt he was gone, accelerating down the twisting track. I only hoped that he would slow down to something like the legal speed limit when he hit the main road. After all I didn't want him to break the law.

CHAPTER 26

In my wildest dreams I could never have imagined it would end the way it did.

But at the time it seemed to make sense. Davis was closer to Raven than anyone else I had met so far and as I didn't have any better ideas I decided to go along with him. I didn't really think he would lead me to Raven. But he seemed just crazy enough to do something violent and I suppose I wanted to make sure he didn't do it to Patricia. I changed into casual clothes and just before seven o'clock that evening found myself back in the quiet leafy street where Raven had his house. It seemed a long time since my first encounter with him, when Raven was still playing the part of a respectable Edinburgh lawyer. And I had been playing the dummy.

Davis was waiting for me by a bench under some trees at a quiet corner of the road, well away from the house but within sight of the gates. There was little or no through traffic in a street of this kind and the only other vehicle was a large black saloon parked outside one of the mansions a little way away. In spite of the warm evening Davis wore his heavy motor-cycle helmet and visor. I suppose he thought it made him invisible. In addition he was wearing the dark leather jacket and the calf-length black boots I had seen earlier, but he had swapped his leather trousers for a pair of jeans. Strapped to the passenger seat I saw there was a spare helmet. I prayed that I wouldn't have to use it. It was a long time since I had been on the back of a bike and the thought of re-learning on Davis's monster didn't appeal to me.

He showed me how to work the mobile and we took it in turn to keep an eye on the house. By nine o'clock nothing had happened and I don't know who was more bored, Davis or me. The problem was that Davis's boredom could become dangerous and I started to worry about what he might do next. I was striding purposefully half way round the block on one of my regular walks when I heard the mobile ring. Davis's voice whispered excitedly in my ear. "The gates are opening. Where the hell are you?" I sprinted back to the corner in time to catch a glimpse of Patricia's white Lancia pulling out of the driveway and the gates closing behind her. Davis handed me the helmet. "Hang on," he said curtly.

Patricia drove sedately out of town in a southerly direction, staying well within the speed limit and stopping dutifully at every traffic light. Davis followed at a modest pace, hanging back a long way to keep out of her vision. Even in the fading light I knew he'd have no difficulty keeping the distinctive sports car in sight. Quite soon I realised that we were heading for the city's ring road.

The big Yamaha hit the dual carriageway and turned east. Traffic was heavy but Davis's powerful machine could more than hold its own with anything on the road. From time to time I felt him accelerate and then tuck in behind the stream of cars. He seemed to know what he was doing and I was actually starting to enjoy the trip, learning again how to adjust my weight to meet the sway of the bike.

As I became more conscious of my surroundings I noticed that we had turned off onto the main highway south. Swiftly we by-passed a series of small towns and in minutes were skimming through open countryside with just enough traffic

229

on the road to make it unlikely that Patricia would notice us. We powered south through the gathering gloom. A lighthouse appeared off to our left, flashing intermittently against the dark sky and I recognised the rocky coastline where the sea takes over almost imperceptibly from the river estuary. The great bulk of the nuclear power station loomed menacingly out of the darkness, then in an instant it was gone.

What the hell am I doing, I muttered to myself, ducking down in the lee of Davis's broad back. Suppose she's heading for Newcastle? Or even bloody London, come to that. She might easily have decided to pack a bag and just take off. I banged several times on the back of Davis's helmet. He turned his head and I gesticulated frantically for him to pull over. At the next lay-bye he pulled in and switched off the engine. He removing his helmet leisurely and shook his bullet head, running his hand over its short dark hair. "Something wrong, pal?"

"Yes," I said bluntly. "How far do you think we can go on this wild-goose chase? She could be heading anywhere south of here. I don't want to end up in London or Paris."

Davis grinned at me wolfishly. "Don't worry about that," he said. "Now I know exactly where she's going!. As soon as she turned down the coast road I knew where Raven is hiding out. There's a cottage on the beach down here that he keeps for his own use. Been having it done up, though it's still fairly basic. That's where she's taking us. Didn't I tell you she was in touch with him!"

I shrugged. Maybe Davis knew what he was talking about. We went slowly on for another couple of miles. Suddenly Davis switched off the lights on the motor-bike and turned into a narrow dirt track that wound downhill towards the sea. He cut the engine and we coasted in silence through the darkness for the next half mile or so, bumping awkwardly on the rough unmade surface of the track. At one point we came to a sturdy metal gate, standing half open. On it was a freshly painted sign saying "PRIVATE-KEEP OUT". Davis ignored it; we squeezed past and carried on down the slope.

Gradually I became aware of solid darker shapes outlined against the night sky. As we approached, they resolved themselves into a group of derelict cottages, scattered about in an untidy square. There was no sign of a light from any of them. "Here?" I said to Davis questioningly. He shook his head and gestured for me to follow him as he pushed the bike.

Behind one of the old ruins we found Patricia's white Lancia. Parked beside it was another car, a big dark-coloured four-door saloon. I walked cautiously across to it. It was another Lancia. There's brand loyalty for you, I thought. Or did Raven negotiate a cut rate deal? Davis hoisted the Yamaha onto its stand and joined me.

"Raven's?" I indicated the new Lancia. Davis nodded silently. "But where--- ?" I started to say. He motioned for me to follow him again. There was another gate and as my eyes adjusted to the darkness I could see beyond it a path, even narrower and rougher than the track we had driven on. It curved steeply down the side of the cliff towards the sea and through the stillness I could hear the regular beat of the water as it surged into a cove below.

"Down there," he whispered. "Raven owns the whole bloody place. Nice and private--- nobody comes here any more." He tapped me on the chest to emphasise his point. "You wait here. I want ten minutes with him alone. Then you're welcome to him." I saw him grin wickedly in the half light. He slipped silently through the gate and vanished into the darkness.

I gave him two minutes and then went after him. I didn't trust Davis. Especially if Raven was down there. I picked my way carefully down the path. It was too early for the moon to be up but in the open there is always a certain amount of residual light and I could see my way well enough. To my left however there was an almost vertical drop into the sea and glancing down I could see the white breakers tumbling in against the rocks. I decided to stick close to the cliffside on my right hand. A look at my watch told me that it was nearing high tide on this part of the coast.

After about quarter of a mile the angle of descent slackened and the track widened to form a low narrow promontory, a natural breakwater running in a long arc out into the sea. Underfoot the rough dirt changed into large flat paving stones, still uneven and in places broken but clearly man-made. Then I saw that the breakwater had a solid sea-wall along its length, effectively turning the little cove into a sheltered harbour. Half way down the sea-wall a trace of light gleaming out across the water. I moved towards it swiftly and silently.

Built into the wall was a large rectangular stone structure, probably an old fisherman's hut and store room, built on two storeys with a couple of steps up to a weather-beaten wooden front door. The door stood half ajar and light glimmered on the stones from a small window where curtains had been carelessly and hurriedly pulled across. As I approached I heard loud angry voices from inside the hut. Cautiously, I put my eye to a gap in the curtained window. My view of the room was half blocked by Davis's broad back. Beyond him and lounging casually against the rough-cast wall opposite, half illuminated by the red flickering glow of a big open fire, was Anthony Raven.

He was quite a contrast to the polished lawyer that I knew; dressed in a rough dark blue fisherman's jersey, heavy trousers and short sailing boots. Strangely, it had never occurred to me that Raven might be a sailor. Then I remembered the high speed motor-boat in the boathouse at Scarisby and the stories of how it had been used. He was leaning back, his arms crossed, a cynical smile on his face. That hadn't changed at least.

Then I saw Patricia, half sitting, half lying, on an untidy

232

pile of blankets heaped on a primitive day-bed. She was dressed simply in a plain white shirt and blue jeans, with ankle-length boots. Her long auburn hair was pulled back and held casually with a tie, revealing the elegant lines of her lovely face. She looked pale and tired. Her yellow eyes were fixed on Davis and there was a look in them that I had never seen before. A glitter of something indefinable. Was it fear or perhaps a strange kind of excitement?

Davis was shouting and waving his arms about. "Don't give me that crap!" I heard him say. "You owe me ten grand. And if you think I'm going to do your dirty work after what you tried to pull, you're off your head!" He stamped about the small room in a rage.

"Tim, dear boy," I heard Raven say soothingly. "You don't think that raid on your place had anything to do with me? You and I are partners. Haven't I always said that? You mustn't jump to conclusions. A lot of people knew about the report--- and who had it. Anyone could have tipped off the police. Or no-one," he went on smoothly. "Maybe the police were simply trying their luck. You know how they operate."

Davis grunted. "What about my ten grand then?"

Even at this distance I felt Raven's mood ease. "Don't worry, Tim. You'll get it, I promise you," he said. "It's just that things are a little tricky at the moment. I have to lay low for a while; keep out of the way until some problems resolve themselves. I know I should have told you about it, Tim dear boy, and I'm sorry about that. I have a lot of cash tied up in projects at the moment. But I'm expecting a big payment very soon. Isn't that right, darling?" He turned towards Patricia. A nervous smile flicked across her pale face.

"Believe me, Tim, a very wealthy client is about to buy something from me that will clear up all the outstanding cash problems. You'll have your money in a week or so at most."

233

Then he glanced knowingly at Davis. "Now, since you're here, why don't you relax and enjoy yourself. Have a drink."

Raven went to a table and lifted a brandy bottle. "I know what you like, Tim." He gave a little twisted smile. "And so does Patricia. Don't you darling?" Her eyes opened wide for an instant. "Why don't you give Tim some of what he likes?"

Patricia shook her head in silence. Her face drained of what little colour there was. "No, please Anthony! I--- I don't want--- ."

In an instant Raven had moved swiftly across to where she sat on the day bed. He took her by the shoulder and I saw his fingers tighten and dig into her flesh. She winced and gasped in pain. "Don't argue dear," Raven hissed. Before I could move, Patricia had obediently dropped to her knees in front of Davis. Her hand reached up to unzip his jeans. I stood frozen in horror at what was about to happen. And yet there was an awful element of voyeurism that held me there fascinated.

The scene was shattered in an instant. Davis swung his hand in a wide arc. "Fuck off, you whore," he shouted. I heard the noise of the blow and Patricia slumped sideways onto the floor, clutching the side of her face. That was enough to shock me out of my trance. I leapt into the hut, threw open the door of the inner room and stepped into the light.

The three figures were immobile as a tableau. Patricia sprawled on the floor, Davis stood menacingly over her in the centre of the room and Raven leaned against the far wall, his arms still folded across his chest. Raven was the first to react. For a split second his face showed surprise. "Lennox! What the hell--- how did you get here?"

I nodded silently in the direction of Davis and turned towards Patricia. "Are you all right?" I asked. She lay staring up at me and holding her face. Her eyes were wide in astonishment and I could see the succession of emotions pour into them and then drain away. Her face, normally pale, was the colour of putty, except for a red weal that showed between her fingers.

Raven looked across at Davis and the air of indifference vanished completely. His mouth twisted into a savage version of his usual sardonic smile. "Davis, you stupid little ass-hole," he snarled. "You brought him here! And you wonder why I want shot of you? Fuck off out of here and take your new boy friend with you. I have more important things to do than piss about with an ignorant little queer like you."

A curious deep throated animal-like noise built up inside Davis. Then a roar of anger burst out from within him, filling the small room with a ferocity that shocked Raven into silence. Davis stooped and pulled a black-hilted long bladed knife from the top of his boot. In the same single swift motion he rose and hurled himself at Raven. From some recess the old training surfaced as by instinct. As Davis lunged past me I grabbed his knife wrist with both hands and pulled him forward, at the same time slamming my right leg hard into a block across his lower body and legs. His wild momentum threw him off balance, his body twisting as he fell. The knife clattered on the stone flags and slithered away towards where Patricia lay.

Davis crashed on to his back, hitting the stone floor with a force that almost made me wince. His reaction was so fast that it caught me by surprise. He bounced up as if made of rubber and with a single stride had grabbed me in a crushing bear hug. His hands locked behind the small of my back and I felt his massive arms and powerful torso tighten.

Suddenly I was powerless to break his grip. I was having trouble breathing and the pressure in my chest was suffocating as he forced my head relentlessly further and further back. My spine felt almost at breaking point. Desperately, I tried everything I had ever been taught. But it was no use. Nothing seemed to hurt him. I struck up at him again and again with my knee. But I was off balance and my blows seemed to have no effect on his strongly muscled abdomen. My arms were pinned tightly at my side. I couldn't move a muscle to free myself, he was so closely locked against me. There was no way I could even get a hand free. I felt my spine begin to creak and a near paralysing pain shot through my lower back. My head begin to swim as the oxygen supply cut off. Christ, I thought. This crazy little bastard is going to kill me. What a stupid way to die!

Suddenly an impact sent our locked bodies staggering sideways. I was vaguely aware of a blur of movement in front of my face and felt Davis's grip relax slightly. I wrenched myself clear, half falling. Davis was on his knees beside me, his solid bullet head drooping and Patricia clung to his back, one slim arm round his chest while her other hand plunged the long-bladed knife into his neck, again and again in a frenzy. Davis toppled forward and his weight pulled him free of her grasp, wrenching the knife from her hand. Then he lay still, the black handle of the knife jutting horribly from the side of his thick neck.

There was blood everywhere. Patricia reeled back and fell onto the day bed, panting, her hair dishevelled. She seemed oblivious to everything, her staring eyes glittered and her lips twisted in a savage grimace. A smear of blood across her face matched the red weal from Davis's blow and there were wet bloody patches on the front of her white shirt, making it cling to her body. Raven still hadn't moved a muscle.

But Davis was tough. As I started towards him there was a sudden convulsion and he half raised himself on his arms. He gasped something inaudible and fell forward again, face down on the rough floor. The blood spurted from the deep wounds in his neck. His legs twitched and kicked for a moment, as if he was making a frantic effort to stand upright. But I doubt if he was really conscious. Then whatever had driven him to that last effort died.

The room was suddenly completely silent. Patricia lay on

the day bed, white and trembling, like some ghastly mad woman from an opera. I bent over Davis and went through the motions of feeling for his pulse. But there was no flicker of life. Davis had been tough. But the shock and loss of blood on that scale would have killed an ox. Anthony Raven broke the silence. "Dead, is he?" he asked calmly. I looked up and nodded. He pushed himself away from the wall and straightened up. A cruel smile appeared on his tanned features and he walked calmly across to where Patricia was lying. He reached down and took her chin roughly in his hand, forcing her face up to look up at him. "Well, you've surpassed yourself now, my dear. Though I suppose I should be grateful to you for getting rid of a nuisance. But it could be very awkward for you. Unless you do exactly what you're told." Without warning he tightened his fingers around her mouth and twisted painfully. Patricia gasped in pain and he pushed her contemptuously away.

I crossed the room in one stride. All my pent-up frustrations went into the blow and all my weight was behind the punch. My fist sank into his solar plexus, where I knew it would give him most pain and do least damage to my hand. He folded up with a choking groan and reeled back across the room, fighting for breath. He hit the wall and subsided in a heap on the floor. It was very satisfactory. I looked around. The room had suddenly been transformed into a casualty clearing centre with bodies everywhere. I was last man standing. But I had to think of what to do next--- and fast.

Raven lay in the corner choking and retching, his face ashen and sweaty. He wouldn't be taking much interest in the proceedings for a while. It seemed that he hadn't been in such good a shape as he looked--- and now he looked terrible. I just hoped he wasn't going to be sick. That would be too much. I crouched down beside Patricia. But she seemed oblivious of me and everything that had happened around her. She was obviously in shock, her eyes stared wildly and blindly from a white face, like yellow coals burning through snow. She shook uncontrollably, her hands clutched together in front of her face.

I pulled a blanket from the bed and drew it over Davis's body. Then I went over to the table and poured out half a tumbler of neat brandy. "Drink this," I said to Patricia and pushed the glass into her trembling hands. I had to help her get the glass to her mouth and hold it there while she took a gulp. She coughed and spluttered but clung onto the glass as if it was a life-raft, holding it with both hands. I could hear it rattle against her teeth as she drank.

I sensed Raven getting to his feet and turned quickly back towards him. But he didn't look like a man who wanted to fight. He clutched his stomach and looked sourly across the room at me. "My hero!" he sneered bitterly. "How do you propose to get my little orchid out of this one, Lennox? You will try of course, won't you?"

He turned to where Patricia was silently holding the brandy glass. "You're certainly going to need help, my dear. But don't think Lennox will do you any good. If you continue to do exactly as I say, I may just be able to fix this for you. After all, Lennox here is the only witness." He turned back to me. "Isn't that right, Lennox?"

"Yes," I said. "That's right. I am the only witness. Which could make things difficult for you, Raven. As a matter of fact, I have a feeling it will. Suppose I tell the police that you killed Davis? You have a much more obvious motive to kill him than Patricia. I imagine they would find that quite persuasive, once the story about you and Davis becomes public--- even allowing for any influence you think you have. Even if the police can't prove it, the publicity will finish off any plans you might have for a major career move." I grinned at him. "Take my word for it. I'm in the business and no-one in the financial world will touch you with a barge-pole now. You'll be lucky if they cash your cheques in future."

Raven's face set in a hard anger. "Christ, you've caused

me so much trouble, Lennox." He spat it out with real hate.

I almost hit him again. "I've caused you trouble?" I shouted. "I didn't ask to get involved in any of this. It was you're idea, remember? You called me and offered me the assignment! And I know why now! You knew I would be fool enough to introduce you to Grieder. But remember this! I've discovered a hell of a lot about you in the last few weeks and if the police are involved I can cause you a lot trouble. How Childs died, for a start, and the jeweller in Brussels. And the reason they died, too. Selling fake antiquities to powerful men is not a good idea, Raven. And sending hired killers after me isn't so good either."

He smiled calmly and shook his head. "You have nothing that will stand up to examination, Lennox. You know that. There's no proof to link me with anything.

"What about McNaughton's death?" I said. "Not everyone is satisfied about that. I wonder where you were that night? It will all add up, Raven. Even if the law doesn't get you, some of your overseas clients will find you a bit of a liability now. I imagine they won't enjoy the publicity."

His dark eyes stared at me coldly. "My, my! You have been a busy little man," he said contemptuously. He smoothed back his hair. "But it may be true that you can cause me more trouble. Perhaps we should come to an arrangement of some kind. What exactly do you want, Lennox?"

It was a good question. What did I want? Justice? That was too abstract an idea to explain what I was feeling. No, it was more basic than that. I wanted revenge! Revenge for being exploited; for having been made to feel a fool.

He gestured towards where Patricia sat, still absorbed in her own shaken world. "Is it her you want, Lennox? Damaged goods, I know. But suppose I disappear completely. Leave her to you." He glanced around the room. "I'll help you to clear up this mess. We can get rid of Davis somewhere. No-one will miss him for a while. But I need time, Lennox. Time and money. There are things happening that will finance me for a very long time. But I need time now." He shot one of his twisted smiles at me. "And whether you want her or not, I'm certain you will want to spare her a murder trial. To say nothing of yourself. After all, you're not the only one who can make wild accusations." He smiled again. "It could be a messy trial, if the truth about you and my wife came out. Not so good for your reputation either, Lennox."

He was right. But now I knew how to handle him. "OK, Raven," I said shortly. "Here's what we're going to do. You can disappear. Vanish. Get the hell out of here--- away from this country preferably. I don't really care. Just go away and keep out of my way. Don't contact me or Patricia ever again."

His lip twisted. "Ah, so you do want her, in spite of all you know! And believe me, I could tell you a lot more! You don't know the half of it!" He threw his dark head back and laughed savagely.

"Get out! Just get out, Raven. Before I decide to kill you," I grated, "and leave you here with Davis for someone else to find. That would make an interesting news story. Get out of here."

The moon was up and I watched him all the way back up the path until he was vanished from sight. I waited until I heard his car engine starting up and the noise as he raced away in an angry screech of tyres and a rattle of stones, the sounds carrying clearly down to me through the still night air.

I stood outside the hut for a few minutes and breathed the clean smell of the sea. Then, before I went back into the hut to do what I had to do, I walked down to the sea-wall and climbed a short flight of old stone steps. I looked down at the water. The tide was fully in and the little harbour was flooded.

On the other side of the wall the sea surged heavily half way up the rocks. Soon the tide would be on the turn and ready to carry the flotsam into the darkness. Or should that be jetsam? I never can remember which is which.

# CHAPTER 27

Patricia sat clutching the empty brandy glass, staring at the blanket covered figure on the floor. I hoped she really was as insulated from the nightmare as she seemed to be. To make sure, I half filled her glass again. Automatically she put it to her lips and gulped it down. The smeared blood on her face was starting to dry and I thought of wiping it away but decided not to disturb her. Wherever her mind was, it was a better place than here. I gently laid her back on the bed and she curled up, her back to the fire, the empty glass still clasped in her hand.

The fire had burned down and a chill was already starting to seep from the ancient stone floor and walls. I heaped on more logs and stirred up the flames until they were burning fiercely. I was going to need a good fire for what I had in mind. With a glance at Patricia to make certain she was still comfortable, I turned my attentions to Davis.

Swiftly I rolled him in the blanket. Pools of his blood had gathered in the hollows of the uneven stone floor but I would have to deal with that later. I found extra blankets and sheets in a cupboard and spread them about to soak up the worst of the mess. Then, surprisingly easily, I dragged his body out of the hut and down to the steps in the sea-wall.

That was when the problems started. The wall was

almost head high on the land side and the steps were steep. Davis had seemed a small man but he was solidly put together and now he seemed extra-ordinarily heavy. Or maybe I was weakening. Somehow I hauled him up the worn steps until I stood panting and sweating looking down into the black waters. Already they seemed to be receding slightly. Good, I thought vaguely. The luck of the Lennox's. It could have been low tide, which would have been much worse. I shook my head violently. Get a grip, I told myself. You're out of your mind doing this. It's certainly a criminal offence. Polluting the foreshore if nothing else. I pulled the knife out of his neck and tipped the body--- that's what Davis had become now in my mind--- over the edge. As the blanket unwound he fell in a whirl of arms and splashed into the sea.

I straightened up and watched for a moment. But where the body had been was already lost in the darkness. Of course it wouldn't float, I knew that. Dead bodies sink. Gradually it would drift down to the sea-bed, tossed to and fro by the tides, dragged out into the deep North Sea on the flood and back again towards the mouth of the estuary on the ebb. Eventually it would rise to the surface, as it decayed and filled with gases.

Then some unfortunate fisherman might find it. But if so, it would be far from here and probably a long way down the coast of England. And after weeks, perhaps months, bumping along the jagged sea-bed and battering against rocks, to say nothing of the effect of the hungry fish, it would be impossible to tell Davis from any of the dozen or so drowning victims whose remains are pulled out of these waters. It was unlikely that there would be enough of him left to tell the coroner how he had died. I wiped the handle of the knife on the blanket and hurled it as far out to sea as I could.

Back in the hut the fire was blazing up nicely. I poured myself a generous brandy and downed it in a single gulp. Then I stuffed the blood-stained blanket into the flames and started to clear up the room as best I could. It was only a superficial clean but it might satisfy a casual inspection. Hadn't Davis told me this was Raven's private hide-away and that no one was likely to come here. Of course, Davis's bike was still standing up above the cove. I frowned. It would have to stay where it was. Patricia was in no state to drive and once I left this dump I had no intention of ever coming near it again. Eventually of course the machine would be found. But even if the hut was examined and traces of blood identified it was hard to see how it would be connected with an unknown body drifting somewhere down the coast. So Patricia was probably safe, as long as she kept quiet. Always providing Raven did the same. But that was a danger I had to risk. I went across to her and shook her gently back to life. "Patricia! Patricia, wake up!"

She came half awake but still seemed dazed, whether from shock or the brandy she had drunk, I couldn't tell. I brought her some warm water and a clean cloth in a bucket. "Patricia, you must wash yourself. Wipe away the--- ," I checked myself and looked her over. She stared back at me stupidly. Her eyes were unfocussed. "Here," I said quietly. "Let me help you."

I unbuttoned the front of her shirt and like a little girl she raised her hands to let me pull it from her shoulders. An ugly claret-coloured patch stained her pale skin where the blood had soaked through and there were dark stains on her brassiere. I turned her around and undid it. Then rolling her clothes into a ball I tossed them into the fire. "Stand up," I ordered her. Once again she obediently arose and turned to face me.

I wiped her down with the damp cloth; cleaning her face and then her smooth shoulders and breasts, trying hard not to think about the last time I had seen them. Then I saw that her jeans were soaked with blood. "Take those off," I told her. Silently she did what she was told, swaying slightly. She stood there almost naked, the flickering firelight playing over her body.

In spite of myself; in spite of everything, I felt my excitement grow. Clothes, I thought. She's in shock. I'd better keep her warm. Besides, if I'm not careful I'll be the one who's in shock. Somehow I had to get her back to Edinburgh without attracting attention and in only a pair of pants Patricia Raven would not be exactly unobtrusive if the local constabulary stopped us. I rummaged in a cupboard and came back with what I assumed was a pair of Raven's old shorts and a belt. "Here. Put these on once you're clean." I kneeled down and wiped away some traces of blood from her legs and thighs. "I can't find a shirt but you can have mine. This sweater will do me for a while." I stood up and stripped off my sweater and shirt.

Suddenly her eyes opened wide. "Oh Terry," she gasped. "What have I done?" She swayed forward into my arms. I felt her damp body as it pressed against me. Her face looked up into mine. "Take care of me," she whispered. "Please take care of me, Terry." Her lips closed on mine and we sank down on to the scruffy day bed.

It was clear she realised now that she had done something terrible and the knowledge seemed to generate a terrible need in her; a need for some kind of animal contact and warmth. Some kind of security, perhaps. I didn't flatter myself that I was the cause of her urgent need. I just happened to be there. In spite of everything I knew, everything I had seen that night, her need aroused something in me. I wanted her, fiercely and savagely, in a way that I had never felt before.

It would be quite wrong to say we made love there in front of the fire, just a few feet from where Davis had died and with the flames of her blood-stained clothes flickering over us. But we did have sex. Somehow nothing mattered. At one point I noticed with a shock that she still had a smear of dried blood on her upper lip, a smear that I had overlooked in my haste. It was Davis's blood. I knew that of course. But even this didn't put me off. I'm ashamed to say that it was one of our most successful bouts of--- , whatever it was.

When it was over we lay for a while in the firelight,

gasping and sweating. I gently wiped away that smear from her mouth without saying a word. "What can we do," she whispered, only half to me. I didn't have an answer. I'm not even sure I knew what the question meant and I had an awful feeling that if I asked her to explain Patricia wouldn't have known either.

Eventually I got her dressed. She found her hand-bag, fumbled in it and gave me her car keys. Then, engrossed in that miraculous process that women alone seem to comprehend, she started to repair her ravaged make-up, peering into a small mirror like a fascinated budgerigar. After all the horrors of that night for some bizarre reason the sight of this shocked me. "Patricia," I exploded, knowing that I sounded incongruously like an impatient husband. "For God's sake!" We stumbled up the path together to her little Lancia and I drove her back to the city.

As I drove she snuggled against me and slept most of the way. I stared into the cone of white light ahead of me and went over and over in my mind what I had done. Where was the loop-hole? When someone found the motor-cycle there would be some interest shown in Davis, always assuming the bike was registered in his name. Then it struck me like a thunderbolt. His keys! I'd left his keys on the body. Along with any other identification he had been carrying. I groaned. I could only hope the sea did its work well. In any case, there wasn't much to connect Davis with me; except for Raven, of course. Which might be the problem. When we arrived at the silent house in the suburbs Patricia opened the automatic gates and I drove straight up to the front door. "Come in with me, Terry," she whispered quietly. "I can't face being alone, not tonight. Stay with me, Terry. Please!"

I didn't much like the idea. But I followed her into the darkness of the big high-roofed sitting-room and up to the mezzanine balcony and into her bedroom. She stepped forward into my arms. "You will stay the night, won't you Terry? I don't want to be alone. Not after what has happened. I know I'll have nightmares--- I'm so afraid."

Ay, there's the rub, I thought silently. There was no chance of Davis dreaming tonight. But I felt uneasy about being in Raven's house, probably ending up in Raven's bed if past form was anything to go by. "What about Anthony?" I asked.

She didn't look up, her face buried into my chest. "He won't come here. He says there are people looking for him. He seems to be in terrible trouble, Terry."

"Who's looking for him, Patricia? Davis and his friends?"

She shook her head abruptly against me. "No. It's someone else. I don't know much about them. But Anthony told me he had to disappear for a while." She looked up at me. "Please stay. It would mean so much to me. Just for tonight." So I stayed with her that night. Well, she had my shirt, for a start.

But I didn't sleep much. I spent the night holding her and drifting in and out of consciousness, occasionally comforting her when she woke in a panic. Though in actual fact she slept better than me. I suppose I must have dropped off for a time at some point because I was suddenly awakened by a bunch of inconsiderate blackbirds outside the window, welcoming the dawn or whatever it is that birds do at that unspeakable hour. It was daylight, although still very early. Without disturbing her I slipped out of bed and dressed quickly. She was awake by then and lay watching me.

I kissed her on the forehead. "I'd better go. After all, I have my reputation to think of." She gave me a brief wan smile. Well, you can't expect much by way of repartee at that time in the morning, can you?.

# CHAPTER 28

I walked through the empty streets in absurdly high spirits. Maybe it was being alive that made me feel so good. When I arrived back at the flat I made a pot of fresh coffee and not the decaffeinated kind. My current life-style seemed to rule that out. Then I settled down on a sofa to review the situation.

My irrational euphoria began to evaporate as I took stock. The worst news was that I had a hired killer chasing me and that three people had already died unnecessarily. I had one client on the run and unlikely to pay my fees and I had involved my most important client in an attempted fraud. Also, Raven now had a new and dangerous hold over Patricia, if he ever needed it and I didn't want to think about what he could do to me if he chose. Meanwhile I had unwittingly helped to remove the threat of Davis for him. So now Raven was free and Davis was dead. Not so good so far. What about the credit side?

I had probably saved Patricia from several years in a women's prison, which she would not have enjoyed one little bit. On the other hand she had saved my life, not once now but twice. I owed her for that. And perhaps, just perhaps, I had upset Raven's nasty little games for good. Although it seemed that his plans had been unravelling before I became involved. But the equation didn't seem to balance very well. Sometimes when the gods have you in their sights the only sensible thing to do is keep your head below the parapet until they forget you and go after some other poor sod. No other great thoughts came to me and after a while the exertions of the night took their toll. I must have dozed off.

I woke to hear a loud ringing noise. The sun was high in the sky, my watch told me it was almost midday and I felt hellish. I was badly slept, unwashed and unshaven. Gradually it penetrated my half-fuddled brain that the noise came from my door bell. I staggered into the hall and began to unlock the door. Too late, just as I opened the door the image of the man Duchene sprang into my mind. But instead, three smartly dressed figures stood in front of me. None of them was Duchene. I blinked at them wearily. Three men in business suits? I shook my head in an effort to clear it. No, it's not the Church of the Latter Day Saints, I thought. They hunt in pair. "Who," I said haughtily, "is it who disturbs me at the crack of noon?" They didn't laugh.

One of them, older than the others, unusually small, dapper and slight, looked almost tiny beside his large companions. But it was he who spoke. He was wearing a dark grey double-breasted business suit and a subdued red tie. Apart from his diminutive size he looked every inch the company chairman. His hair was almost grey but it had been jet black at one time and he wore it brushed straight back from a high forehead, exaggerating the naturally oval shape of his face.

"Mr Lennox?" was all he said. But that was enough to tell me he was an American. I also heard the note of doubt in his voice. In my unkempt state I must have looked more like the caretaker or a handyman. He studied me with a pair of coal black eyes of that disconcerting kind that seem to have no pupils. A chilly smile flitted across his olive-coloured face. "Mr Lennox, the management consultant?" he enquired.

I nodded to him sadly. "I realise it seems unlikely. But I was not always as you see me now." Oh God, shut up, Lennox!

This is how I lose clients, I thought desperately. But last night must have left a touch of hysteria in the air and somehow I didn't care. The small dapper man ignored my words. He simply frowned and continued to stare up at me with those black eyes. I glanced at the other two. They were younger and much bigger, both of them about my size and weight and they looked fitter, not to say much better dressed than me. Not only did they not seem to understand what I was saying but they didn't seem to care. Instead they examined me with the kind of professional detachment I imagine a brain surgeon feels when he encounters an unpleasant but relatively routine tumour.

I smiled at the small man. "Sorry. Bad night last night, I'm afraid. Looking after a sick friend--- not much sleep. What can I do for you?"

He produced a business card and handed it to me silently. It was stylishly embossed and said simply, "Ernest Colmo; Vice-President (International); European Property Development Group; Amsterdam".

"Colmo?" I said, looking down at him. "Isn't that Italian for height?" There are days when I just despair for myself.

The little man gave another fleeting smile, more frosty than the first. "Literally, it means the summit, Mr Lennox. But you are correct, Mr Lennox. It can mean height. As in the height of folly. Perhaps my colleagues and I can come in? There is a matter of business I wish to discuss with you."

I hesitated. "Well, you have caught me at a bad time. But do come in. You can join me for coffee, if you don't mind."

I showed them into my sitting-room and excused myself while I prepared another flask of coffee, decaffeinated this time. The other stuff was playing hell with my nervous system, I decided. When I rejoined them they were sitting primly on the edge of their seats, like patients in a dentist's waiting room. I placed the tray of coffee on a side table and wandered casually across to the window. In the street below, parked on a yellow line, was the same big black saloon car that I had seen in the road near Raven's house. "If that's your black car down there," I said helpfully, "you had better not leave it too long. The wardens are very down on illegal parking around here. "

Colmo ignored me again. "Your sick friend, Mr Lennox. I hope he is not too serious?"

I shook my head. "I'm afraid we don't have a lot of hope for him. He didn't look at all well when I saw him last."

His small black eyes fixed on mine. "Sad," he said. "But then none of us live for ever, Mr Lennox." He gave another humourless smile. One of his companions sniggered quietly. "As I said, there is a matter of business I want to discuss with you."

I poured out the coffee and took a sip from my cup, watching him over the rim as I did so. His minders seemed to have no real interest in me. One of them sat back studying the curtains intently, while the other stared into his coffee cup as if it might contain the secret of the universe. I picked up his business card and examined it casually before tossing it back on the table. "European Property Development?" I enquired. "Sounds vaguely familiar. Are you part of a larger group?"

"We are a wholly-owned subsidiary of the Property Investment Bank, based in the Caymans," Colmo said briefly. "What I want to speak to you about is a more personal matter." He paused. "I would like our discussion to be entirely confidential. It is a matter of some delicacy." That usually means it's of no delicacy whatsoever, I thought. But I decided Colmo was probably not up on his Oscar Wilde epigrams. I simply nodded and waved my hand graciously, hoping he would take that for agreement. He went on quickly. "We understand that you are an associate of a lawyer called Anthony Raven. That you have on occasions acted for him?"

"Yes, I do know him," I said cautiously. "But I would not say that I was an associate. Although I have acted for him--- in certain respects." My vague feeling of hysteria began to resurface. "Yes, I have acted for Mr Raven on occasions," I said solemnly.

"Good," said Colmo. But it didn't sound good to me. "Perhaps therefore you can tell me how we can contact Mr Raven. There are some financial matters outstanding between him and our organisation and we are very anxious to locate him. He seems to have--- ." Colmo pondered for a moment or two to find the right phrase. "Gone away," he said simply. "We need to speak to him urgently. We understand that you may be able to help us--- that you know his whereabouts?"

I shook my head. "No. You've been misinformed. I have no idea where Raven is. Try his office. If they can't help you I wouldn't know what to suggest."

Colmo sighed. "Naturally we tried his office first, Mr Lennox. But they seem to have no knowledge of his movements. Nor does his wife." He stared at me. His dark eyes looked like black pebbles at the bottom of a cold stream. "There is a considerable sum of money involved, Mr Lennox. Cash that your friend Raven was handling for us. We do expect to recover that money, one way or another. We expect you to tell us what you know of Raven's whereabouts. Let me be frank, Mr Lennox,"

I still wasn't in the mood to take him seriously, which, as it happened, was a mistake. "That's fine by me!" I said brightly. "I thought you were Ernest. But you be Frank and I'll be earnest." I stood up and looked down at him. "Watch my lips, Frank. I do not know where Anthony Raven is," I said very slowly.

Colmo stared at me. "We were told that you were an amusing fellow, Mr Lennox. And also stubborn." He nodded his head towards his two companions. The one holding the cup jerked his arm and threw the hot coffee in my face. I gasped, blinded for a moment, and felt myself spun around and my arm wrenched up behind my back. My cup and saucer crashed onto the table and smashed the cafetière. At the same time a thudding blow hit me in the lower ribs and the pain shot through my body.

Colmo stood up and came towards me. He took a handkerchief out of his pocket and reaching up wiped away the coffee from my eyes. I re-focussed, blinking and shook my head. "So you don't like decaff," I croaked. "You should have said." The minder who was holding me gave my arm an upwards jerk and I gasped in agony. Colmo was studying me impassively.

"Please tell us what you know, Mr Lennox. It will save everyone a lot of time and trouble."

My sense of humour was starting to flag. "Listen shorty," I spat out at him, "I have no idea where Raven is and--- " Before I could finish he motioned to the bigger man and two more thudding blows crashed into my ribs. I winced with pain and felt my head start to reel. There was a strange far away ringing sound in my ears and I decided to keep quiet. They obviously didn't like my sense of humour any better than they did the coffee.

Then from the hallway I heard the rattle of a key in the lock, followed by the noise of a door closing. A few seconds later Tom Drever strode into the room clutching a suitcase in one of his great hands. "Hello, hello!" he boomed. As always he seemed to fill the room instantly.

Colmo and his two men had frozen in their places around me. Tom reached the centre of the room, still grinning broadly. He was wearing his usual outfit; a pair of countrified brown corduroy trousers, a checked cotton shirt open at the neck, a homespun grey woollen pullover and a tweed jacket of uncertain

253

colour that I think I recognised from his university days. He beamed amiably at everyone, looking for a moment like the village idiot who had wandered by mistake into the laird's sitting-room. But his shrewd brown eyes took in the scene instantly. "Lennox, you old bastard," he said cheerfully and leaned forward to place his suitcase on the floor at Colmo's feet.

Then as he straightened up, without any warning he hit the minder in front of me with a clubbing blow just beneath the heart. Tom's ham-like fist swung up in a wide arc with all his weight and power behind it. The minder was a big man but the force of the blow lifted him off the ground and hurtled him across the room. He struck the arm of a chair, toppled over and lay draped across it, unconscious.

Almost in the same movement Tom seized Colmo by the collar of his neat double-breasted suit with one huge hand and with the other grabbed his waistband. Then he lifted him off the ground and turned him sideways, holding the little man in front of him like a shield. "What do you want me to do with him, Terry?" He jerked his head towards the tall windows. "Shall I chuck him out?"

I felt the other minder slacken his grip on my arm slightly. Colmo was wriggling and cursing in two languages, suspended in mid air. "I really think you should let go of me," I said quietly, over my shoulder. "It costs a fortune to replace these Georgian windows." Tom's grin widened even more and without apparent effort he raised Colmo high above his head, like a weight-lifter completing a clean and jerk.

"For Christ sake," screamed Colmo. "Let him go! Before this maniac---."

Tom stood with the wriggling Colmo over his head, looking longingly across at the big windows. Then he nodded to the minder. "Aye, I think you had better let my friend go."

As the man hesitated I stamped the heel of my shoe hard into his instep, pulled myself away and pivoting, struck hard backwards and upwards with my free elbow. There was a satisfying crunch as I hit him under his chin on the soft part of the throat and he dropped choking to the floor.

I rubbed my shoulder. "Mr Colmo," I said, looking up at him suspended high in the air over Tom's head. "It seems that we have got off on the wrong foot. Perhaps we should start again. Let me tell you once more, I don't know where Anthony Raven is. But I'm no friend of his, I can assure you. So maybe we can be of assistance to each other. I have scores to settle with him too. Apart from anything else, he owes me money as well."

I gestured to Tom. Reluctantly he placed Colmo gently back on his feet. The little man, looking like a badly ruffled bantam-cock, indignantly straightened his clothes and stared around him. His minders were picking themselves up slowly from the floor and it was clear that the one Tom had hit wasn't going to take an active part in events for some time. Colmo's black eyes were cold with rage. But I was counting on him being more of a businessman than a hoodlum. "Take a seat," I added casually. "More coffee?" Then I turned to Tom Drever. "Good of you to drop in, Tom. Coffee for you?"

Tom shook his head disdainfully. "No, no," he said scornfully. "All that caffeine is terribly bad for you." He heaved his suitcase on to a chair and threw it open. He rummaged under a heap of socks and underwear. Then he grinned and straightened up holding two whisky bottles. "Highland Park!" he exclaimed. "Twelve year old! That's what we need to settle the nerves!"

I cleared away the wreckage of my coffee pot and cups and found some glasses. By this time Tom had helped the two minders into seats and was chatting genially to Colmo about life in the islands and the problems of running a rural newspaper.

255

Colmo sat staring at him as if Tom had been beamed down from another planet. I didn't blame him. Sometimes I thought so too.

Colmo wouldn't take a drink. But his minders both needed one and so did I, while Tom Drever virtually ran on the stuff. "Suppose we level with each other," I suggested to Colmo. "I'll tell you what I know about Raven, for a start." I pulled out the information Donald Lynch had sent me about the Islands Development Trust, carefully removing the details about the Property Investment Bank. I took him through all that had happened in the past two weeks, leaving out only the events of the previous night. Tom Drever listened as intently as the rest of them. When I mentioned the man Duchene a flicker of recognition appeared in Colmo's dark eyes. I sensed the other two men exchanging glances.

"You know the French-Canadian?" I asked quietly.

Colmo hesitated and then nodded. "Yes, we know Duchene. We know him well." He looked at me appraisingly. "He works for us on, let us call it, security work. But we didn't know he was doing private work for Raven. That's something we don't allow." He smiled grimly in the direction of his companions. "We'll have to have a serious discussion with him about corporate ethics."

He turned back to me. "What you're telling me makes some sense, Mr Lennox. We knew that Raven would have to raise money quickly. But we did not know about this Trust." He paused. "A great deal of cash he was in custody of has failed to reach its destination. When we investigated, we discovered that Raven is heavily committed in some property schemes of his own--- schemes that have gone financially badly wrong."

"What kind of schemes?"

"He has been involved in financing a series of hotel and leisure complexes, here in Europe and also the in Far East. He's

256

made a lot of good contacts on that side of the business through his work for us." Colmo looked at me stonily. "But not good enough, it would seem. We understand he has run out of funding." He shrugged. "There is a general slump in property values, so balance sheets are starting to look sick and banks are reluctant to lend on underlying assets that are doubtful. We think he has been diverting our cash to plug the gap. To meet period payments on construction projects and interest on his loans." Colmo shrugged and gave me a cheerless smile. "As you can imagine, we don't allow that. Presumably this necklace was a gamble of his to raise enough cash to keep us off his back. But he's in trouble, any way you look at it."

"Doubling up on your bets when you're losing is always a high risk strategy," I said. "Usually a quick way to the bankruptcy courts. But it fits with what I know about him."

Colmo stood up and his two followers immediately did the same. "I can't say it has been a pleasure to meet you, Mr Lennox," he said dryly. "But it has been interesting. If you are right and this brooch is a fake," He paused and almost smiled. "Then it looks as if Raven will come up short yet again." He glanced at me. "And we don't like it when there are deaths involved. The publicity is not something we welcome." He smiled thinly. "Except when it is unavoidable. I'm sure you understand." I nodded silently. "So if you do learn anything about Raven's whereabouts, Mr Lennox, if he should turn up here for example, I would like to hear about it."

I smiled blandly. "Put like that, Mr Colmo, how can I refuse? It's a pity we got our discussion off on the wrong foot."

What might have been a real smile flitted across his swarthy features. He picked up his coffee stained business card from the table and stared at it disapprovingly. Then he scribbled something on the back and handed it to me. "These are two telephone numbers where you can contact me or my people at any time, day or night. If you hear anything about Raven, let us know."

"And in exchange?" I asked politely. "What about this man Duchene? You say he works for you?"

Colmo nodded. His eyes stared into mine for a second. "We will de-activate Duchene. I don't imagine Raven has been able to pay him real money yet--- and Duchene would not come cheap. Even for something as simple as killing you, Mr Lennox." I saw his lip quiver slightly. "But we'll deal with him. In the meantime I advise you to be careful, Mr Lennox. For Duchene can be very dangerous."

I showed them out of the flat. As they left, he turned and looked coldly at Tom Drever. "And you sir, I advise you not to visit Amsterdam for a while."

Tom beamed at him. "Oh, that's not likely," he boomed. "I hate that Dutch gin. It gives me a terrible hang-over." Colmo was shaking his head as I closed the door behind him.

The rest of the day was lost in a haze as I tried to convince Tom Drever that his theory about McNaughton's death was wrong, while at the same time trying to match him drink for drink. "I know all about the break-in now," I said. "That was Raven, too."

Tom frowned. "But why? I don't see what he had to gain."

"You saw the set-up at Scarisby. It's clear Raven was using the place to entertain some of his gay friends; the ones with exotic sexual tastes."

"In return for favours?"

"It looks that way. Though what the favours were we probably will never know for certain. Then the stories about a

258

"magic circle" of powerful men started to circulate. Now that was a two-edged sword as far as Raven was concerned. On the one hand it made some of them shy away from him, for fear of the publicity."

"Which meant a loss of influence for him."

"Just at the wrong time, when he needed all the help he could get with his property schemes running into cash-flow problems. That was probably when he began to divert Colmo's money to tide him over." I paused and shook my head. "Not a good idea."

"But the break-in?" Tom frowned at me. "Why?"

"My guess is that Raven learned from his legal contacts that there was an unofficial report into the "magic circle". He had to get hold of it for two reasons; to stop it leaking out prematurely but also because he realised that he could use it for his own purposes."

"So he arranged for one of his associates to "liberate" it?"

I nodded. "Again, it's only supposition. Someone on the inside wanted it made public and thought he would do that for them. But what he did in fact was to make it disappear for good. But in doing that he stirred up the muddy water quite deliberately and just enough to scare his old mates back into line, at least for a time. I think he was always desperately playing for time. But now Raven had the report and, unofficial or not, accurate or not, it was potentially dynamite in his hands."

"Blackmail, you mean." Tom grunted.

"Oh sure. But blackmail of the most subtle kind. You can imagine! All Raven had to say was that he knew who had the report and also how the individual could be bought off. But only via Raven, of course. Which was more control for him. It's all about control, Tom. Then he decided he didn't need Davis and tried to shop him to the authorities, who were still anxious to shut the story down for good. But that plan went wrong and the truth about the break-in started to come into the open when people like Ray Morrison got their teeth into it. Which was bad news for Raven."

"Wasn't it was risky for him to turn in this guy Davis? He knew a lot about Raven. Why would he take that chance?"

I thought for a moment. "I'm not sure. But my guess is that Raven loves taking risks. For a start he can't resist the urge to destroy anyone who happens to be in his power. Even if it means a risk to himself."

"Or maybe because of the risk," Tom said ruminatively looking into his empty glass and reaching for the bottle. He splashed out two more helpings of Highland Park. "You were right, by the way," he added. "Raven was in Orkney the night Childs died. I persuaded someone to check the passenger list for me." He stared at me. "Childs was seen at the airport that evening too. Presumably he went there to meet someone. But no-one recalls seeing him with anyone."

I sat back and considered the latest news. "So Raven could easily have killed Childs; shoved him off the cliff and returned to Edinburgh in time to call me and make his trip to Asgard. Tom, the whole thing revolves around that Norse artefact, the Gripping Beast. Raven organised that fake--- I'm certain it is a fake now. He killed McNaughton or had him killed, I don't know which. Then he eliminated van Heulen the maker and then finally Childs to remove the last evidence. Remember it was only Childs' provenance that linked the brooch to the tomb and the McNaughton family."

"He'd have to kill McNaughton to gain access to the estate and to set up the Trust," said Tom reluctantly. "Aye, that makes sense, I suppose. So Childs was in it from the start?"

"Maybe not McNaughton's murder," I shrugged. "It might have been presented to him simply as a fraud. But the clever scheme turned out to be fatal, for him and for McNaughton." I smiled at the doubtful look on Tom's face. "You will have to write another chapter for your book after all!"

"But was Raven anywhere near Orkney when Archie died?"

"Tell me the date of McNaughton's death."

Tom screwed up his face. "From memory, McNaughton died on the twenty-sixth of October last year."

"Right," I said. "I can find out where Raven was that day. Leave it to me." The last thing I remember before I staggered to bed was Tom's voice, slightly blurred, telling me to come to Orkney with him. "It's time you laid low for a while, Terry old son. You're making a lot of unnecessary enemies around here. It's starting to seem dangerous. Come up and spend a while with me, out of harms way. We'll do a bit of sailing and have a few drams."

Oh God, I thought as I faded out.

# CHAPTER 29

I woke early next morning in better shape than I deserved to be. But I decided to skip my exercises again. My ribs ached where Colmo's pal had pounded me and my back still creaked from Davis's attempt to twist it into a pretzel. I moved quietly about the flat while I made coffee, not wanting to disturb Tom Drever from his slumber. But I needed some music to get the day underway. A Requiem Mass seemed most appropriate under all the circumstances. The choir had just started to boom out "et lux perpetua" when the telephone rang. I said something irreligious, turned down the music and picked up the receiver.

"Terry," she whispered, "I need to see you." She sounded desperate. "I need you. Everything is going crazy. Maybe I'm going crazy."

After what had happened at the cottage I wasn't surprised. "Try to forget it, darling," I said soothingly. "I know how awful it is. It was a shocking thing to happen, but --- ."

"It's not that," she snapped aggressively. Then her voice softened again. "At least not just that, horrible as it all was." Then the steel return and she added tersely, "Don't forget I did it to save you, Terry! But that isn't what I'm talking about. Anthony's in serious trouble and I don't know what to do about it. Some men have been here to see me--- ."

"Colmo?" I interrupted.

"Who? No--- . Look, I don't know what you're talking about, Terry. Please listen to me," she said peevishly. I decided to listen to her. "I had a visit from two men from the Law Society. They were looking for Anthony."

"Isn't everyone?" I said.

She gave a bitter laugh. "Not me, Terry. I'm finished with him forever, I hope."

"What did they say to you?"

"I didn't understand it all. But it seems there is a problem over clients' cash. They say the firm is to be put into administration pending an investigation into Anthony's financial affairs."

I whistled. The legal establishment wasn't losing any time in putting a 'cordon sanitaire' around Raven and his affairs. "I can't say I'm surprised. But that sounds serious."

"Yes, yes, I know," she said impatiently. "But that isn't why I need your help. Grieder has just called me. He wants me to go back to that strange place of his in Switzerland. He's sending his private plane to take me there, to Asgard. Terry, I have to go. He still has the necklace and he says wants to buy it. But even if he doesn't buy it, I'll have to get it back. It may be all I have left---- the only thing of value from this nightmare."

I stared at the receiver. Why would Grieder still want to buy it? Had his experts been fooled? Did he prefer to believe them rather than me? That would certainly be in character. Or was I wrong about the object. Could it be genuine after all? I'd been wrong about a lot so far. Either way, I was beginning to doubt whether I understood Grieder. Or Patricia, come to that.

"Patricia, you do realise that necklace is almost certainly a forgery? That's why van Heulen was killed in Brussels. If I'm right, he was the jeweller who made the damned thing. Grieder knows that perfectly well."

"Terry!" she cried out, almost in pain. "That can't be true! Surely not! Grieder wouldn't want to buy it if it was a fake. You must be wrong."

I breathed a deep sigh. "I don't understand that one, I have to say. But what exactly is it you want me to do?"

"I want you to come to Asgard with me, Terry. Please! I--- I can't face him on my own. He looks at me so strangely. I don't trust him and I'm afraid of what might happen without Anthony there." I suddenly realised, with a sickening wrench, that she didn't trust herself either.

"No, I don't trust him, Terry," Patricia said again. "Please help me." She hesitated. "Anyway, I told him you would be coming with me--- as an advisor."

"You told him?" I exclaimed. Then I stopped myself. "Listen," I said calmly. "I'm sure you have nothing to fear from Grieder. He's the soul of--- ." The right word didn't come to me. "He's highly ethical." I said lamely. No, he's not, I thought. He's a ruthless bastard who gives no quarter to anyone who is in his way. "How did he react when you told him about me?" I asked curiously.

"He didn't seem surprised."

I recalled that telephone conversation with Patricia from his London flat when I had suspected that he had been listening in. No, he wouldn't be entirely surprised that she wanted me there. But what was he up to?

"All right," I said. "I'll come with you." Well, Tom had advised me to lay low for a while and keep out of trouble. Where safer than Grieder's mountain fastness? In any case, I wanted to know what he intended to do about the necklace.

Patricia gasped with relief. "Thank you Terry. It will be wonderful to have you there. Will you meet me at the airport at two o'clock? You don't know what this means to me. I'll feel so much safer with you there."

Safer, I thought. What was it that Patricia really feared? I started to throw some clothes into a suitcase. What do you wear on a kamikaze mission?

## CHAPTER 30

But the trip began well enough. Grieder's sleek little jet was waiting for us on the runway and a couple of hours later we were wafting through the valleys south of Bern in the type of chauffeur-driven limousine I had only ever seen delivering clients. My luggage looked scruffy by comparison and I hoped the uniformed driver would mistake me for a rich eccentric. But somehow I don't think he was fooled.

Patricia, on the other hand, looked every inch the limo type. She had that amazing knack of knowing just what was right for any occasion and as usual she looked like a million dollars. Which, as it happened, was about the price Raven wanted for the necklace. She wore a chestnut-coloured roll-necked sweater of fine cashmere under a brown and white hounds-tooth checked jacket, a dark brown mid-length pleated skirt and a pair of tan leather boots that probably cost as much as a plane ticket to Bern.

We didn't say much to each other as we glided past the neat fields, the chocolate-box model chalets and the occasional group of painted cows peacefully chewing unnaturally green looking grass. Then I was aware of the high mountains ahead of us, like a low cloud on the horizon. Soon we were close in beside them, looming over us, their sheer bulk foreshortening the sense of distance as the limousine ran smoothly through a series of picturesque little villages by the side of a long lake. Then it turned into a side road, narrower but well maintained. I noticed there were no weeds growing by the side of the road, only a trim strip of grass even in this remote stretch. I mentioned it to the chauffeur. He shook his head. "No sir," he said simply. "It is not allowed for weeds to be left by the roads."

"Is that government policy? Or does Herr Grieder insist on it?" I asked him politely. I heard a stifled snort from Patricia beside me.

The driver stared stolidly ahead, concentrating on the road as it unwound and steadily climbed out of a tree-filled valley. "No weeds are allowed on any road, sir," he said firmly, as if that settled the matter. I opened my mouth to ask why, but then thought better of it.

By now the trees were thinning out as we reached the higher slopes and on each side were towering jagged mountains, much closer to us now, their north slopes thick with snow. A mile or two beyond another picturesque village the car began to slow down. A large yellow security post with steel gates blocked the way ahead and a uniformed guard emerged to check the car. He and the driver exchanged a few brisk comments in German that I couldn't follow and the gates were opened for us.

A few hundred yards further on the car stopped again and the driver leapt out. He opened the door for Patricia and pointed us towards an open-sided wooden platform where the glass-enclosed gondola of Grieder's private cable tramway stood waiting. "Your luggage will be brought to your rooms, sir." He spoke briefly into a telephone set into the wall and then he snapped a smart salute in my direction. "You will be met at the house," he said crisply.

The aerial tramway carried us away silently through the

tree tops. We climbed steadily for about twenty minutes, watching the terrain change from forest to high meadow. Patricia glanced at me. There was a strange excited look in her eyes. "Asgard is quite a place, Terry." She said. "Not like anything I've ever seen before."

I was having trouble making sense of this situation. Here I was about to enter the hallowed ground of Asgard with Anthony Raven's wife. To do exactly what? How would Grieder feel about having me there--- the hired help? Patricia leaned forward and kissed me lightly on the mouth. "Don't look so worried Terry. I'll protect you," she said mockingly. It was as if she had read my thoughts. "Haven't I've done a good job so far?"

It was a surprise to me that she had recovered so swiftly and completely from the events at the harbour. But I had to admit that if it hadn't been for Patricia I would probably be dead by now. Though, but for Patricia I probably wouldn't have been involved in the first place.

The cable car topped a rise and there, sprawling over the crest of the mountain like a gigantic animal, dominating the skyline was Asgard. It had one soaring central tower, built of the same stone as the mountain, so that it seemed to rise from its very core and was crowned by a lofty glass-domed atrium. Two wings flanked it, curving along the natural line of the mountain top. The wings had steep sloping copper-clad roofs and walls divided by row upon row of tall windows glittering in the sun. Wide terraces ran the length of both wings and looked south across the valley below. The cables that carried our gondola seemed to disappear into the base of central tower.

We closed rapidly on the house and with a jerk came to a stop within a brightly lit underground cable station. Yet another uniformed guard opened our carriage. Ignoring me he said to Patricia, "Mr Grieder is waiting for you." He showed us towards the doors of an elevator. Like the one in Grieder's office in

268

Brussels there were no controls. It could only be operated from above.

A few moments later we emerged into a vast circular hall that occupied the entire space of the tower. Light, glass and stone were the dominant impressions. Far above us was the domed atrium roof and immediately in front of us, rising up to meet the roof, was a sheer semi-circular wall of stained glass that formed the northern side of the tower, flooding the area with brilliant colour. High up in the walls were niches in which stood life sized bronze figures dressed in what looked like medieval armour.

Striding to meet us across the flagstone floor came Hans Grieder, tall, elegant and athletic, his blond hair glinting in the blaze of light. He wore an immaculate business suit and an ice-blue tie that seemed to emphasise the colour of his eyes. How had they matched the false one to the real, I wondered? He ignored me and drew himself up stiffly in front of Patricia. Taking her hand he bowed low over it with that old-world gesture I had seen when he first met her at the Club in London. For a moment I thought he was about to kiss her hand. But instead he straightened up and stared at her. An almost fanatical light gleamed in his good eye. "Mrs Raven, I cannot tell you how much pleasure it gives me to see you here again, so soon. It is more than I dared to hope."

I looked on in amazement. The intensity of his emotion was bouncing off the walls. I glanced at Patricia to see the effect it was having on her. She stood frozen into silence by his greeting. This was definitely not a Grieder that I had ever dreamed existed. I was starting to have the uneasy feeling that, whatever Patricia said, I was very unnecessary. I cleared my throat loudly.

Slowly, as if reluctant to take his eyes from her, Grieder turned towards me. What passed for a smile briefly crossed his face. "Ah, Mr Lennox. How good of you to come," he said graciously. "How convenient that Mrs Raven should ask you to advise her in this matter." He paused for effect and then went on, "Though I am a little unclear as to what your precise role is." He laughed abruptly and fixed me with his icy stare. "I assume that, after all, you are still acting for me, are you not? I assume there is no conflict of interest?"

I tried to summon up an affable grin for him. "Please don't worry on my account, Mr Grieder. I'm rarely clear about my precise role." He smiled slightly uneasily, sensing probably that I had made a joke of some sort. "And even when I am clear, I rarely stick to it." Grieder's gaze became even more glacial. "Still, I think you know my thoughts on the object in question," I ended pointedly.

"Indeed," he said curtly. "You were kind enough to make that clear."

"I suggest that you regard me simply as Mrs Raven's--- ," I hesitated, genuinely trying to find the right word.

"Companion and advisor," Patricia said coolly. "I hope that will not be a problem, Mr Grieder."

He smiled and bowed graciously to her again, waving to a young housekeeper who was hovering in the background. "Show our guests to their rooms. They will wish to rest after the journey. Then perhaps you would care to join me on the terrace for a drink at about seven o'clock this evening?"

The housekeeper lead us through a pair of enormous oak doors and into the east wing of the house. The long curving corridor stretched away into the middle distance before us and on our right there was a succession of doors. The north side of the corridor consisted of one unbroken wall of glass that offered a stunning view across a spectacular mountain range to the north. I stopped and stared out in amazement.

270

"The Eiger and the Jungfrau," the girl said with a shy smile and opened one of the doors for me. "This is your bedroom, sir." Then she turned to Patricia, "You are here, madam, in the next room. Your bags will be with you shortly."

I stopped her as she turned to leave. "Where is Mr Grieder's room?" I asked her curiously.

"This is the guest wing," she said with another smile. "Herr Grieder's apartments are in the west wing, near the business offices and the computer centre."

"Of course they would be," I said, and walked in to my room. It turned out to be more of a suite, with a spacious sitting room that opened through a pair of sliding glass doors to the wide terrace, and a bedroom with enough space to dance in if you were that way inclined. The walls and ceiling were finished in a simple roughcast and painted in a virginal white. Apart from the general luxury of the furnishings the place had the air of a monastic cell--- except for the view and the amount of space and the prospect of drinks on the terrace. I wandered around getting my bearings and opening doors. One door lead into a marbled bathroom with an Olympic-sized bath and enough mirrors to satisfy Narcissus. So maybe it wasn't much like a monastic cell.

The bathroom had a second door. I pulled it open, expecting to find a cupboard filled with towels. Instead I found my self in another identical bathroom, the mirror image of mine. It must be Patricia's. I called out, knocked on the inner door and walked straight into her bedroom. She was bent over the bed unpacking her suitcase. "Hi," I said casually. "I'm the handyman. Your plumbing seems fine as far as I can tell, madam. And by the way our rooms are connected," I added.

"Now that is handy," Patricia said dryly. Then she looked sharply at me. "I wonder how much Grieder knows about us?"

I shrugged and sat down on the edge of her bed. "There isn't much Herr Grieder doesn't know about most things. Remember information is his business," I said shortly. "Listen Patricia, what exactly do you expect to get out of this trip?"

She shot an almost contemptuous glance at me. "Money, Terry. Money! What do you think? I have to have money. If Anthony is really finished I need to save something from the wreckage. I can't survive without money." She glared at me, "Can you?"

"But you realise the Gripping Beast is almost certainly a fake, Patricia," I insisted. "You know what happened to van Heulen and Childs. I've explained all that to you. What's more, Grieder knows the whole story. So there's no way a man like him is going to buy the necklace." I paused. "I suppose you could sell it for what you can get. But that wouldn't be much more than the value of the gold. Which is something, but not enough to keep you for long."

She stood staring down into her empty case. "I wonder if you really know what kind of a man Grieder is," she murmured softly, almost to herself. Then she smiled ironically. "But in any case, Terry, I don't seem to have many options," She stared at me distantly, "I suppose I shall have to see what Grieder has in mind. He seems to have taken a fancy to me, don't you think?"

I seized her by the shoulders and spun her round to face me. "What are you talking about?" I said harshly. "You can't be thinking of that. The man has ice-water in his veins."

I felt her shiver under my hands. She looked at me defiantly and her mouth twisted into a half smile, "Are you so sure, Terry. Haven't you seen the way he looks at me?" She tried to pull away from me. "You really are a fool, Terry," she hissed at me. "What do you expect me to do? You know how I live. And you don't want me now, do you?" She shook her head to answer her own question. "No, not now you know about me."

272

Shocked in spite of myself, I let go of her and stood back. "There, you see, you know it's true," she spat out viciously. "I don't owe you a thing, Terry. Not a thing! Just remember that if it hadn't been for me you'd be dead by now."

That was true, for sure. Whatever we had once been--- and I had never really known what that was--- it was over now. The strange gripping beast had finished it.

# CHAPTER 31

Just before seven o'clock I stepped out onto the terrace and found Grieder was waiting for me. "Ah, Mr Lennox! I'd like to have a word with you. Champagne?" he enquired, beckoning to one of the staff.

"Now that's a word I enjoy having with anyone," I said lightly.

Grieder frowned and looked puzzled for a second. Then he nodded. "Ah! I see. A joke! You can be quite an entertaining man, Mr Lennox." I took a tall cold glass from the silver tray held out to me and made a silent mock bow in his direction.

"Mr Grieder, I can see how awkward my presence here is for you." Under his ski-ing tan, I had the satisfaction of seeing a red flush rise. "Let me make it clear. I am here simply as an old friend of Mrs Raven's, at her request. I gave you my best advice on the object. Now I have no further interest in the matter."

He stared at me. Even after all this time I couldn't remember for certain which eye was the real one. "And let me make it clear to you, Mr Lennox, that I have no need for your advice in this matter." Then his tone softened. He sipped the champagne thoughtfully. "However, since we are speaking frankly, perhaps you can confirm something for me. I understand that Mrs Raven's husband is in financial difficulties. Moreover I'm told that he has not been seen for some time and that no-one, including perhaps Mrs Raven, knows where he is. Is this the case?"

I stared at him bleakly. Then I nodded. "As far as I know, that seems to be the situation."

Grieder smiled. "Thank you," he said coolly. "Finally, Mr Lennox, I should make it clear that I am aware that in the past you may have been something more than--- did you say an old friend, to Mrs Raven?" I started to interrupt but he held up his hand. "Please hear what I have to say. Whatever you may have been is now immaterial. You have probably realised--- you are a perceptive man--- that I find Mrs Raven a most attractive woman." He paused. "I may tell you, more so than any woman I have ever known." He glanced cautiously at me. "If Raven has indeed vanished it seems that she will need a great deal of support. It is my hope that she will come to depend on me. Moreover, I intend to do all that I can to ensure that she does. Do I make myself clear, Mr Lennox?"

Before I could answer--- or even hit him, Patricia stepped out on the terrace, dead on cue. Grieder swiftly moved to greet her and I was instantly forgotten. The rest of the evening was like a bad dream. Oh, the view from the terrace was stunning and the food was wonderful. Patricia looked even better, like something out of a fairy story. She had changed into a long golden-yellow silk dress, tight waisted and full skirted, sleeveless and low cut enough to reveal her shoulders and hint at her breasts without being too obvious. She wore no jewellery but she didn't need it. Her auburn hair set off the dress to perfection and her tawny eyes seemed to glint with the same golden colour. The wines were good too, except they were Swiss rather than French.

But it was obvious that I was surplus to the evening's

entertainment. After dinner Grieder suggested we take our coffee inside. "Perhaps you would like to see some of my paintings," he said. "I'm afraid I restrict them to the private wing." He smiled at Patricia. "It's selfish of me, I know. But I rarely have a guest to whom I care to show them." The old etchings gambit I thought. I had hoped never to hear it being used. But Patricia didn't seem to notice.

He led us into the corridor in the west wing of the building. But here the walls were not bare. Instead, they were covered with paintings. I wandered down the passage, studying them curiously. The artists were all twentieth century and mostly German; Klee, Max Weber and Ernst were the ones I recognised. The only other feature was that they all hinted at something primitive and savage and ugly. I looked at Grieder with renewed interest. Apart from anything else, these paintings represented a considerable fortune that had been well invested. Patricia looked even more impressed. When she recognised some of the artists Grieder looked impressed too. So now we were all impressed. "Let us take coffee in the great hall," Grieder announced abruptly.

We went back to the huge entrance hall. At the far side an area had been set out as an informal sitting room, with large comfortable chairs and low tables dotted about under the great stained glass windows. On the table I saw a magnificent rosewood box and as the lackeys poured our coffee, Grieder stood up and raised the lid of the box. There lay the necklace, its ornate gold glinting in the dying light from the tall windows. Patricia leaned forward and I sensed her excitement. The weird troll-like creature stared up at me, its body writhing and twisting and its mouth savagely grinning. It was like something out of a nightmare, matching Grieder's taste in art.

Grieder picked up the necklace and moved round behind Patricia. "May I," he said quietly. She automatically swept aside her hair as he fastened the Gripping Beast around her neck. Suddenly I knew why she hadn't worn any jewellery with the yellow dress tonight. Now she was complete. We drank the coffee in silence and I began to feel more and more an intruder. Grieder saw me studying the bronze figures in the niches above us. "Heroes from German history, Mr Lennox," he pointed out. "The Knights of the Holy Grail. You may recognise them. Parsifal and Lohengrin."

"Not family then?" I said politely.

Grieder ignored me. "Cognac, Mrs Raven?" I looked across at her. Patricia had drunk a lot of wine at dinner and she was beginning to show it ever so slightly. Though still apparently cool and poised as ever, I could hear the voice become a fraction louder and see that her gestures were a fraction less controlled. But Grieder didn't seem to notice. Perhaps I had more experience of drunken women than he did. The brandy didn't help her at all. Grieder leaned forward towards her. "Usually I like listen to music at this time in the evening," he murmured. "But it is exactly as you prefer--- ."

Patricia gazed at him, "I'm in your hands," she said quietly, with a look that I seemed to recognise.

"Not Wagner, I hope," I said brightly.

Grieder stared at me and merely shook his head sadly. Then he rose and pressed a few buttons in a small electronic console set in the wall. The soaring notes of Tristan and Isolde filled the great hall. In that setting I had to admit the effect was magnificently theatrical. But I was feeling more and more as if I had stumbled into a social evening at Berchtesgaden. As Isolde's love song died away there was a moment of silence. No one spoke or moved. Then the faint and gently beautiful sound of the Siegfried Idyll drifted over us.

I looked towards Grieder. He was sitting bolt upright in his chair, his eyes closed. A single tear trickled from the corner of one eye and fell across his cheek. Patricia sat with her eyes fixed on him, a look of complete fascination on her face. Neither of them noticed when I stood up and went to my room. Half-an-hour later I heard a movement in the corridor outside and the sound of Patricia's door opening. She moved about in her room for a few minutes. Then I heard her door gently close. I peered cautiously into the corridor. There was no sign of Grieder but as I watched, Patricia crossed the wide flagged floor of the hall and disappeared into the private wing. "Let's talk about art--- maybe," I said and went to bed.

For some reason I didn't sleep too well that night. I woke very early too and lay for a while thinking of my next move. Then I decided my best move was to get out of bed and have a shower. I'd already knew I must leave Asgard immediately. From what I'd seen, Patricia obviously didn't need any help from me. I was tossing my clothes back into the suitcase when I heard someone moving around in the next room. Then there was the sound of bath water being run. I went to the connecting door and knocked gently. "Come in," she said. Her voice sounded hoarse and strained.

I walked into her bathroom. She was lying in a deep tub of hot water, soap bubbles piled high around her neck and shoulders. A heady aroma of perfume filled the air. Her hair was tied up out of the way and rivulets of sweat trickled down her face. She looked pale and there were dark shadows under her eyes. I looked at her silently. She stared back at me sullenly. Then she moved slightly and the water splashed aside the thick bubbles. That was when I saw the ugly red marks on her neck and shoulders. "Christ," I said in disgust.

Her smile was more of a grimace as she reached up with her hands in an instinctive, futile gesture to rearrange her damp hair. Around both wrists were livid lines of red bruising where she had been tied too tightly. My face must have said it all. She looked at me sadly, her eyes strangely dark against the pallor of her face. She gave a faint shake of her head. "What the hell did you expect, Terry?"

I went back to my room and finished my packing. Yes, what the hell did I expect? There was no sign of Grieder but one of the underlings produced a car and driver for me and promised to relay my apologies for such an early departure. I somehow doubted that he would be surprised when he heard that I had gone. I persuaded the driver to take me directly to Zurich Airport. It was a long drive but I figured that Grieder owed me something. From there I caught a flight to London and it was still only mid-afternoon when I arrived back in the flat.

Tom had gone but he had left a note repeating his invitation for me to stay with him in Orkney. After what had happened at Asgard I decided it was indeed time for me to escape for a while. But first I had unfinished business; a question that still nagged at me.

CHAPTER 32

I changed into my best business suit, the one I wear when I want to look like a management consultant, and made my way through the sunlit streets to Raven's office. Whatever else had happened to Raven, his entrance hall and the elaborate Georgian ceiling with the decorative plasterwork looked as impressive as ever, though it seemed like a long time since my first visit. The two wooden columns were still standing there trying to look like marble. I mounted the staircase and found the middle-aged receptionist was still there too. Somehow she was managing to look worried and bored at the same time, so I decided to brighten up her day. I leaned down and gave her my best smile. "Hello," I said. "Lennox? Remember me?"

She took off her spectacles and patted her hair. "Oh yes! Mr Lennox." She smiled back at me. "I'm afraid Mr Raven is away."

I nodded. "I know. I've just come back from a business trip on his behalf--- with Mrs Raven."

She looked at me sharply. "Oh yes?" This time the words had a subtly different meaning.

I went on blithely, "and I need to check something about the estate at Scarisby. You remember the work I was doing for

Mr Raven? I believe he had a meeting there last year sometime. I think it was possibly in late October. Can you confirm the exact date for me? It would save me a lot of time. I'm not certain when I'll see Mr Raven again."

She looked doubtful. "Mr Raven keeps his own private diary," she said. "And we have some gentlemen from the Law Society who are," she hesitated, "helping Mr Raven at the moment. They have his main office diary with them in the boardroom at the moment." I must have looked disappointed. "But," she carried on, "I do keep a record of all Mr Raven's trips in my own office diary."

I beamed at her. "Of course you do! I wouldn't have expected anything less from you. Is it handy? Or," I jerked my head towards the boardroom door, "do they have it?"

She shook her head primly and reached down into a lower drawer. "No they don't have it. I have it here. When did you think he had this meeting?"

I gave her the date of Archie McNaughton's death and waited while she leafed through the big desk-diary. Her finger scrolled down a list of dates. "Ah yes," she said triumphantly. "Here it is! Mr Raven travelled to Orkney on the 25th of October last year--- by car. Yes, I remember it now. The flights didn't fit in with what he wanted to do. Does that help?"

I smiled and told her it had helped a great deal and that in my opinion she was probably the most efficient secretary in the world. She was still laughing as I left.

When I reached flat I looked out the number that John Boyd had given me. This time I got through to Norman Orr without difficulty. I told him he wouldn't have any more trouble from Tim Davis. "I understand he's gone away on a very long journey. In fact, it's not likely he will be back."

Norman sounded surprised and relieved. "But there are still some people who want me out of the way," he said. "Pretty influential people at that."

"So maybe it would be a good idea if you went on a long trip for a while as well." I certainly intend to, I thought. "Just tell me something, Norman. Do you ever remember Archie talking about a piece of old jewellery that he owned? Something possibly Norse in origin? Something very valuable?"

He was quite definite. "No," he said with a laugh. "If there was anything really valuable Archie would have sold it long ago!"

"OK," I said slowly. "Then let me tell you something. You were quite right. Archie didn't commit suicide."

"So he was murdered! But who,---" he started to say excitedly.

"I'm not certain. Perhaps we will never know for sure. But I do know that Raven was in Orkney the night Archie died. Did you know that?"

I heard a sharp intake of breath. "He wasn't at the house. I was there all that day; the day the news came. I know Raven didn't come to the house. So where was he? And what was he doing?"

"I don't know for sure, Norman. But I suspect he had something to do with your friend's death. It's probably too late to prove it now. But I thought at least you should know."

There was a silence at the other end of the line. "I knew Archie didn't kill himself," he said quietly and I couldn't tell if he was glad or angry. "You see, he had no reason to do that. He was---, I mean, we were happy." Then he hung up on me. I stared thoughtfully at the telephone. Terry Lennox, bringer of truth and joy.

# CHAPTER 33

I had been glad to escape from Edinburgh. My recent memories were pretty bad, what with Grieder and Patricia and Tim Davis and young Norman Orr, to say nothing of Duchene and Anthony Raven. They all made it seem a good place to get away from. So I took Tom Drever's offer to use the boat, hoping that in Orkney the winds and tides would blow the bad dreams out of my head.

I booked into the hotel by the harbour and sailed every day for a week. The weather was superb and the islands were a paradise of blue seas and the clear skies. The fields were full of wild flowers and the old cottages covered with perfumed shrubs that looked as if they had never heard of gales and horizontal rain. Which partly explains why I was taken so completely by surprise when the fog silently rolled in that day just off South Ronaldsay.. For in the morning, rigging Tom Drever's little day-racer, the sun had been hot on my back and Orkney was looking more like the Greek Islands than usual. Of course I should have known better. But that was something I seemed to have been saying a lot recently.

It was the sudden blast of a foghorn, unexpected and curiously unconvincing in the bright sunlight, that first alerted me to the danger. Then away to the west I saw a solid white wall of fog blanketing the entire horizon. My first reaction was to outrun it and instantly I put the helm over and the boat came about, graceful and responsive. It was approaching high water and there would be a strong tide running into the North Sea which would get me clear.

But the fog was closing faster and faster. Still, even with light breezes Tom's yacht moved beautifully and I wasn't really worried. I could clearly see the tall grey cliffs of Hoxa Head only a mile or two away to the north-east and I knew that once past the Lowther Beacon and its awkward reefs I had only to clear Old Head and I would be safe. From there it was an easy sail to Tom's mooring. I took time to glance across the dark waters to the cliffs where the Scarisby tomb lay. It was hard to believe that only a few weeks ago I had known nothing about the Tomb and its story of death.

Then I realised that the fog was moving faster than I thought and in just a few minutes the first wisps drifted into the boat. The sunlight faded rapidly and the air became damp and chill. I started to shiver and cursed myself, remembering the sweater I had left behind. What had possessed me to set out on these waters wearing only light cotton trousers and a shirt under my life-jacket?

But when I had slipped off the mooring that morning I had managed to convince myself that all was well with the world. A week with Tom Drever and his collection of malts had put me in a mood to relax. In spite of everything, I had completed another assignment for Odin Investments--- almost certainly my last. The agonies had all dissolved and the dramas had resolved themselves like the plot of a Wagnerian opera. The beautiful love goddess had found her hero; the magic necklace was won and the villain was cast down. So it had all been a morality tale? Well, that would be going too far. But at least I had survived, more or less intact.

I crouched over the tiller and peered across a glassy swell of water into the steadily thickening mist. The cliffs and hills faded, reappeared briefly and then vanished totally. Visibility was down to a few hundred yards and getting worse. I looked up at the tell-tale ribbon on the mast-head. It fluttered fitfully as the wind alternatively gusted and died away. Worst of all, the sun was reduced to a pale watery globe drifting vaguely in and out of low clouds of fog. Then it disappeared entirely and in an instant my world was reduced to the wooden rail of the boat and a few feet of heaving dark water. I was completely folded in a cold white shroud.

Now I was worried. I had been heading roughly south-east when the world disappeared. But in fog the wind can change direction and I knew that I could no longer trust it. No sun and only a fluky wind! All I could hope for was to hold my last known course as best I could as I tried to recall exactly how the currents ran around this dangerous coastline. On the flood-tide I would be pushed south into the Firth and out towards the open North Sea, which would be fine, as long as I was lucky and didn't hit something hard like the Lowther Reefs or run onto any one of the smaller islands.

If I was unlucky--- well, I didn't like to think about the rocks that lay scattered around these waters. I cursed myself again. I could have been cruising around San Francisco Bay on my step-father's boat. Or even better, sitting on the deck at Sam's in Tiburon drinking a beer and watching the sun go down behind Mount Tamalpas.

Still, I thought cheerfully, the first step towards solving a problem is to know that you have one. At least that's what I tell my clients. Well, now I knew I had a problem. What I really needed was a solution or a bit of luck.

That was when I heard the sound of the motor-boat coming towards me through the fog. Hallelujah, the luck of the Lennoxs has worked at last, I thought. But of course I was wrong. The breeze was coming in fits and starts now, clearing away the fog to reveal a dozen or so yards of greasily heaving waves which were almost as quickly hidden again in a thick white blanket. I wasn't sure the approaching boat would see me in this visibility unless it was fitted with radar. I turned Tom's little yacht into the wind and let her sails rattle free. She lost way quickly and began to drift in the current. I stood up and began to shout.

No more than fifty yards away the dark bulk of the other vessel loomed out of the mist and the sound of powerful engines throbbed out across the water. I waved my arms in delight and started to call out a greeting. Suddenly the low steady note of the engines changed as the throttle was opened. The boat surged towards me out of the mist, its white bow-wave spurting as it gathered speed.

My wave of greeting turned to a frantic gesture of warning as the long sleek shape closed on me with frightening speed. Then I knew we were going to hit. At the same instant, in a flash of recognition I realised that I knew the boat. It was the big semi-displacement job I had seen in the Scarisby boat-house. I scrambled for the lines and hauled in the jib and main sails together, hoping to catch the wind and get me underway.

But it was too late. The fast moving speed-boat struck the yacht with a grating crash and I was thrown into the bottom of the boat, cracking my head on one of the heavy wooden cross-thwarts. Dazed, I staggered to my feet and saw the other boat veering off into the mist. By sheer luck the yacht had been turning head on to the motor boat's line of approach when we struck, so that the blow had been a glancing one. It had barely scratched the two-inch teak planking of Tom's boat. But I knew that if he had hit me sideways on at that speed I would have been swimming by now.

I heard the note of the engines change again to a low ominous throb as it circled out of my sight in the fog. Hastily I tightened up the sails and steered to take advantage of a breeze that had sprung up. The little yacht glided deeper into the covering mist. What had been my chief problem moments earlier was now my only hope of survival.

Did he have radar? Or had he found me by chance? For I had no doubt who was in the speed boat. I tried to recall the details of the boat I had seen lying in the shed but all I could think of were the two powerful in-board engines. They would hurtle that machine along at thirty knots or more. I hadn't been able to tell if they were diesel or petrol driven. But that didn't seem to matter much now.

I ghosted silently along, listening to the eerily regular throb of those engines, like the purr of a giant beast of prey prowling invisibly around outside a camp. Did he know where I was? The engine note grew louder. Now there was no doubt. He had radar and he must have me in his sights. The sound came closer through the mist. I thought frantically about my options--- and decided that I didn't have any.

With a surge of fear I saw the dark outline appear out of the fog directly astern of me and the engines roared into life again. I had time to thank my lucky stars that once again he wasn't coming at me from abreast as the big motor-boat bore down on me at high speed. I held to my course desperately, knowing that to turn either way too soon would lay the little yacht right across his path and lead to disaster.

But this time I had some way on the boat and more control. Watching him closely over my shoulder I waited until the last possible moment. Then, from almost under his sharp bows, I threw the yacht into a tight turn at the same time hardening up the sails to keep as much of the wind as possible. At all costs I had to maintain my manoeuvrability. It was my only defence now, except for the fog.

He missed me by no more than a foot. As the motor boat flashed past the yacht's transom I saw Anthony Raven's face quite clearly, turned towards me, white with hate, his teeth clenched, his dark hair torn by the wind. Then he vanished into the thick clouds of mist again.

I bore away as far as possible from the direction he had taken, burying myself deeper and deeper in the fog. But where the hell was I now in relation to the land? If the wind had stayed in its original direction I reckoned that the shore must be quite close. I listened anxiously for a sound that would give me a clue. But all I could hear was the steady slap of waves against the side of my boat and that regular menacing throb from somewhere out in the whiteness that surrounded me. Even the sea birds seemed to have fallen silent.

The noise of Raven's engines grow louder and louder. Before I even saw the shape of the boat its engine note increased again as he revved up more power. It flashed through my mind that either he had me lined up exactly or he was completely off his head with jealousy and hate. How ironic, I thought. How very ironic!

Then the sheer black lines of Anthony Raven's speed boat appeared, bearing down on me. He was going to hit me dead amidships on the port side this time. In the same moment I was half aware that to my starboard side a tall, weird shape with long stork-like legs had materialised out of the drifting fog. It was the Lowther Beacon and less than twenty yards away! Almost before the fact had time to register I had turned instinctively to meet Raven's charge. Once again the little yacht responded, spinning her slim bows to meet the collision. There was a horrible crunching blow and she lurched sideways, pitched violently and almost rolled under as the impact sent me sprawling into the bottom of the boat again.

I struggled up and automatically steered into the cover of the thickening mist. Behind me I heard a long ugly scraping, grinding noise and then a loud metallic crash that rang out over the water. The beacon was completely hidden by fog again and it was as if it had never been. For a moment there was complete silence. Then I heard the explosion, a deep woof like the bursting of a very large paper bag. At first imperceptibly the fog turned gently from white to pink, rather like a sunset after rain. Then it became a dark angry red colour and finally it was split by leaping tongues of bright yellow flames. So the engines had been petrol after all, I thought, as I tried to turn the yacht around. Diesel doesn't burn like that.

At least now I had no trouble finding the Lowther Beacon. My problem was to get there. The tide was running strongly and I had to fight my way back in a series of blind tacks towards where Raven had struck. I cruised around for a long time but as each minute passed I had to fight a stronger current and the light wind just couldn't cope.

There wasn't much I could have done anyway. The hulk of the motor boat burned fiercely and soon it would be little more than another wreck covered by the rising tide. There was no sign of Anthony Raven. If he had survived the crash and the fire he would most probably be drifting out there somewhere in the Pentland Firth. I hadn't noticed if he was wearing a life-jacket. But even with one it was unlikely that he would last for long in these cold waters.

I gave up and went with the tide until I saw the dark bulk of Old Head and could fight my way out of the main tidal stream and into the shelter of the islands. As if by magic the fog thinned and the sun burned through. Looking back to the south I watched the bank of fog drift slowly east and disperse in the wide waters of the North Sea. Suddenly it was as if the danger had never been. I shook my head and steered for Tom Drever's mooring. Maybe Raven would bump into Tim Davis out there. They'd have a lot to talk about.

The damage to Tom Drever's boat turned out to be mostly superficial and the story I gave him seemed to make up for it. I reported the accident to the coastguard and said I thought I had recognised the occupant of the boat. Then remembering my promise to Ray Morrison I called him to let him know the truth about Raven. When I had finished recounting the events to him over the telephone he said, "By the way, how did you get on with Tim Davis?"

"Ah," I said. "We never actually met. He must have had a better offer."

"Well," said Morrison, "I'm not that surprised. He seems to have vanished altogether. Probably didn't want to be involved in Raven's problems. You realise that the gay angle to the story is untouchable now? There are writs threatened and an official investigation into the police. So it's all subjudice. Even the details of Raven's finances are under wraps while his firm is in professional administration. The lid is very firmly on." Morrison's story came out under the headline of "Edinburgh solicitor lost in sea tragedy." At my request he didn't mention my name.


A pile of mail was waiting for me at my flat and a fax from Donald Lynch. The fax said, "Where the hell are you? Had a useful meeting with Grieder. What a charming man! Now negotiating a Scheme of Arrangement. But you won't understand that. Will call to explain." I looked it up in Palgrave's Dictionary of Money. It said that a Scheme of Arrangement was a clever and flexible way of merging two companies under section 425 of the 1985 Companies Act.

Donald's call came through as I was reading. "Hi Donald," I said casually before he could say a word. "A Scheme of Arrangement, eh. That sounds like a clever and flexible way of amalgamating the assets of the two companies. Did you think of that on your own?"

There was silence for a moment at the other end of the line. "You looked it up," he said accusingly. "You must have looked it up. You wouldn't know anything about a Scheme of Arrangement!"

"Just the broad principles," I said smoothly. "I leave the boring details to the likes of you."

There was a sharp intake of breath. "You are a very lucky man, Lennox. I've pulled a solution to your problem with Grieder out of the fire for you. He was sick to death with those boring actuaries you've been putting forward. He leapt at my proposal."

"Hey," I said, "I thought it was you and the Irving Group who had the problems."

He ignored me. "It's all agreed in principle. We still have to go through a balls-aching series of meetings with the main Irving shareholders. But at least we only need a simple majority of the votes. Unlike a reconstruction using section 110 or a full bid under 428."

"Ah," I said. "That sounds good."

Donald rattled on cheerily, "The bottom line is that Grieder will take over Irving's retail business and consumer finance operations at a price that is better than book value."

"The Irvings will like that," I said. "But why is he prepared to pay over the odds? That doesn't sound like the Grieder we know and love."

"The condition is that I come along with the businesses," Donald went on calmly. "My first task will be to sort out the retail side and sell off the properties for what we can get. At the same time I'm going to integrate their crappy finance operation with Odin's existing money broking and fund management activities to create a new division with me as Chief Executive. Oh, and I'll also be Grieder's Executive Assistant with a strategic trouble-shooting role throughout the entire Odin Group. Did you know he's planning to get married?" he ended inconsequentially.

All I could think of to say was, "What's the salary?" Donald named a massive six-figure sum and I mentally calculated my fee. It was the only good news I had heard for some time. "So the Irving family gets rid of the bits of the business they don't like," I said, "and loses you at no cost at the same time."

"And me too," admitted Donald. "But they can bear the loss. While Grieder gets a star performer," he added modestly. "And you pick up a big fee for doing next to nothing."

"Listen," I said seriously, "I hope you know what you're doing, Donald. Though I suppose a couple of years with Grieder will look good on your c.v."

After he rang off I sorted through the rest of my mail. There was one envelope that was bulkier than the rest and I opened it first. Half a dozen 8x10 glossy prints fell on to my desk. All of them were well photographed and showed a woman in a variety of sexual positions with a group of young men. The woman's face didn't show up too well in all the shots because of the interesting angles the photographer had used. But in one or two it was clear enough who she was. All the prints had the same single processing fault, a faint line down the extreme right edge of the picture--- the one that appeared on all of Raven's prints.

What a sweet guy, I thought. I wonder if he sent a set to Grieder? And I wonder what Grieder thinks about them?

# CHAPTER 34

It was well into August before she called me. I had made some coffee and I was sitting staring into my mug, thinking about San Francisco, when the telephone rang. The voice was soft and low and unmistakable. "Terry," she said. "It's me."

"Mrs Raven," I said ironically. "Or have I got the name wrong?"

"Terry, please don't be difficult. I need your help," she said urgently. "I have to see you." She sounded desperate.

I took a deep breath and tried to stop the room from whirling around. "Where are you?" I asked cautiously.

"I've just arrived at the airport. I have a car and I can be with you in half-an-hour or so. You don't--- you don't have anyone with you, do you?"

What did she mean? Then I realised it was her way of being discreet. "With me? No, I'm alone," I said quickly. "But what can I possibly do for you now, Patricia? I thought--- "

"Yes, yes, I know what you think." For an instant there was an edge in her voice. Then it softened again. "But I do need to speak to you. You won't believe what has happened."

Twenty minutes later she was with me. When I opened the door she was standing there, tall, slim and beautiful, the long auburn hair falling free over her shoulders, the eyes glinting like yellow topaz against her pale face. She gave a self-deprecating little shrug but didn't move towards me.

"I've turned up again. Like a bad penny," was all she said. She was wearing something red, checked and tweedy and it didn't suit her. Red wasn't her colour.

"Rather more expensive than that," I said ungraciously and motioned to her, "Come on in."

I gave her a mug of coffee and she sat bolt upright in a chair, nursing it in her hands, her knees together like an awkward schoolgirl.

"Terry, I know you have every reason to hate me." She looked quickly up into my eyes and stared at me intently. "I can't blame you if you do. But Terry, you know I'd still come to you if you wanted me." She must have seen the look on my face and her voice faded away. Looking down at the coffee mug again she went on sadly, "No, you do hate me." She covered her face with a hand and I saw her shoulders shake with a sob. "But everything I did he made me do. He made me do it all."

In spite of everything I wanted to take her in my arms but just in time I stopped myself. "Who made you do it, Patricia?" I asked her softly. "Anthony? Or Grieder? And what exactly are we talking about?"

She straightened up and brushed away a tear with her sleeve like an unhappy little girl. Automatically, I fished out a handkerchief and tossed it to her. She fussed briefly with her hair and gave me a fleeting smile. "I know what you think, Terry and I'm not surprised you feel that way. But whatever I've done, I truly need your help now." She leaned towards me and placed

294

her hand on my knee, looking into my eyes pleadingly.

I couldn't forget what she had done for me in Brussels. I owed her for that, if for nothing else. "What's the trouble, Patricia? What has happened now?"

She took a deep breath and said simply, "Anthony is alive."

I stared at her. "That's nonsense," I said. "How can he possibly be alive? I saw the boat explode."

Patricia shook her head. "I don't know how he did it. He's like a cat somehow. He always survives. But he has been in touch with Hans. He's still alive and he wants money. He says he needs cash and if Hans gives it to him he will go away again. Disappear for ever this time."

"Where has he been since the accident? How could he have possibly survived?"

She shrugged desperately. "I know what the papers said about it. But the fact is he did survive. He somehow swam ashore and then slipped away off the islands. Now he needs money to vanish finally," she repeated blankly.

Well, Raven was certainly a survivor if ever there was one. Wasn't that the very quality he admired in his orchids? "Let me get this clear" I said. "He's asking Grieder for money in return for keeping out of your life, is that it? So that you and Grieder can marry?" She nodded mutely. "And you want me to help you?" I laughed in spite of myself. But whether it was at her or at myself I wasn't really sure.

She opened her handbag and pulled out a large thick envelope. "There's $45,000 here. Anthony says that's what he needs to get away clear. To start a new life in Thailand or somewhere." She looked at me pleadingly again. "But he wants me to deliver it to him personally."

"And Grieder has agreed?" I said grimly.

"Well, only after I told him you would come with me. He says it's cheap at the price, if we can get Anthony to disappear."

Much too cheap, I thought. It had to be another set-up of some kind. But who was setting up whom? Patricia always knew when I was weakening. "He wants to meet us at our old house at three o'clock today," she added quickly.

It was barely mid-day now. I thought for a second and then nodded. "All right," I said. "I'll come with you. I saw the start of this thing. I suppose I may as well see the end."

As we stood up she swayed easily into my arms and kissed me on the mouth. It didn't feel at all bad. But not like that first time. Not that very first kiss. And it certainly didn't change my mind--- about anything.

"Tell you what," I said slowly. "Go away now. Do some shopping or something. I have some calls to make-- business to deal with." I suppose the truth was that even now I didn't trust myself to be alone with her. She went reluctantly. But I could see from the faintly mocking look in her eyes that I wasn't fooling her one bit. Though I really did have a call to make and it was one I made without a second thought.

## FINALE

Raven had asked Patricia to meet him at three so I decided to be there early, just in case he had any more surprises in store. But I didn't want to be too early. I wanted my own surprise to have time to work. We arrived at the house about ten minutes before the hour. Patricia was driving and I told her to park in the street near the big iron gates. They were open and I smiled grimly. Someone was there before me. I took Grieder's envelope from her and stuffed it into my jacket pocket.

"Wait here," I said to her.

"But Anthony said--- "

"I know what he said. Just wait here," I repeated. "I want to look the place over. I'm afraid I don't trust your late husband."

Patricia nodded obediently and I slid out of the car and walked up the overgrown path to the house. A few weeks neglect at the height of summer had reduced the garden to near chaos, with already a look of decay about it. Entropy, I thought. Entropy always gets you in the end.

I paused at the front door, which stood slightly ajar. Someone had definitely arrived before me. I pushed the door wide open and cautiously went into the tall silent hall. It was as quiet as an empty crypt, the only motion coming from slanting bands of dust motes drifting in the light from the high windows. I moved quietly down the hall towards the door into Raven's orchid house. Some instinct told me that I would find him there. I pushed opened the glazed inner door and stepped into the half darkness of the corridor.

Then I froze. In front of me stood the tall slim figure of Duchene, with a long-barrelled automatic pistol dangling from his right hand. I rapidly calculated the odds, estimating the distance between us. Then I gave up on the idea. He was just too far away to jump and I registered mechanically that the automatic in his hand was fitted with a silencer.

Duchene raised the pistol and waved it casually in my direction. He smiled. "Ah! The late Mr Lennox. For once you are early! But at least we have a chance to meet face to face at last." He read the expression on my face and laughed lightly. Then he slipped the gun inside his jacket. "Do not concern yourself, Mr Lennox. Everything is in order. Mr Colmo asked me to say that he is grateful for your telephone call."

Then he had glided past me before I could react and in an instant was gone. Looking back, I caught a glimpse of him moving swiftly across the hallway and vanishing into the garden. I pushed open the green metal door into Raven's inner sanctum. After the semi-darkness of the corridor it took a moment for my eyes to adjust to the blaze of sunlight that streamed into the conservatory. Then I saw the scene of devastation. There were withered and dying orchids everywhere. Raven's little pets had wasted away.

He was sitting at the table where I had seen him working on his plants. But this time he wasn't working. He wasn't doing anything much. Instead, he was slumped forward with his head cushioned on one arm, the other arm hanging down by his side. He might well have been asleep except for a neat bullet hole with a ring of powder burns behind his right ear. On the floor beside his dangling hand lay a revolver. I bent down and felt his pulse. Anthony Raven had died only minutes before.

I walked thoughtfully back to the car and slid into the seat. Patricia looked anxiously at me. "Did you see Anthony? Is everything going to be all right?"

"Let's get out of here," I said shortly. As she drove me back to the flat I thought about the best thing to do next. All it needed was an anonymous telephone call to the police saying that I was a neighbour who had heard a shot from Raven's house. I had a feeling they would be happy enough to write Raven's death off as suicide without too much investigation. There were things about Anthony Raven that a lot of people in this town wanted to forget. So no-one would look too closely at this incident.

As I got out of the car Patricia sat gazing up at me. She repeated anxiously. "Everything's going to be all right, isn't it?"

I leaned back into the car and kissed her cheek. "Yes," I said to her gently. "Everything is going to be all right. You can tell Grieder that everything is going to be just dandy." Then I slammed the car door and walked away.

I sent a fax to my step-father to say I was on my way and next day I was on the mid-day flight from Heathrow to San Francisco.

There was plenty of time on the way across to the West Coast to think about winners and losers. By any reckoning Anthony Raven was a loser. Of course Grieder and Donald Lynch were winners, as usual. They both got exactly what they wanted and I suppose Patricia got what she wanted too.

Raven's law practice was quietly subsumed into another larger firm, where his tangled finances and other problems were made to disappear. Grieder paid his fee for Donald's appointment, promptly as ever, though I noticed that the envelope was quite empty apart from the cheque. There was no friendly hand-written note of congratulations and personal thanks. I'm touchy about things like that. After all, it's the little things in life that make it all worthwhile.

But ironically what I called The Gripping Beast affair turned out to be one of my most successful assignments. In some respects I suppose honour, if that's the right word to use under the circumstances, was satisfied on all sides. Certainly Grieder's $45,000 just about covered the fee I didn't collect from Raven. Of course I never heard from Grieder again and I never had another assignment from Odin Investments.

I blamed Donald Lynch, of course. But he denied any responsibility and afterwards actually had the gall to say I owed him a good dinner to compensate him for the emotional trauma he suffered working for Grieder! He survived three years, which is more than most people managed. But as I always tell him, I am sure the experience was character forming.

I haven't heard from Patricia again. But one of these days I probably will.


THE END